Bottled Butterfly

A Novel
By

Penny Lauer

ArcheBooks Publishing

Bottled Butterfly

By

PENNY LAUER

Copyright © 2007 by Penny Lauer

ISBN-10: 1-59507-177-6
ISBN-13: 978-159507-177-4

ArcheBooks Publishing Incorporated

www.archebooks.com

9101 W. Sahara Ave.

Suite 105-112

Las Vegas, NV 89117

First Edition: 2007

Dedication

To my husband and two wonderful daughters for their love and support and especially to my mother and father who taught me that nothing is impossible if you want it badly enough.

Acknowledgments

This book could never have been completed, or the writing of it such an enjoyable experience, without the insight and encouragement of so many friends. Special thanks to my initial readers, Sandy Streicher, Emily Brasfield, Jean McKenzie, and Judy Lindstrom, who provided outstanding feedback. Brian and Joan McFarlane read and critiqued the book and truly understood what I wanted to say; I can't thank them enough for that understanding. Mary Lind, a prolific writer and outstanding editor, helped me believe that I was writing something worthwhile and encouraged me to get better. Her input was invaluable. Many thanks to John Johnson for his patience and photographic skills. JoAnn Remington provided marketing ideas and direction, and Cindy Denney and Kathy Moroscak trusted me and helped launch the book. What would I have done without my exercise friends, book club and bridge ladies who asked daily about the novel and encouraged me to keep at it? Finally, sincere and special thanks to my husband "agent" for getting me organized and insisting that I start "the next big one." He is my rock.

Bottled Butterfly

This gift of life is precious, and I chose early on not to be meek about living it, but to grab hold of all it offers up to me with joy and passion. I hope that at the end of my story you will understand. I want so much to be understood.

NELLIE

To Marge — My lovely vivacious butterfly friend. Enjoy! Tommy

PART 1

I hit at the screen door as hard as I could and thumped out of the house shadows into the sunshine, careful not to let the screen slam back against the house. "I hate her," I whispered and plopped down a little harder than I had intended and adjusted my behind on the splintery steps. I knew she'd follow me out.

She stood at the screen with her hands on her big hips. "Just look at you, lollygagin' around like there's nothin' to do around here, and me working my fingers raw for you and the rest. Get on in here, Nellie, and help out, or you'll be real sorry."

I turned to her and used the same bossy voice she just used as I backed down the steps away from her. "You're not my boss. You're not my mother. I done what I needed to do. Mind your own business. And don't start preachin' at me neither. I don't want to hear it."

I ran down to my swing at the end of the lane, half expecting her to come after me. She knew I could outrun her, though, anytime. She banged out the door and marched out onto the steps.

"You're a lazy, stupid, selfish..." She ran out of bad things to say to me. Her choice of words was pretty small, once she stepped out of her Bible passages. "Hmph," she said. "You're not worth the words and the time it would take to describe you."

She was always preachin'. My older brother John said she acted like she had God in her back pocket. Phoebe was different from the rest of us. John and my other older brothers respected the faith 'cause they respected Mama. My younger brothers and sisters was too young to have an opinion about all of that, and Daddy, well, he just went along with Mama so far as I could tell. Phoebe was the oldest, the first-born, and she acted like that gave her some kind of right to act all high and mighty; then, too, she thought she had more religion than the rest of us and that should give her the upper hand in things.

Phoebe's God was mean, not like Mama's. Her and Pastor Fredericks told us how God would come back to earth some day and would strike down sinners and destroy parts of all the stuff He created and rip up people and set them on fire. He said God's son Jesus died for our sins so we could be cleansed and forgiven, but then him and Phoebe said that we all sin and will go to damnation for all the bad stuff we do. Somehow Phoebe didn't put herself in that category of people who would burn in Hell. I don't think Preacher did neither.

"Dammit," I whispered. I liked using a word the women in my family would go into a tizzy over; all the women, that is, except Aunt Lizzie and my cousin, Little Edith. I liked "dammit" and I loved "oh, hells bells," which I learned from my three older brothers. Where they found out about them, I didn't know. Had to have come from some men in town. Daddy didn't cuss. Least, I'd never heard him.

I turned back to the noise coming out the door. It was creeping its way into my brain and was messing with my thoughts. The whole family was home today, even Daddy. He'd been gone almost a month this time, and my heart was so full of gladness when I saw his wagon pull up in the morning, it almost hurt. I was his favorite. He never really told me that, but I knew. Mama was always telling me to "slow down, Nellie; you're not going to a fire!" Daddy would say, "Run, Nellie, you can jump higher. I know you can." He called me "spunky," and he grinned that special way he had when I got a little sassy. Phoebe said I was a tomboy, which was a real sin in her book. She said that boys had their ways of behavin' and girls should have theirs. Me, I liked doing things that everyone in my family liked doing, the men and the women members, except for housework. I didn't like that. I promised myself from time to time I'd try real hard to be more like Mama and Phoebe, but I just couldn't.

I got ants in my pants when I heard the birds in the morning or the crickets at night, and I had to find some way to get out there with them. I'd look at those big trees out there on top of our hill and get such an urge to be up there in the middle of all those branches, I'd have to work real hard to calm myself down. And the wind, let me tell you, there wasn't nothing that felt any better than havin' the wind blow through your hair. Daddy understood that. Mama and Old Phoebe hardly was ever outside except to work in the garden or ride into town.

I turned back to the house. The ruckus inside was picking up every minute. My whole family was nutsy with Daddy being home and all. You see, he worked the coal mines down in the Hocking Hills. I didn't know exactly where that was, but it was still in Ohio, but down south somewhere. Daddy went back and forth 'cause he didn't want to make us all leave the farm, and, besides, the shanty towns was no place for us to live, he said.

I overheard Mama and Grammy talk sometimes about how dangerous mining was and how they hoped Daddy could get different work close by, instead of having to go so far and work so hard. I thought I'd like to visit Daddy there from time to time. The town sounded pretty exciting to me. Daddy told us about the fights that broke out down there between the Ohio workers and the men from down south, and he explained how some of the men made moonshine to add a few dollars to their family income. Daddy knew how to make it, he said, and he brought up from time to time how he could make us some money makin' it. Mama didn't approve of makin' moonshine and said we didn't need any trouble in our lives. That was the end of that.

Daddy seen a lot of the world. He didn't talk about it. I heard it from Aunt Lizzie who really wasn't my aunt. She was Grammy's best old friend. Her and me, we was real close. I'd go to her house, which was just down the road a little, and we'd bake fruit pies and molasses cakes and peanut butter fudge. I'd help her out with the baking and all, and it didn't seem like work, not like it did with Old Phoebe and Mama. Aunt Lizzie was always laughin' and tellin' stories.

Skinny as a beanpole with a voice that screeched like a hoot owl, was the way Daddy described her. Oh, boy, would she let things fly. Why, she'd say anything that came to mind, and she'd laugh so loud and hard that you couldn't help but join in, even if you didn't really understand what she was laughing about. And she sure loved my daddy. "How's my Johnny," she'd say when I was visiting, and I'd fill her in on everything I knew. Daddy liked her too. Him and Aunt Lizzie played gin rummy together. Mama didn't approve 'cause playing cards was a sin.

I was over to Lizzie's house one day when one of her friends was visiting, and I found out a lot I didn't know before about my daddy.

"Yep, John was dirt poor when he married Rebecca and certainly had no prospects for a house," Lizzie was saying to her friend. "He was living with his folks when him and Rebecca met."

I was playing in the sheets on the line out in her yard, and she thought I couldn't hear the talk going on. I hadn't paid much attention 'til I heard my daddy's name, and then my ears sure zoomed in on the rest of their conversation.

"You know Johnny ran away from home when he was just fifteen. Yep. No one heard from him for over a year, and then he just sauntered back into town and told his mama he had gone right out and enlisted in that Spanish American War. Got a touch of Malaria or something in Cuba and was sent home."

Well, that part of the story made me feel real proud. I could just picture Daddy out there by himself, seeing the world, tall and brave. And so young. Yep, he was my hero all right.

"His family was poor as church mice," Aunt Lizzie added. "Came back to help out his family. Was going to leave again soon as he got things squared away, but then he met Rebecca."

I was dying to hear more, but I missed most of the rest of it, because the danged wind picked up just then and hurled the sheets all over the place. They made such a racket banging into each other and me that I couldn't hear much of anything else. But I did catch little snippets here and there about him changing his ways and being a hard worker and something about sowing wild oats and a roving eye. Didn't make much sense so I stopped listening altogether.

I swung a little on my swing, trying to get my madness back, but all of the thinkin' and rememberin' I just done made me forget what Old Phoebe had said to make me so mad and why I'd stomped out to the porch in the first place. I decided to give it up and head out to the back of the house to our summer kitchen. Now, I have to tell you, that was my favorite place on our farm at this time of day, when the sun was big and low in the sky and the shadows was long. Truth is, I knew all along that was where I would end up when I ran away from Old Phoebe and her complaining.

The summer kitchen was just across the yard, behind Mama's flower and vegetable garden. As I walked up to the door, I took note that the sun was in perfect position so that it could just flow in through the side window. And I knew that, as soon as I walked in, the room would be magic. I looked around to make sure no one was following me, and I opened the door real fast and closed it behind me real quiet.

The coolness hit me quick. It felt so good. See, there was a cold stream that ran right underneath the stone floor there, and it made the little room feel chilled and fresh like the great outdoors. We kept milk and eggs right there in the stream to keep them from going bad. It was called the summer kitchen 'cause it's where we stored the food we'd put up in the summer and where we all ate when it was real hot outside.

Anyway, I went right over to the middle of the small room and just stood there, leaning against the long wooden table and looking over at the window where the sunshine was pushing its way through. The sun's beams was warm, and they moved around on my face and neck and arms. I closed my eyes, turned around real slow, and then opened them gradual-like, to see what I had really come in there for.

Sure enough, that old sun did it again. Mama's canning jars was all lined up real tidy on the shelves on the wall across from the window, and when the sun's rays came through that window and flowed across the room, they broke into hundreds of pieces of light as they hit those jars, sparkling yellow and green and pink and even blue. Them sparkles bounced over to the other walls and onto the table and the floor, and I felt like I was standing on top of the sun itself.

I was sparkling too.

Right then the music came into my head, and I let myself start swaying with it, and just like that, I was back there in my make-believe world, dancin'. I held up the hem of my beautiful blue silk gown so it wouldn't get dirty from the castle floor, and I said, "Why, thank you so much," when people told me how lovely I looked and what a fine dancer I was. Mama's wooden table became a golden trunk, and I reached inside and pulled out gifts for everybody there. There was toys and candies and cookies for the little boys and girls, and for the mamas I had soft, snow-white hankies and perfumes that smelled like roses. I gave the daddies fine shirts and gloves and hats so they'd be warm when they was working at their homes in the cold times. And everyone hugged each other and was happy until I said, "I'm so very sorry, but I must return now to my own family because they miss me very much," and, with a flick of my head, I just flew away.

The time always went by so fast when I was alone in that summer kitchen that it took me some time to get myself back to what was real. This day I said goodbye to it only because I was afraid that maybe Phoebe might be out looking for me. If she ever caught me there, dancing and pretending, I'd be in a heap of trouble. According to Old Phoebe, what I'd been up to was sinful, even though it was all just pretend.

That night me and Phoebe helped clean up the kitchen and get the youngins ready for bed like we always did, and then we all went outside and chased after lightning bugs and talked Daddy into telling us some spooky stories. After that, we sang some church songs with Mama, and she led us in prayers, and before we knew it, it was time to turn in for the night.

We all almost always went to bed at the same time 'cause us kids slept in the same room. Us girls slept two at the head of the bed and two at the foot. Little Grace was always next to me 'cause she was a little afraid of Old Phoebe too. The boys slept the same way. Baby Faye's crib and baby Rowe's cradle was still in Mama and Daddy's room.

Somehow sleep just wouldn't come to me that night. I was thinking too hard about how nice it was to have Daddy home and how Mama was smiling more. And I was thinking about what Old Phoebe had said about me earlier and was wondering if it was true. Then I thought about how beautiful the stars must be outside and how good it must smell out there, and just like that I decided to get out of bed and go out for a little fresh air.

I sneaked out at night from time to time. Didn't go nowhere. Just stood out in the backyard, letting the dew cool my bare feet and letting the chatter of the crickets settle me down. Sometimes I'd find a place to sit over by Mama's garden and watch the heavens. The glitter and huge-ness of it almost hurt sometimes. I'd look up at that big old sky and want to reach out and bring it all right up to me and put it around me like a blanket so that I could sparkle too. I'd think about far-off places and imagine me going to them sometime. I'd never been any farther than Frazeysburg, but I had my dreams.

This night I tiptoed out through the parlor where Grammy slept. Everything was quiet inside, but out on the porch there was the soft glow of a lantern and the sound of folks whispering. I found my way out the back door and around to the dark side of the house and saw it was Mama and Daddy sitting on the swing, talking soft to one another. I kept my back against the wood of the house and tried hard to make my breathing slow down 'til I darn near made myself pass out.

They was talking about when they was young and had just met each other. Daddy was sayin', "I remember I heard a bunch of girls gigglin', and when I looked up to find out where all that fun was comin' from, you was the first person I seen. You was the prettiest girl then, Rebecca, and you still are."

"Well, the years have brought on their damage, that's for sure." Mama answered, but Daddy said that wasn't true, that she was still a mighty fine looking woman. It was a while before they went on.

"They all thought you were awful handsome too." She laughed soft-like and said she remembered how her and her friends got all excited and grabbed onto each others' arms and prepared to strut by Daddy that first day they'd had a chance to really get a look at him, and how the other girls was so taken by his good looks that they could hardly walk they was gigglin' so hard.

"Not you, Beck," Daddy said. "Remember how you looked right up, direct at me? You said, 'Hi, stranger, who are you waitin' on? Wish it was me.' And then you and your girlfriends took off running."

I had to hold my mouth shut real tight to keep the laughter from pouring out. I couldn't imagine Mama talkin' like that. I'm just real glad no one saw me that night 'cause I must have looked like a crazy person out there in the dark, standing in my nightshirt, back up against the wall, just grinning away to myself.

"It's been fifteen years, Beck," Daddy said. "Fifteen years today. I know they haven't been easy, but we've had some good times, haven't we? Lots of good times." I waited for Mama to say somethin' back, but she didn't right away. That's when Daddy said, "I love you, Rebecca. I've always loved you."

"Do you, John? Then why...I mean...I still don't understand."

Mama was having trouble saying what she had to say, and that surprised me. She usually always knew how to speak her mind.

"Never mind," she said. "There's nothing left to say that hasn't been said before. It will be better now that you're going to be home more, won't it?"

I didn't want to hear no more. Knew I shouldn't. Their talk didn't sit just right, and I turned around and hurried back to my bed and had a lot of trouble falling asleep.

The next day was real busy, and the last thing I had to do that afternoon was get the table ready for us to eat our supper. I didn't actually mind that job so much. I was good at it, if I do say so.

I had a little time left before I had to put the food out, so I took a short walk and ended up at my swing again. I started swinging real easy and closed my eyes and dreamed again about places I wanted to go: far-off places that teacher talked about, places you could only get to on trains. Then I swung real hard and leaned way back on the way down to see how close I could get my head to the ground and pretended that I was about to fly. I could just picture myself swooshing out over the road and then soaring over the trees that made up the thick woods that started over there. Sometimes, when I was walking across the farm, I'd get to the top of a hill and open my arms out as far as I could and run back down lickety-split. I swear I could fly. I didn't tell anyone about it. That one, they'd never understand.

I was just dreamin' away and thinkin' about this and that, when my eye caught a movement behind one of the trees on the other side of the road. I figured it was a deer out there about to peek its head out to see if there was somethin' better to eat on my side. The woods was so thick, there wasn't any real good place for people to get in or out of it, but a deer wouldn't have trouble with that. I sat real still, hopin' it would show itself, but after a while I gave up and figured I scared it somehow.

I took one more good swing, almost up to the branch where the rope was held on, and I was almost stopped when I saw the leaves move again, right across the road from me this time. I stared across at the trees, waiting for the deer to cut through, but when the leaves broke apart, a face covered with thick black hair was looking back at me. The hand holding back the branches was huge and hairy too.

I froze.

Neither me or whoever it was on the other side of that narrow road moved. It felt like we was attached somehow. I wanted to jump off that swing and run into the house, but I couldn't get my legs to do what my brain was telling me. The face smiled ugly for a second, and then it turned away and disappeared.

I ran into the house and told Mama and Daddy about it. I must have

talked awful loud, because when I stopped, the whole family was standing there. Daddy told me real calm-like that the sounds I'd heard
probably was from a deer, just like I thought at first, and my imagination just took over after that. Well, that was the last thing he should
have said in front of the boys and Old Phoebe.

"Nellie saw a boogeyman," they all said together. " Nellie's dreamin'
again. Hey, Nellie, did your spooky man have antlers?"

Then Phoebe chimed in and said if I'd pay attention to the house
and do my chores the way I was supposed to, instead of lollygagging'
out on that swing, things would be a lot better around there. Daddy put
an end to the whole situation by telling everybody to get out and wash
up for supper.

Little Grace hung onto Mama, saying, "Did Nellie see the Boogeyman?"

"No, honey," Mama told her. "You know there's no such thing as a
boogeyman. We've talked about that, haven't we? It was just Nellie's
imagination. Right Nellie?"

She didn't really want me to answer. I knew that. I didn't know just
then what I would have said anyway. I do know, though, that before
everyone got themselves all sat down around the table, Daddy walked
out to the end of the lane, there by the swing, and stood a while lookin'
into the woods.

I made myself go back out to my old swing a couple times after, but
it didn't feel the same any more. Being afraid takes away a lot of your
joyfulness.

In the end, I just stopped swinging.

I have to tell you that there is not a more beautiful place on this
earth than Ohio in late September and October, and the fall of that year
was extra special. Daddy said we'd had just enough rain that summer to
allow for the trees to change their colors just perfect and hang on to
them a while. What a show they put on for us. The whole valley glowed
bright golden-yellow and pumpkin orange and deep red and even pur-

ple, as far as your eyes could see. The days stayed warm, but some coolness creeped its way in on the breeze at night and carried the earthy smell of those bright leaves out over all the fields and through peoples' windows. Slowly the leaves gave way to the wind and fell real slow to the rich earth. Wherever you looked there was color. It felt like God was putting on a big party for us right before He had the earth go to sleep, and the falling leaves was His confetti.

It was our Indian summer.

Me and Little Edith climbed as many trees as we could get to the next few weeks and raked up one pile of leaves after another and laid there on top of them and looked for pictures in the clouds. I would have treasured those days even more if I had known what was coming.

Right out of the blue one morning, Mama asked, just like it was the most common thing in the world, would I like to ride into town with her.

"Just you and me, Mama?" I asked.

"Just you and me, Nellie. Daddy and the boys are going to kill some chickens and fix some things out in the barn. Phoebe has some Bible studying to do here, so she and Grammy will watch over the little ones while we're gone." She must have seen the worry on my face because she added, "Don't worry, Nellie. They'll be fine."

You see, Grammy's eyesight wasn't real good. She could get around and all okay, but she mostly saw things shadow-like. Least that's what she said. She wore glasses, but they was just plain glass and wasn't meant to help her see. She just looked better with them on because her eyes was always kind of pale and cloudy looking and the glasses covered them up a little.

Quilting was 'specially hard for her these days. Phoebe and me had to cut most of the cloth pieces for her and stack them up by color. When she sewed, Grammy had to bring the quilt pieces up so close to her eyes in order to see them, they'd almost touch her glasses. I tried to do that a couple of times myself, but it made my eyes cross, and I was afraid they'd stay that way, so I quit.

"Nellie." Mama brought me out of my thinking, and when I looked up at her, she was shaking her head at me. "Oh, Nellie." She clicked her tongue up on the roof of her mouth the way she always did when she was exasperated about something, and I felt bad that I was upsetting her. "Do you want to go in and wash up so we can leave soon?" she said.

Did I ever. Having her all to myself was special and, besides, I'd have a chance to see some other people and roam around a little by myself in the store while she shopped.

I rushed in and filled the cleaning bowl with water and scrubbed my face like crazy so I'd look good for Mama and all those people I'd see. Then I pulled out the dress she had made for me early spring. I loved that dress. It was blue, my favorite color. Blue with little white flowers like daisies on it. I brushed my hair real good, too, and hoped Mama would let me wear it down today. When I went out on the porch where she was waiting for me, I knew I'd pleased her, but she still pulled my hair back with a single braid. Loose hair in public was not a thing Mama tolerated.

Her own hair was always pulled up in a knot on top of her head. I wished my hair was blond like hers. The boys and Phoebe had real dark hair like Daddy's. Little Grace's was the color of lemonade, and I loved hers the best. Mine was brown with lots of red in it, and I was the only one in the family with hair that color. Mama called it auburn. Actually, I didn't look much like anybody in my family, and Phoebe kept reminding me how I didn't act like anybody in our family either. Sometimes all of that worried me, but I kept pushing back any bad thoughts I might have about it.

Daddy gave me a boost up into the old buggy, and I took my place next to Mama. Daddy said a few words about being careful with Glory, our old horse, reminding us about how easily spooked she was these days. I'd be spooked easy too if I was that old. Actually, I think I'd just sit myself down in that straw and refuse to come out of the barn, let alone be hitched up with all that stuff in my mouth and around my neck, more than a little lame, and still expected to bring supplies in and out of town. But not old Glory. She came out into the field without any fuss, like she knew all about responsibilities. I concentrated on keeping myself still on my seat and tried to float a little so she wouldn't have quite so much weight to pull.

Just as we was about to get started, Grammy poked her head out the door and told us to take protection from the rain. Mama and me looked up at the clear blue sky.

"What rain, Mama?" my own mama asked.

"Rain's a-comin', sure enough," Grammy said. "Best take your umbrellas." She could tell we had our doubts. "Look at Gertie."

Gertie, our cow, was facin' the direction where the little breeze was blowing from, and she had her tail up in the air, a sure sign of rain according to Grammy. Mama usually paid attention to Grammy's signs, but this time she just said that we'd be back in plenty of time before any rain came and that Grammy shouldn't worry about us.

Grammy shrugged and said, "Suit yourself. You'll see." I didn't know which way to go with that one and so I just kept still about the rain issue.

Well, anyhow, Glory got Mama and me going, and we headed into town. The sun was high overhead, and the trees caught its rays on their leaves and held them tender-like. We slowed down and watched yellow and blue and black butterflies play around the cat-tails and goldenrod and Queen Anne's Lace at the side of the road, and we said how pretty those butterflies showed up against the brown and yellow and soft white, and I thought about how clever God was to have made so many different plants and creatures and have them blend together so good. Sometimes a butterfly came up close to take a good look at me and Mama, and I sat real still, hoping maybe it would settle somewhere on me. I never reached out to catch butterflies because I was afraid I would hurt them. They are the most fragile creatures and, in my mind, the most beautiful.

We went ever so slow, Glory's only speed. We didn't talk much. Mama never talked much, but I kept looking at her sideways so she wouldn't see me watching her, and I could see she felt the same happy way I did. Once she caught me lookin', and she smiled a big smile and put her hand over mine and patted me. Then she asked me if I'd like to hold the reins, and I was so happy I thought I'd burst.

As we got closer into town, that peaceful feeling left, and the excitement took over. Mama was on a mission. We went right to the General Store, and I had plenty of time to meander around and touch all the pretty things while she got her chores done. I picked up ends of bolts of fabrics and ran them through my fingers to test the softness of them. And I looked into the shiny bottles of creams and opened the jars of perfume and took little sniffs of the good smelly stuff in them. I wanted to put a little on my wrist, but no one was allowed to wear perfume in our house. I just closed my eyes and took several real deep whiffs of the one I liked the most so I would be sure to remember it. It smelled like lilacs, and I wondered why Mama didn't wear something like that. I had a feeling Daddy would like it.

The Sears Catalogue and *McCalls* was the only things I could find that day to look through, so I took *McCalls* off the rack and held it real tight against my chest and walked away so Mama couldn't see what I was up to. I turned the pages real fast to see all the pictures I could find of all the pretty men and ladies in the ads.

When Mama called out to me, I froze. I couldn't turn around, 'cause she'd see me so I pretended I was looking out on the street through the big window facing me.

"I'm here, Mama. I'm coming." I made a dash over the few feet of space to the counter where the magazines was and put mine back in its spot. Then I went to the back counter and stood behind her while she finished up.

Mama was asking the new man in charge if he would put what we owed him on her bill. He pulled a couple of sheets of paper out from a box he had sittin' there on the counter and took his time looking at them. He appeared a little flustered.

"Well, now, Ma'am, let's see here. Looks like it's been a while since you've put down anything on what's owed. You have quite a tally here, Ma'am. I'm not sure..."

I walked around Mama and stood at the counter with her.

"Well, hi there, young lady," the man said. I gave him a big smile and said "hi" right back. "What's your name?" he asked.

"Nellie," I spoke right up. "What's yours?"

Before the man could answer, Mama put her hand on my shoulder and instructed me to be polite. I could feel the heat rise up at my neck and turn my face red, and I apologized to the man for being so impolite and asking him his name.

"Oh, my, that's okay, Ma'am," he said to Mama. "My name is Mr. Connors and I'm the new owner of this place. Nellie, you're a very pretty young girl. What a lovely smile. Why don't you just come on over here and pick out a piece of candy. You like chocolate?"

I looked up at Mama real fast to see if she'd give me some idea about how I should answer his question, but she was just looking straight at the wall behind Mr. Connors, and so I ventured out on my own and said, "Yes, sir. I do."

"Well, then, come on over here. My treat," my new friend said.

I hoped my smile didn't take up too much of my face. The only time any of us ever got candy was at Easter time and Christmas, so this was a major event going on in the General Store. I looked back at Mama, and she was lookin' right back at me this time.

"It's okay, Nellie," she said. "Be sure to thank the nice man."

Mr. Connors and Mama watched me pick out the piece of chocolate like it was the most important choice that would take place in the store the entire day, and after I settled on what I wanted, he looked back at the paper in his hand and said, "Well, I think we can take care of this today, Mrs. Ruthford. Glad to have you as a customer." Him and Mama shook hands, everybody thanked everybody, and we headed out towards Glory.

Well, I'd thought the ride into town was pretty wonderful, but the ride back home was even better. I asked if Little Edith could come over to our house soon, and Mama said that would be fine. Then I told her how one time this last summer Little Edith and me climbed up the back hill to the berry bushes and picked and ate so many blueberries that Edith got tummy cramps and had to stick her finger down her throat to up-chuck. I told how she made horrible gaggy noises, and how her mouth was all purple, and how I couldn't stop laughing for some reason.

That made Mama laugh, and it was a good sound.

Usually Mama didn't laugh much. Didn't have time. She had us ten kids and Grammy and Daddy, when he was home, to clean, cook, can, and wash for. Once when Daddy was still at the mines, I woke up in the middle of the night and tiptoed out to the kitchen and found her sitting at the table with her head down on her hands. I was scared at first, seeing her like that so late and still dressed with her apron on. She was so quiet, except her shoulders was quivering just a little, and when I whispered her name, she jumped and brought her head up. But she didn't look at me right away.

I said, "Are you all right, Mama?" And she just nodded like she couldn't say nothin'. "Are you crying?" I asked her.

She turned around, wiping her face off with her hands, and said she was just fine and went over to the washboard and the stack of clothes lying there on the floor and got back to work.

I wanted to keep thinkin' about Mama and how I might be able to help her out more, but I kept getting interrupted by other thoughts. The pretty things at the general store kept flashing up in my mind, and my nose wiggled every time I remembered the smell of lilacs. Then I started thinking about how Mr. Connors had said I was pretty. Mama clearly didn't like him saying that, I know, but he did say it, and he didn't have to. He could have said, "Well, you are a nice, friendly girl." Or he could have just said, "I'll bet you like candy." But he had definitely said that I was pretty. I tried to think if anyone else had said that to me before, and I was sure that no one had.

Mama broke into my thoughts and told me to reach into her purse. She said she had a surprise for me. I brought her purse up on my lap and reached in.

"An orange!" I shouted the words right out. "You got us an orange!"

She made that wonderful happy sound again and told me to break it open so, if we wanted, we could have it right then. We cut it into four sections and took our time eating them.

When we was finished, she said, "Now, Nellie, you'd better not tell the others about our special treat. I couldn't buy enough for everyone, and I just thought we should have a little something for doing our errands."

I loved having a secret between just Mama and me, and I hoped that there might be a lot more coming. Maybe the two of us was on the verge of getting real close.

I wondered how Old Phoebe would take to that, and I figured it wouldn't be good.

We almost made it home before the rains came. Got to the bridge no more than a half a mile from our place when it came out of nowhere. Just a shower really, but it pretty much soaked us. We parked Glory and the wagon under the oak tree out front and made a big dash up to the front porch. Darned near ran right into Grammy and some other people as they was coming out the door.

"Didn't expect you back this soon," Grammy said. I knew she wanted to say something about us being soaked, but she contained herself. "This here is the Jefferson family. They was getting ready to leave when the rains came. How was your trip to town?"

While the grownups talked, I took a good look at the Jefferson kids out of the corner of my eye. The girl was younger than me. Her hair was the color of Little Grace's, and she had the bluest eyes I'd ever seen. She looked so fragile and fine that I felt big and rough next to her. The boy was a lot younger and was antsy to get going.

When Mr. and Mrs. Jefferson started in talking about how nice our farm was, Mama interrupted them, which took me by surprise because she was always sayin' how it was impolite to do that. She told everyone there how me and her was soaked to the bones, and how we should get inside and dry off. We all said how nice it was to meet each other, and Mama directed me through the door.

"Who are those people, Mama," I said. "What are they doin' here?"

But she was back to bein' like her old self and told me to never mind. "It's nothing for you to be concerned about, Nellie," she said real agitated like. "Grammy has some business with them. If she wants to tell us about it, she will."

I knew not to ask any more questions.

The church always had a social every year to celebrate the last harvest. Families from town and from out on farms like ours got together on a Sunday that Preacher thought was the right one to mark the end of the harvesting, and everybody that one day acted like they was the best of friends. I never cared much for those socials because I ended up spending most of my time just wanderin' around tryin' to look busy.

See, I didn't know the girls my age very good even though I saw them at church and prayer services most every week. I never could find much to say to them. Matter of fact, I wasn't much in the way of conversation with too many people my own age, not even at school. I felt better around adults. Grammy said I was just at that awkward age and that I'd blossom sooner or later.

When the day of the social came up—the fall one I'm talkin' about—I was sure I was about to start blossoming, and I took more time than usual to get ready to make sure I looked as good as I could and checked myself out in front of our mirror. I was thinkin' again how Mr. Connors thought I was pretty, and I was looking to see if it might be true. Old Phoebe walked in just as I was putting the brush through my hair one more time.

"Enough of your preening, Nellie," she told me, frowning like I'd done something really wrong. "Vanity is the devil's poison to pull you from Jesus. Cast it away and think not of yourself, but of the Lord's work."

"I can't see what Jesus would find harmful in a person's tryin' to be their best."

"You don't know a thing, sister. You'd just better guard yourself against the evils of this world or you will surely have trouble all your life."

I didn't like to be too close to Phoebe when she was in one of her preachin' and foreseein' moods, so I dodged past her and muttered that she didn't know as much as she thought she did and maybe she should take the brush to her hair and try to make the best of what the Lord had given her. I just couldn't let her have the last word.

At five we all headed for the church down the road toward West Carlisle. The yard was packed with families, and the long trestle tables was covered with food the women had brought. We got there just in time for Preacher's speech about our little community and the importance of church-going. Then he said a prayer and thanked the Lord for all of His blessings and reminded Him to continue to send us a lot more. After that, we all said our "Amens" and dug right in.

The same people brought the same things every year, so you knew that Mrs. Fisher had made the lemon meringue pie. The cherry pie with the fancy lattice crust came from Mrs. Cooper, and the German potato salad was Mrs. Tilson's. Mrs. Taylor, from town, must have been very rich because she always brought a huge pot of beef and noodles. We brought several jars of Mama's apple butter and blueberry jam and a big basket of fried chicken. Most farmers brought fried chicken, but Mama's was the best.

Daddy was always in the thick of things with the men. I felt real proud the way they all listened to him and laughed at his jokes. He usually won playing horseshoes, and he was always the pitcher at the softball games. I wanted to hang around with Daddy, but Mama said how that would not have been appropriate.

When the boys went off and played pitch or horseshoes, I took hold of Little Grace and meandered over to where some of the girls my age was jumping rope. After we stood there for a while, Janey, who I knew a little from church prayer nights, motioned for me to come on over. Well, I wasn't so sure I wanted to join all those girls, who I didn't know all that well, and, besides, I had Little Grace to take care of so I just looked at her, trying to think what to say.

"Nellie is the best jump- roper," Little Grace said. She put her little hand on my arm and pushed me toward Janey. "Show her, Nellie."

I wanted to dig a hole and climb inside it. "Don't say that, Grace. It's...it's not nice to brag and, besides, I'm not that good." I thought I sounded a lot like Mama just then, and I knew she'd be proud of me bein' humble.

"Well," she said, "it's true."

Well, what could I do? When my new best friend asked me to play again, I said okay, and Grace sat down close by, folded her hands, and smiled so sweet.

"Jump good, Nellie," she said.

I stood in line and joined in singing the songs we all knew to help us keep the rhythm, and when it was finally my turn to jump, I started out doing what the others did before me, and I sang real nice. But then I got a little bored. See, you kept your turn so long as you didn't tangle your foot up or get too tired, and I hardly ever did either thing, ever. So I started doing some fancy things like turning around and doing some side jumps, and Little Grace kept saying, "Good, Nellie! Good!"

My new best friends got excited right along with me and turned the rope faster and sang louder and faster and we was all laughing and having such a great time and everybody was liking everybody else, and we was having so much fun, and then...and then Mama appeared and the singing stopped and the rope fell.

"Nellie, that's enough." She was whisperin' and fixin' my hair. "Look at you." She put baby Rowe down in the grass. "Your hair has come down and you were singing so loudly." She looked at the other girls and smiled at them real sweet while she told me that it was time for us to go and that I should thank the girls for being so nice.

Then she picked up baby Rowe and took hold of Little Grace's hand and stood while I stepped out of the rope. I managed to mutter, "I'm sorry I was so loud. Thank you for letting me play with you."

As I walked away from the silent faces, I willed myself to hold back the tears that was stinging my eyes and wished again for the thousandth time that I wouldn't get so red when I got embarrassed.

That very next week, Mama's two brothers and her sister and my cousins from Zanesville and Newark came for a visit. Family reunions was usually in the spring. Fact is, we'd had our reunion with all of Mama's side of the family in early June that year. Grammy said that this event coming up was just a little extra family get-together and that my aunts and uncles wanted to come back on out to the country and get away from town while it was still nice out.

"Seems like a long way to go for a casual visit when they was just here," I said, trying to figure out why there was such an interest in visitin' from my city relatives. Mama and Grammy looked at each other like they was waitin' for the other one to say something and then they both told me to nevermind.

This visit, things started out a little slow, with us all standing in a circle and everybody kind'a grinning funny-like. The moms and dads gave each other stiff hugs and quick hard raps on each others' backs, and us kids just stood there, taking a lot of interest in our feet and the grass.

Then someone said, "Well, aren't you kids going to say hi or something?"

My brothers was absolutely gaga about Uncle's new car, a shiny black Model T, so it was easy for them to break away from the circle by asking if they could go sit in the thing. When Uncle Bill said they could, they took off. I wanted to sit in it too, but when I started to follow, Mama suggested that maybe Little Edith and me and cousin Jane could go play at something while the grownups visited.

I looked around for something interesting to do, and all I could see was the swing hanging all lonely like from the big old elm tree across the lane.

"Want to go swing?" I asked with way too much enthusiasm.

So we went over there, all three of us, and I tried to figure out who should get on the darn thing first. Edith came to the rescue and said that Jane should go first. Well, standing there watching Jane swing was about as much fun as peeling potatoes. Edith came to our rescue again.

"Nellie and me can swing double," she said to Jane. "Do you want to?"

Now, I couldn't see going double with Jane so soon when we'd just met again, so to speak, so I pretended to be all unselfish-like and said that her and Little Edith could go first. Watching the two of them

23

swing together wasn't much better than watching Jane going alone, and I was thinking hard about what we could do next when I saw the boys heading for the barn.

"Hey," I blurted out, "want to go to the barn?" That brought the swinging to a stop pretty fast, and the three of us ran to catch up.

Well, we never even got to the barn before we was all laughing and talking like we really liked each other, and we had lots of fun from then on. All of us cousins tromped up to the top of the hill behind the barn, laid down in that sweet-smelling grass, tucked our hands up behind our heads and rolled down clear to the bottom, squealing all the way. We all tried to stand up together, but we was so dizzy we bumped into each other and laughed harder. Then brother John asked us girls if we'd like to have a ride on Gertie, our old cow. Well, we did, naturally, and so he pushed all three of us up on that big old back of hers and led us around the field. Jane got a real kick out of that, and I felt good to know that we was doing things she couldn't do at her place in the city.

The best part, though, was in the barn itself. We played hide and seek for a while in the empty stalls, and then me and my brothers decided we should all go up in the hayloft. Next thing we knew, all of us cousins was all bent over and climbing up the rickety stairs, one by one, holding tight to each step in front of us. Those stairs went up real high real fast, and just to climb up was a double-dare kind of thing.

It was beautiful up there in the loft. The first thing your eyes saw when you straightened up from the last step was hundreds of sun streaks climbing down through the little open spaces between the wood beams of the roof. And each one of those streaks was holding up tiny specks of hay dust everywhere, and everything was golden and you knew you was going to walk right into all of that light and color and movement. It was magical, just like my summer kitchen. You had to get used to the smell of the hay up there, it was so strong, and you had to make up your mind that you wasn't going to allow yourself to itch. It was a little too much for anyone not used to it, and my cousins was pretty anxious to head on out to somethin' different.

The last thing we did that day was play softball together. It was understood that Daddy would be the pitcher. Uncle Jim and Uncle Bill kind of organized the two teams and told us where we should play. My brothers didn't need any coaching, but they let it pass. For a while the women and Old Phoebe sat on blankets and chitchatted while we played, but then pretty soon Old Phoebe rushed over and said she wanted to join in the game.

Everybody was pretty surprised, but Daddy put her in the line-up, and when it was her turn at bat, she actually got a base hit. I'm sure Daddy was a little slow on purpose to pitch the ball to first just so she'd get on base and I was going to complain, but I bit my tongue. No sense stirring things up.

Jesus help me, but watching Old Phoebe run was something to behold. Her round tummy and big bosoms bounced up and down so, I wondered how in the world she could keep herself balanced. I didn't have any bosoms yet to speak of, and I just prayed that when I did get some, they'd be a whole lot smaller than hers because they was just downright embarrassing.

Anyway, except for them and her tummy, Phoebe was stiff as a board while she ran to first base, and by the time she got there, her neck and forehead looked like she'd just taken a dive in the creek down the road. She seemed to be havin' fun for a change though, and I was hopin' that just maybe that would be the beginning of a new Old Phoebe. That was just wishful thinking.

We took our time over supper, and when it was time for our family company to leave, we all hugged and promised to get together again real soon. The grownups said something about how they was going to miss this place, and I wanted to tell them that, shoot, they could just stop by any time, but I decided it wasn't up to me to say. Me and Grammy waved a long time there at the end of our lane 'til we couldn't see anyone anymore, and we walked back real slow and stood a while in front of the house, just lookin' and thinkin' about how much we loved the place.

She put her arm around me and sighed. "Well," she said, and that was all. There was a sadness in our walk into the house, and I didn't understand why. I'd know soon enough.

Grammy hurried to finish the quilt she was working on before the cooler weather swelled up her fingers and made them stiff. I helped her as often as I could between my chores and my school. We talked a lot while we worked. I liked to hear about the old days when her and Aunt Lizzie was young and what Mama was like when she was my age. Grammy liked to hear about what me and Edith did when we was together, and I tried to make my stories interesting for her. She got tired from time to time, and sometimes when she'd take a break, she'd tell me to come on over and sit on her lap and give her a hug.

Grammy had the biggest lap in the world, and I loved sitting on it. I'd outgrown Mama's and Daddy's laps a long time ago, but I don't think I could ever outgrow Grammy's no matter how old I got. She was a big person, and soft all over. Her hair was white, and she wore it in a huge braid that she pulled right up to the top of her head, which made her look taller than she was. Her eyebrows was white too, and when I asked her what color her eyes used to be, she said they had been blue. Her bosoms was huge, huger than Old Phoebe's, and when she put her arms around me to give me one of her hugs, it felt like I was leaning against two really soft pillows.

One day when I was sitting in her lap, I asked her to tell me another story about Mama.

"She sang or hummed no matter what she was doing," Grammy said. "And she had a lot of friends, and she was pretty. She was real smart, too. Why, she could 'a done so many different things. She could've made something really good of herself."

"What do you mean by that?" I asked her, thinking that was a funny thing to say. Didn't Grammy think Mama was really good? I knew she did. Why, nobody was any better than Mama. We all knew that.

"Oh, I just mean she could have maybe been a teacher or a nurse or something because she was so smart," she said, giving me a little hug. "But the best thing she could 'a done was be a mama to all you children, and that's just what she did."

Grammy couldn't talk much about Daddy's family. She said she never really knew them and that they'd left for somewhere else early on after Daddy and Mama was married. I got the impression that Mama had it pretty much made on this farm with her little family when she was a young girl but that Daddy didn't have it so good when he was young.

"Your daddy brought his good looks and his great personality into our lives," Grammy said. She didn't add anything else.

I knew she was thinkin' hard about something, because she was still staring out at some of her memories, and she had quit rubbing my hand. Finally, she looked back at me and gave a little laugh.

"I'll never forget, a year or so after you was born, your daddy had a great idea to buy a small drill of his own to dig water wells out here and around the countryside nearby. He thought that maybe if he could start his own business drilling wells, he wouldn't have to keep looking for work in the mines. I had a little money put aside at the time so I gave him what I had and we borrowed a little to buy us a rig.

"Well, he was excited. We all was. He went out and found the rig he could afford, and the first well he dug was the one right out there in back. Worked real good. Then he got a few jobs out at some of the neighbors' places and things was lookin' up."

She shook her head and chuckled a little.

"Well, one night he was comin' back late from a job he had just finished," she went on. "The rig was all tied up on a wagon he put together himself for carrying the thing all over the county. I told him when he built it and put the rig on it the first time that it looked awful top-heavy, but he was in a hurry, as usual, and said it would work just fine. So he left it like it was. Anyway, that one night it was real late and he was excited to get back home and show us all the extra money he'd made. He was just going lickety-split down that road, pushing Glory fast as she could go, and was almost home when he rounded the curve too fast up by the bridge yonder. Old Glory slipped a little, or the wagon in the back veered off, I don't know which. Anyway, the wagon and your daddy and our horse ended up in the creek. Wonder they weren't hurt real bad. That's how Glory got lame, you know."

She stopped there, but I had to hear the end of the story.

"What happened after that?" I said.

"Well, your daddy made sure Glory was going to be all right and got her unhitched from the wagon and rode her back here to the house. You should have seen him. Soaked all over, cussin', and just carrying on. Lordy, Lordy. I'd never seen him so shook up. It wasn't just that the horse was lame, you see. The rig was way beyond repair."

She sighed a real heavy sigh.

"Just one more idea shot to hell," she said.

I snuggled down into her arms again and felt her sadness creep into my own heart.

"Your daddy is a good man, Nellie," Grammy told me, and I could feel the effort it took for her to put some happiness into her voice. "He had some great ideas, but... Oh, Nellie, why am I rambling on like this? Things are going to be just fine, honey. Now, tell me what you and little Edith are going to do tomorrow."

The days was getting shorter, and we knew cold weather would be settin' in soon. Daddy and us big kids helped Mama clean the house and summer kitchen from ceiling to floor. We called it our fall cleaning. Mama harvested the rest of the vegetables from her garden and finished canning. When she wasn't canning and making jelly to sell, she was sewing, getting our winter clothes ready. The pretty glass jars came down from the shelves of the summer kitchen and went to stay in kitchens in town.

My special place for dancing and pretending would soon be shut up tight.

One day, in the middle of all that cleaning and sewing and canning, Mama called me into the kitchen and sat me down at the table. "Nellie," she said, "I have to talk to you about something important, and I need you to listen real close, all right?"

I nodded and said that sure, I'd listen, and she got right to the point, which was her way.

"For the next several days, maybe a week, I'll be going into Newark to do some wall papering for some people. If I can, I'll come home a couple nights, but you shouldn't count on it. What you need to promise is that you'll be real good and help out here as much as you can. Will you do that for me?"

I nodded real hard to tell her that I would be really, really good, and that she didn't have to worry. But already I was worried. Mama had never gone away before to work, and I couldn't think why she'd have to do it now, and I couldn't imagine how we'd get along without her.

"I have a real special job for you," she told me. "Real special. We have a lot of jars of jelly that we can sell—more than ever before. And what I thought your job could be is to set up a stand on Saturday like we've always done down at the end of the lane and see how many jars you can sell for us. People will like buying our jelly from you."

I sat up a lot straighter and tried real hard to keep from smiling, except it came anyway, all crooked-like.

"You and Phoebe should make a nice sign and write down on it how much each jar costs," she told me. "It will be up to you to arrange them and make them look real pretty out there. You're good at that. Make it all tidy, just like you do when you set the supper table for us. Nellie, did you hear what I said?"

"Yes, Mama. But do I have to be out there all by myself?"

"Well, someone will be in and out to check on you, of course. The boys will be in town most of the day, doing some things with Daddy, but Clyde will be here and Grammy getting things cleared up here in the house."

"Where's Phoebe going to be?"

"Phoebe's going into town with me to help out with the wallpapering."

"What about school?"

"Phoebe can afford to miss a few days of school."

I didn't say anything. I hadn't decided yet what I should say or how I should say it. Mama didn't understand why I was so quiet, and she didn't like it.

"Nellie, I really need you to do this for me," she said.

Of course I could do it, but I was thinking about being out there not too far from my swing, across the road from where I saw the face peering out of the woods.

"I'm just thinking of that man out there," I said in a very little voice, half hoping she wouldn't hear.

A little look of worry brushed across her eyes, but she only said, "Honey, have you seen anyone out there since then? It's been over a month, Nellie. Trust me. It was nothing. Daddy has asked around to see if anyone else saw someone in the woods. There's no man out there, Nellie. I'll make sure that someone keeps checking up on you. All right?"

She put her hands around mine, and we looked down at the four of them holding on to each other tight.

"Nellie," she said softly, "I need you to be a big girl for me. This is very important. I can make us some extra money in town to get some things we really need."

Another few seconds went by, and she finally looked directly at me.

"We're a little short right now, honey. Daddy didn't get his full pay from the mines, and I don't want him to go back there. I need him to be here. He needs to be with us. There's not much work around town. Lots of people are having trouble. If all of us pitch in and work real hard, your daddy can stay here with us. The boys are doing some odd jobs in town after school too. I like to wallpaper. Hopefully this job will lead to some others."

"Don't you worry. I'll sell lots of that jelly. I'll miss you, Mama."

She told me she'd miss me too and gave me a quick hug.

My thoughts was all jumbled up. I didn't want to be scared, but I was, and I wanted Mama and Daddy to understand how I felt, and I wondered why they didn't. And I already felt lonely just knowing Mama was going to be gone. And I didn't like all that talk about people in trouble and Daddy not being able to find work. There was just too much happening too fast. We was in trouble, and I didn't know what to do about it.

John and Old Phoebe came right into the kitchen then, and I knew without a doubt that they had known about Mama's business in town a long time before today. I wondered why I was the last one to be told. I was going to make a fuss about it, but I decided to keep still. I knew, without even knowing how I knew, that something important had just started in our family.

I made myself go down to the end of the drive and set up the table the next day, all the time trying to keep one eye on the woods and the other on the house. I was scared, and because my mind wasn't on what I was doin', setting up took way longer than it should have. After a while, though, I figured that Mama was right, and that thing in the woods had just been my imagination.

I sold thirteen jars of Mama's hard work that day, and I figured I had made close to three dollars. Me and Grammy counted the dimes and nickels and quarters out loud together, and when we was done, she slapped the table with her hands and shouted out a big "hurray" and gave me a tight hug.

"You made two dollars and ninety-five cents," she said. "Oh, Nellie, your family will be real proud of you."

Mama and Old Phoebe was always sayin' how being proud is a sin, and I wondered if maybe we all just might go to hell over the sale of those jars of jellies and preserves, but Grammy's excitement made me want to sell even more the next time.

I can tell you one thing. I didn't like it one bit that Mama wasn't with us. The whole place took on a weird feeling. We was all going around living our lives there, but it was all somehow whopper-jawed, and we all seemed a little like strangers to each other. We just wasn't the same people without Mama.

After the third day she'd been gone, I went to Grammy because I thought I'd pop if I couldn't talk to someone about how I felt.

"None of the other mothers around here have to work," I said. "I don't see them going off to Newark to get more money. Why can't Mama and Daddy both just work on the farm like everybody else?"

"Honey, the people you're talking about are real farmers."

"Well, so are *we* farmers," I said way too loud.

"Well, not exactly, Nellie," she explained. "We have a farm, but we don't really farm it. I mean, we've got our cow and our chickens and our gardens, but those things hardly put food on our own table. We have to find other ways to keep care of our growing family. Awe, shucks, honey, you'll understand soon enough. Right now you just need to be a good girl and help your mama and daddy however you can."

She gave me a big hug, and I knew that was the end of the conversation.

Mama came home mid-week, and we all gathered in the parlor like always for our songs and Bible reading and storytelling. But before we got started on that, we talked about how hard we had all been working. We was all puffed up with ourselves. Even Old Phoebe was being proud, smiling so when she told us how she had cleaned out the cupboards and beat the rugs and finished washing the clothes at the Jones' and how they told her she was the best help they'd had in a long time. Daddy praised me real good when it came my turn to tell what I had done, and everybody seemed pretty happy that we was two dollars and ninety-five cents richer.

I'll tell you, I sang those old church songs real good that night. Daddy picked at his guitar, Mama played her mouth harp, and Old Phoebe banged away at Grammy's organ. We sang Mama's favorite songs, *In the Sweet By and By, Rock of Ages,* and *When the Roll is Called Up Yonder, I Will Be There.* We could have gone on all night, but Daddy said we all had to turn in so we could be ready for the new day. Then he said his evening prayer and asked God to watch over us during this difficult time and to allow Mama to stay here at home with us again real soon.

There it was again, that talking about bad times. My happiness fluttered away, and that fearful feeling popped back up and made a little hole in my heart.

Mama left again on Friday, and Saturday morning I was determined to sell more jelly than before, so I set off down the lane like I meant business. I had a real mission. I was quick to set things up that time, and when I was done, I stepped back and looked at how good the jars looked the way I had lined them up. There was lots of people on the road, heading back and forth from town, but I didn't wait for the wagons to stop on their own. No sirree. I called out to the drivers and asked them if they wouldn't like to buy some of the best jellies you could find anywhere in Broomstick Valley. I did such a good job that by noon I had just a few jars left, and when Grammy called for me to come in for lunch, I yelled back and told her I wasn't hungry, that I'd come in, in just a little bit. I wanted to sell every last jar and make my family happy.

I went out on the road then and looked up and down to see if anyone was coming, but no one was in sight so I decided finally to go back in the house and see if there was any more jars left to sell. No one was around in there, so I just grabbed the couple of jars I could find and picked up the butter and sugar sandwich Grammy had made for me, and I ran back out so that I wouldn't miss any customers. I kept looking up and down the road, waiting for a buggy to come by, but there was no one around. I got real fidgety and decided to pick up some pinecones and kind a' forgot everything else. Someone close by said my name.

I looked up real fast and stumbled a little when I turned around to the voice and was mixed up 'cause I didn't know the huge man standing over there at my table. He was bigger than anyone I had ever seen, and he didn't look right.

He walked toward me real slow and kept looking up to our house, like maybe he was lookin' for someone else.

I tried to think how he knew my name. "Sold 'most all of your Mama's jelly, have ya', Nellie?" he said.

I couldn't get my voice out to answer him.

"You're pretty little to be out here all by yourself, ain't ya'?" he said. "Well, maybe you aren't so little. Let me see."

He looked at me all over and smiled, and I saw that his teeth was all yellow and brown and oily looking, and they made me feel queasy. He had on a big brown hat with a brim that was crumpled down and hid his eyes, and his face was mostly covered with a black beard like before.

"You're a big girl," he said, and his voice took on a deep breathless sound. "And you're pretty, too. Anybody ever tell you that?"

I wanted to move away from him, but I couldn't. I held my breath and prayed someone, anyone, would come and help me get away from him.

He looked away from me up to my house again, and said, "Where's your mama and daddy, Nellie? Ain't they at home? What's the matter? Cat got your tongue? Come here and tell me about what you're selling."

I didn't want to go to where he was, but Mama always told me to be polite to grownups so I did what he said.

"Tell me about this one, honey," he said, picking up one of Mama's jars. It looked real small in his hand. "Is it real good?"

His plaid shirt was unbuttoned to where his overalls buckled, and black hairs peeked out from his neck and chest. Pieces of broken leaves stuck all over him. His body was like another big world I lost myself in.

"I don't have money, Nellie," he said, putting his hand in his pocket and pulling out something. "But I have some special treasures here I think you'd like. I'll give you my treasures for a jar of jelly. Come on over here and look at what I have. See how pretty they are," he whispered hoarsely.

When he grabbed my wrist, a sob came up in my mouth and got stuck there.

A voice inside me said to yell for Daddy and to pull away, to hit and scratch, but I was frozen into myself and my body wouldn't do any of it. I was flat up against him, my face in a place it shouldn't be. He moved backward, out toward the road away from my table and he was groaning. My feet wasn't touching anything and I was having trouble breathing.

Time slowed down and stopped and all I felt was his arms holding the top of my body tight, squeezing the air out of me. The grit on his overalls pricked at my face when he grabbed my bottom and pulled me up to where his private parts was. There was something big and hard pushing against me and I knew what it was. He stood there groaning, moving back and forth, back and forth, and his hand slipped between my legs.

34

And then somewhere, someone was calling, "Nellie, Nellie, Nellie, Grams says…" The words trailed off in the wind, even though I tried hard to hold onto them.

The man stopped moving and let me slip a little.

"Nellie? Hey. Wait. Nellieeeee. What's going on down there?"

I heard someone scream "Daddy! Help!" More people was yelling and getting closer, and we stumbled, that man and me, and I fell to the ground.

Other arms lifted me again, and they belonged to George. "You're going to be all right, Nellie," he said. "You're going to be all right."

Daddy's big voice was screaming terrible things. George and me looked up to see him running fast as he could into the woods.

My brother screamed out to him, "Daddy, don't go in there. Please don't go."

I don't remember much else 'til I found myself on Grammy's bed where I stayed the rest of the day. That night I slept with Grammy too.

That's when the dream started.

It was nighttime.

I was alone in a shiny black buggy pulled by a monstrous black horse. The horse foamed at the mouth and its eyes was all white and huge with fear. We raced down a dark and narrow road with black trees, dense, on both sides.

There was no sound. The silence was deafening.

We careened around a big curve, and just then the moon came out bright and shone down on a white figure standing there in the middle of the road. It had the shape of a person, but it didn't have any face, and the body was white and quivery looking. I knew we was going to hit the thing, and I tried hard to stop the wagon, but there was no reigns for me to pull. I screamed with no sound and put my hands up to hide my eyes.

There was a horrible thump underneath me.

That's all I heard: not the wind, not the horse's hooves, nothing but the thump. I turned around in slow motion to see what I had run over. The white thing stood up from where I had run over it and turned around. Now it had black eyes, and they stared at me. I pulled myself away from those eyes, but when I got myself turned around, there was the same white thing standing in the road in front of me again. The wagon hit it again, and there was the same thump. It happened over and over again until my own sobs woke me up.

Night after night the dream came back. I laid in my bed, and I tried hard to keep my eyes open so that I wouldn't fall asleep and see the white thing I killed. I was afraid to sleep. But the dream took over even my wakeful hours, popping up whenever it wanted to.

Preacher was always saying how the devil takes over if we don't follow Jesus' rules. He said we have to be vigilant and cast out our sins or we'll be damned forever. I was afraid the devil was inside me, and the man and the dreams came because of my damnation.

Mama and Grammy said I needed to talk about everything that had happened. They told me the man would never come back, that the sheriff and the police would find him and put him away in jail and that he'd never bother anyone again. They said they was sorry they'd doubted my story in the first place, and they would never forgive themselves for taking it so lightly.

But the trouble was, I couldn't talk about it. No one wanted to talk about it. Our house grew quiet, quieter than it had ever been. Finally, the preacher was called in. I stood by the window the day he came, and the sight of him walking up our lane, dressed in his black suit and black hat, scared me so that I ran to the bedroom and locked the door behind me. For the first time in my life, I refused to do Mama's bidding: I would not talk to Preacher. She shooed all of the kids out of the house, and the four grownups sat down in the kitchen and whispered while I sat on the floor in the corner of my room, wrapped in Grammy's quilt, determined to stay put. But I had to know what everybody was sayin' about me, so I tip-toed to the kitchen door and put my ear against it.

"I understand your anger, John," that preacher was saying, "but you must let the authorities do their job. What's important now is Nellie. She is a lamb of God, but the serpent is always close by, tempting even the little children, the same as he tempts us all."

"Are you blaming my daughter for all of this?" I heard Daddy say.

"I'm not blaming anyone, son. I'm just suggesting that maybe you need to rein her in a little. Teach her Godliness. Have her attend prayer meetings, and..."

"Don't you even begin to suggest any of this was that little girl's fault. You listen to me, dammit."

"Hold on, John. Let's put it this way. That man was evil, no doubt about it, and the authorities will deal with him as will the greatest authority of all. I have no doubt he will burn in Hell. I'm just saying that you've got to rein the girl in."

I could hear Daddy muttering something that sounded a lot like cursing and Mama making those noises that she always made when she wanted him to settle down.

"You take her hunting. You allow her to climb trees. When she comes to church, she dozes until the singing starts," the preacher said, "and then she belts out the songs like she was at a picnic. She's headstrong and she's so friendly with everyone that..."

Someone pushed a chair back.

"You're crazy as hell, you know that? I want you out of my house."

"Get control of yourself, my son. Get control. Nellie is a child of God. I'm not saying otherwise. I'm just saying that she is strong spirited and could easily be misunderstood. Watch her closely. Bring her up to be a woman of God."

There was a commotion on the other side of the wall then, and I ran back to my room. The last thing Daddy yelled as he bolted out the front door was, "And you are so full of shit."

Now the thing is, I knew where Daddy stood, but I wasn't sure about Mama. She had been so quiet that I had the horrible feeling that maybe she thought Preacher was right. After all, she knew more religion than Daddy did.

I couldn't sleep because of my dream. I couldn't eat. My brothers and sisters stayed clear of me because I couldn't talk. Old Phoebe was the only one left with a voice.

"I warned you," she said, "but you wouldn't listen. Give yourself up to Jesus before it's too late. Trust in Him and He will deliver you from Satan. Are you listening, sister?"

She grabbed me by the shoulders and pushed her sweaty face right up to mine.

"Confess your sins at prayer meeting Friday night, Nellie. Pray for forgiveness, and peace will come to you. Turn everything over to the Lord, and he'll protect you from yourself."

I wanted peace. I wanted to start out fresh. I wanted to be good. I promised her I would go up to the altar at church that Friday night and ask Preacher to help make me clean.

As usual, the church was full for Friday's prayer meeting. Phoebe held onto my arm and told me in a low voice that I would walk out of that church that night a whole new person. She was so excited for me that she was breathing hard and sweating buckets. The singing was loud and the prayers was long. Preacher looked directly at me during his sermon, but I didn't hear any of it. I was waiting for the part when he would invite sinners to go up to him so he could cast out the evil in them.

The time finally came. The congregation rose up and said their "amens," and the preacher stood there with his arms stretched out to all of us and begged the sinners to come forward. Mrs. Potts, the piano player, banged out the hymn, and everyone shouted out the words and swayed back and forth with their arms up in the air, pleading with Jesus to forgive all of us. Phoebe pushed me over to the aisle and whispered that now was my chance to find salvation.

I was sweating too by then. I knew my time had come, but I didn't know what I was supposed to do. The "halleluiahs" and the "amens" got louder, and Preacher's voice roared over it all. I prayed the devil would leave me once I got up in front of all those people and Preacher laid his hands on me. I walked up slowly with my eyes on Preacher. I heard him and Daddy say my name at the same time, and I stood still for a minute, looking back and forth between the two of them. And then I just kept on the way I had started.

"Brothers and Sisters, praise God," Preacher called out. "Here is a lamb of Jesus. Our own little Nellie come to be saved. She has felt the sting of Satan in the worst possible way."

The place was quiet for the first time that night, and I felt everyone's eyes boring into my back. They already knew what had happened out there at my house with the big man, and I felt myself shrinking from their pitying looks. I knew what they was thinking.

"Are you ready to turn your life over to Jesus and cast out evil, Nellie?" Preacher wanted to know. "Are you going to give up vanity and honor your precious mother and behave like Jesus would have you behave, full of piety and love of Him?"

He put his hands on my shoulder then and turned me around for everyone to see. "People, pray for this Lamb," he shouted. "Pray that Jesus will enter her heart and that she will accept Him so that He can cast out the devil inside her."

Then he began to twist and turn me like he was pulling me away from something, and he kept saying Jesus' name over and over, and the people in front of me raised their hands and closed their eyes and rocked back and forth and said "Amen" and "Praise God." I tried hard to feel Jesus come into me and push Satan out. I gritted my teeth and closed my eyes and got dizzy with trying, but I didn't feel nothing.

Didn't feel Jesus' spirit move in me at all.

I was damned forever. I broke away from Preacher and ran down the aisle and out into the cool night with his voice ringing out behind me.

Daddy appeared out of nowhere. He picked me up, and I wrapped myself around him and told him how sorry I was that I embarrassed my family so much back there and how sorry I was that I couldn't be saved. And then he told me that neither one of us would ever, ever set foot in that place again. He cussed somethin' awful and said how the inside of that place was like a carnival. I buried my head into his big shoulders and allowed myself to feel all empty.

The next day no one would look at anyone else. Finally, just before it was time for me to go to bed, Mama and Grammy told me that maybe a change would do me a world of good. That was how it happened that I moved in with Aunt Lizzie for a while.

Aunt Lizzie's log house was tiny: just one room divided into parts by furniture. One part was the kitchen with a round table, two chairs, a wood burning stove, and a washtub. The sitting room was the middle part of the room, and in it was her big stuffed rocker, a settee, and a table with her lamp and books. Her bed and nightstand took over what space was left. In the back was a few stairs that went up to a little attic where my bedroom was supposed to be. There was a bed up there and a small bureau. A bright rag rug was on the floor, under the tiny window that opened up to the back field.

Mama helped me put my clothes in the bureau and stayed for an early supper and then left so she could get back before dark. Lizzie and me helped ourselves to another piece of cake and ate it out on her steps outside, chitchatting about this and that. But it felt awkward 'cause we was trying too hard to appear happy to each other, so I told her I was sleepy and asked if I could just go on up to bed.

I couldn't take my eyes off the open window. I needed to know if someone was going to try to climb in after me. I tried real hard to be good and stay there, but I just couldn't. The owls and the wind in the trees spooked me, and my body got stiff with every creak the roof made. And so I tiptoed down the stairs and stood by Lizzie's bed. She was awake, and it seemed like she was expecting me.

"Can't sleep, Honey?" she said, pushing the covers down beside her. "Why don't you just climb in here with me for a while. See if this is better. It's cold up there in the attic and not very hospitable. I never liked it much up there neither. This will be better."

Her bed was the softest thing I had ever settled down in, and I told her so. She explained that it was made out of goose feathers, and we talked a while about that. I snuggled up against her skinny body and felt cozy. Later in the night I ventured over to the other side there and stretched out and realized for the first time how good it was to lie down where there was room for me.

She tucked me into her own bed every night after that and sat and talked with me about whatever came into our heads: like how we liked lemonade, and how the sheep was sheared in the spring, how she beat Daddy at cards, and how her husband died so many years ago from an accident on the farm. I laughed at all her stories except the last one, and then she told about all the things her and Grammy did when they was young. Sometimes I fell asleep in the middle of one of them stories, and when the dream came she was right there and shushed my crying and said that I was safe, that no one would ever hurt me again.

The sun found its way through the window beside Aunt Lizzie's bed every morning, and its warmth on my face woke me up. I took my time getting out of that good place, stretching my legs and my arms out as far as I wanted. And I thought about how when I grew up the first thing I'd get for myself was a big old feather bed just like that one. I'd think about how nothing could be better than that bed, but then I'd smell the bacon and eggs frying in Lizzie's big iron skillet, and that smell pulled me up and over to the old oak table where she'd be waiting for me.

Each day, we spent some of the hours baking, and she taught me how to make her special German Chocolate Cake. We meandered over soft hills, around the sheep, and up into the woods where the mushrooms would pop up in the spring, and she promised me that we would pick them together then. She grabbed her sheep and had me feel their soft wool that was long now, and she read me stories and cut out paper dolls, and we drew dresses for them on pieces of colored paper and cut them out too. She was surprised that I never did that at home. I made believe the dolls was me and my friends going to birthday parties.

Lizzie taught me how to play gin so I could play with Daddy sometime when we was alone together.

Then one day she brought out her Ouija Board.

"Now, I'm going to teach you how to use this thing, 'cause it's helped me a lot in the past, and I figure someday it could help you too. You can't tell your mama or your grammy that I taught you, though. I'm not sure they'd approve, 'specially your mama."

I asked what it was used for and when Aunt Lizzie said that you ask it questions and it gives the answers, I wanted to know how it did that.

"Spirits," she said. "Good spirits that want to help us out. You could call them guardian angels. They move our hands to give us the answers."

"You mean the spirits is here, right where we are?"

"Yep." She saw me look around the room. "'Course you can't ever see them. Spirits are invisible. That's why they call 'em that. But don't worry. They're good ones."

"What about Jesus? I thought we was supposed to pray to Him and He'd give us all the answers we need."

"Well, these spirits kind 'a work for Jesus. Think of it that way. Just trust in it. Concentrate real hard and believe in it, or it won't work."

Then she showed me how we had to put our hands lightly on the thing that moved around over the board and just allow it to go wherever it wanted to. She said it would move to "yes" or "no" or would spell out answers, depending on the questions we asked.

Aunt Lizzie had a lot of questions to ask, and the board gave her all the answers, and she seemed happy with them. I kept quiet and decided I'd just wait a while to talk to the spirits. She told me we'd try it again in a few days when I was ready.

I was confused.

Jesus was standing out there somewhere waiting to be called upon to help, according to Preacher, and there was His helping spirits, according to Aunt Lizzie, talking to people through a piece of wood. And then there was Satan, powerful as could be, lurking in the shadows ready to take people into the depths of hell if they didn't behave proper or had bad thoughts. This was all too complicated to reason through, and I didn't feel quite ready to talk to the Ouija.

Things got even more confusing.

Aunt Lizzie liked to sit in her rocker and let me brush and pin up her hair fancy. Sometimes it looked real good, but sometimes when we stepped back and looked at it, we couldn't stop laughing, she looked so strange. We always ended those hair sessions with a Sen Sen from the little box she kept right there beside her chair. We both liked the strong taste of the little black pieces of breath refreshers and how they made our tongues tingle.

Anyway, I couldn't help but notice that when we was finished with our little treat and she got up from her chair, she held on to the back of it and stopped it from rockin'. I asked her about that.

"Well, honey, when a rocker is allowed to go back and forth on its own with no one sitting there, it's kind'a like inviting spirits to come in and sit a spell. Now, you never know if those spirits hanging around is good or evil so it's always best to just stop the rocker and play it safe."

"So," I said. "If there's good and bad spirits all around us, what keeps the bad spirits from telling you the wrong answers on the Ouija?"

She thought about that for a second and then said that only good spirits could get to you through the Ouija. That's just the way it works. Everyone knew that.

I wanted to work through that some more, but I decided not to right then. I needed to have more faith, the way Lizzie said I should. I took to stopping the rocker, too, when I got out of it, and I walked a little more careful around the cabin, makin' sure I didn't run into one of them spirits by mistake. I sure didn't want to get one of the bad ones riled. I wasn't afraid, exactly, because Aunt Lizzie wasn't, but let's just say I became more aware while I was there and paid more attention to the air around me.

The dream didn't stop coming, and one night when it woke me up again, and Lizzie came over to me, I flung myself into her arms and began to cry buckets. Once I started, I just couldn't stop. She held me tight and told me to let it all out because that was how I'd get well.

"Sometimes," she said, "if you tell a person about what you're feeling, if you open up your heart and share your thoughts, that other person can take some of the hurt away and maybe find a way to put an end to the bad things. Tell me about your dream. Let's talk about the bad man. Maybe I can help it all go away."

I told her what happened, and I told her how I should have run away from the man. I told her how I was too friendly, like when I was in town with Mama and was talking with Mr. Conners. I even told her how I liked to dance in the summer kitchen and how I dreamed about flying. I admitted that I didn't like to go to church, and I even told her how tired Mama looked and how I hated it when she had to go away and work. I blurted out how hungry I always was and how great her pancakes and sausages and cakes was and how I liked the quiet there.

And she listened. She didn't give me answers; in fact, she didn't say much of anything. She just let me go on talking. After a long time, I ran out of things to tell her except to say how much I loved her.

And she said, "I love you so much, too, Little Nellie." And that's all she needed to say.

She said that what we both needed right then was a huge piece of cake and some milk, and while she was getting it ready, I curled up again in that soft bed of hers and laid down. And the next thing I knew it was daylight.

I had slept through the night without another dream.

After breakfast, she combed the tangles out of my hair and put a real pretty pink bow around my head, the way the girls in town wore theirs, and she asked me if I'd take a little walk with her up the back hill.

We walked real slow and kept quiet for a while, and it felt good.

She said, "You know, Nellie, I been thinking about everything you told me yesterday. You told me a lot of important things, and they've weighed heavy on my heart. I'd like to tell you what my thoughts are about all of that. Is that all right with you?"

I told her it was fine with me, and I was amazed that a grownup would ask me if she could speak her mind.

"Then, why don't we just climb up there to the top and sit down a spell," she said. "I think better when I'm sittin'."

So we finished our climb up the hill and found an old log to rest on while Aunt Lizzie talked.

"The first thing I want to say is that you are not a bad girl, Nellie." She slapped her knee to show she really meant it and started to stand up but decided against it. "You're a good girl, a damned good girl. Fact is, they don't come much better than you. The devil isn't in you, honey. No indeed. And anyone who tells you that kind of nonsense, well, you just don't pay no nevermind. Why, a young girl like you is supposed to be happy. You're *supposed* to run. Run as fast as you can and keep practi-cin' to get faster. If you feel like singing, by golly, you should sing at the top of your lungs. And if you think you can fly, why, you just go ahead and do it. Bein' happy is what the good Lord wants for us. Why would He put us here and create all the beauty in the world if He didn't want us to enjoy it? All that hell-fire and brimstone they preach down there at that church, why, it's just a bunch of nonsense."

She had started out calm, but as she talked her voice kept going up higher and louder, and I took a quick look around to make sure no one else was there to hear her say the preacher was full of nonsense.

"Who else besides that crazy preacher is telling you about the devil and how bein' young and happy is a sin? No, nevermind, I don't want to know. Now you listen to me and listen good. You had nothing at all to do with that horrible man and what he did. You was just in the wrong place at the wrong time. That's all. And God will see to it that He pro-tects you better from now on. I'm prayin' on it, and so are a lot of other people."

She stood up then and put her hands on her skinny hips and the way she looked, well, I was prepared to believe every word she said. "Now, just because the Lord wants us to be happy don't mean life is going to be easy," she explained. "It ain't always a bowl full of cherries. That's for sure. Every single person in this whole wide world has troubles from time to time. And there are those who can deal with trouble and there are those who can't."

Aunt Lizzie was getting herself real worked up, I could tell. She looked out across the field like there was other people out there listenin' to her.

45

"The real test in life is to be able to cope with hard times," she said. "Some people just can't deal with what is dealt them. But you're not one of those weak ones, Nellie. I know that. And so do you."

She was right, I thought. I didn't think I was weak. I knew I wasn't, but that was part of my trouble. I was too loud, too boisterous, too friendly, too...everything. I wondered if I could get rid of some of all that and still be strong, still be me

"Here's what I want you to do," Aunt Lizzie told me, bending down to put her long, boney hand on my shoulder. "In times of trouble, you make yourself dig way down deep inside you where your strength is, and you tell yourself you don't intend to be sad or hurt by anybody or any thing, and, by golly, you'll survive. We have to have fortitude, Nellie. We have to find ways to be strong, to get down there to where our in-ner-most being is and say, 'I can face this. I can see it through. I can rise above it.' Do you understand, sweetheart?"

I told her I thought I did, but she could see something else on my face because she said that she'd really got herself in a twit, hadn't she, and she just burst out laughing, and before I knew it I was laughing, too, and we couldn't stop ourselves, and it felt wonderful.

When Lizzie finally caught her breath back, she started a chant, "Fortitude. Fortitude. Fortitude." And I joined in. I got up off that log and held her hand and marched down the hill to her little house, saying "Fortitude!" all the way, and when we got there, we raised our hands up together and gave each other big hugs and shouted, "Hurray."

I didn't count the days I was there with Aunt Lizzie, but after our big talk, I started missing my family and my farm. The dream still popped into my head whenever it wanted to, but I was learning how to shove it out with other thoughts, thoughts about how I was supposed to be happy, just like Lizzie said to do. It was easier now because she kept telling me what a clever and good girl I was. One morning after break-fast, I asked her if I could go home.

There is nothing better than going back home, even if the place you're going away from is pretty wonderful. It had been so good to be at Aunt Lizzie's house. It was quiet and orderly, and I could move around in it without bumping into someone. But my family wasn't there. I promised Jesus that I would never complain again about my brothers and sisters and their noise and them bossing me and teasing me because I loved them. I loved them so very much, and I couldn't wait to get back there in the middle of all of them.

They must have felt the same way because when me and Aunt Lizzie pulled up to my front porch that day, everyone poured out of the house and told me how happy they was that I was back. Little Grace finally pushed her way through everyone and looked up at me with the most beautiful smile, and when I pulled her up to me, she put her little hands around my face and brought hers real close to mine and whispered, "Are you going to be all right now, Nellie? Did Aunt Lizzie make the dreams go away?"

I told her that I was going to be just fine and that I wouldn't ever leave again.

Soon after I came back home, Grammy finished her quilt, and the day she said we could see it, we got ourselves together in the parlor before supper and spread it out on the floor in the middle of the room. She'd made a ring pattern, one of the hardest ones to do, and the colors blended into each other perfect. We said we thought it was the prettiest one yet, and we meant it. I couldn't wait to hear which one of the beds she would put it on, and I crossed my fingers that it would go to us girls.

I didn't want to seem too pushy or too greedy so I kept quiet, but then I couldn't stand it any longer and asked what we was all wanting to know. "Grammy, can you tell us now who you're going to give your quilt to?"

We all got real quiet, waiting for her to speak.

"Well," she said, "I've decided to do something different this year. I'm selling this quilt." She said it real fast and then rushed right on like she didn't want any discussion. "All of our quilts are in pretty good shape, and you all have been working so hard wallpaperin', cleanin', fixin' up around here that I decided that I can do my part to help out my family by selling this. I think it should bring in a good price. One of the ladies at church knows someone who has a booth at the county fair. She's going to take the quilt for me and see if she can sell it."

Daddy spoke up. "Your quilt is beautiful, Hannah. It's a real generous thing you're doing, and we all thank you, don't we, family?"

What's he talking about? I thought. We never have ever sold one of Grandma's quilts. Why now? And then I knew. She was selling it for the same reason Mama was hangin' paper and Phoebe and the boys was workin'. We was out of money, and we didn't have any other way of getting more. I felt something pass between the three grownups. Couldn't say what it was, but I felt it, and Little Grace felt it too, I think, because she looked real hard at Grammy, crawled up on her lap, and snuggled against her.

The days passed quick with all of us working so hard to get ready for winter, and when the breeze turned cooler, a sadness sat down on us. The sun still shined bright most days, but the leaves that was left on the trees was fading to brown, and we had trouble remembering how pretty things had been not so long ago. Daddy made bonfires for us on weekends when we didn't have school, and he told us stories at night before we went to bed, but he didn't make them as exciting as before or maybe we was just too tired and too hungry to listen close. During meal times, we silently fretted over what wasn't bein' put on our plates and tried hard to not let our disappointment show.

The summer kitchen, my place of make believe, was empty, but I felt a need to go to it one last time before the snows came. I sneaked in one afternoon right before supper. The sun was too low and weak to make a show of coming through the window, but there was nothing for it to climb into and sparkle through anyway. The jars was gone. I stood and waited for the urge to dance and pretend again. But the feeling didn't come to me.

My dancin' days was over.

None of us wanted to go to school, not even Old Phoebe. Every day we all came up with excuses not to go, but Mama wouldn't have any of it. An education was important, she said, and we just had to deal with what we was going through.

One night late, when I was worrying hard about things and sleep just wouldn't come to me, I decided to just get up and walk the worry off. I climbed real quiet up over Little Grace at the left side of the bed and tip-toed out to the hall. There was a light on in the kitchen, and I could hear Mama whispering.

"I'm afraid they won't let us buy anything more," she was saying. "I had to practically beg him to let me sign again. He told me he'd let me this time, but he was low on cash, too, and just couldn't afford to let people charge any more. I felt bad for him. I did, John. But what are we going to do?" I heard fear in her voice, and it didn't sound right coming from her because she was the strong one.

"Don't worry, honey," I heard Daddy say. "Don't worry. I promise I'll figure something out, see if I can't take on some more work in town."

"Me and the girls can bake some pies and cakes to sell," Grammy said. I was surprised that she was in there because she usually didn't stay up that late. "I'll bet Mr. Conners would let us sell them in his store. But we'll need money to buy the ingredients."

Someone went over and picked up the kettle and poured from it. They was having more coffee, just like they always did when they was having serious talk.

"Here's what we're going to do," Grammy said. "I still have a little bit put aside for an emergency. Kept it a secret so we wouldn't be tempted to use it. It's my 'rainy day' money and the situation we've got here is more like a storm. It's a good time to use it, that's my opinion. Got some odds and ends of stuff stashed away up there in the attic, too. Stuff I never even get out any more. I was going to give it to the girls some day. But shucks, when the time comes, they probably wouldn't want it anyhow. Yes, sir, we're going to sell it. Sell it all. With that little stash of money we've got and what we can get from that junk up in the attic, we should be able to hold on 'til those people make up their minds about this place."

Mama and Daddy both said "No," and started talking at her at the same time, but she told them to hush.

"We're going to pay back part of what we owe Mr. Conners and then we're going to bake," she said, all determined-like. "Won't make much, but it will help, and we'll be able to walk around town without people talkin' about us. I have never owed anyone a penny in my life, and I'm not about to start now. We're going to dig in and get over this. The kids will have to help, too. Phoebe and the older boys can work after school, and Nellie will help out more around here. Things may be hard right now, but we'll all be okay.

"We're blessed in so many ways," Mama said. "I just pray this next one is as easy as the others."

I could not believe the talk that was goin' on, on the other side of that wall. Next one? What next one? And what does she mean that people are thinkin' about this place?

"Let's get some sleep now," Grammy said. "I'll pull my stuff together in the morning. You can take it into town soon as we get it all bagged up. The sooner we get this going, the better."

Concentrating at school the next day was harder than usual. I couldn't get my mind away from making up pictures of Mama and Daddy selling Grammy's treasures, and I felt more mad than sad. And I pictured Mr. Conners telling Mama that she couldn't buy anything more. And I looked over at Phoebe and Clyde and George and Homer, and I worried about them having to go off to work every day.

Dammit, I thought, *this is just too much.*

I realized too late that I had just banged my book down on my desk and that Miss Jensen was standing over me with a worried look on her face.

"Do you need to go outside, honey?" she said in a low voice.

"No, ma'am," I whispered. "I'm going to be okay."

And I meant it. Right then and there I decided that I was going to have "fortitude."

John was hired on by a dairy farmer to work after school and help haul the milk to the dairy on Saturdays, but the other boys couldn't get work, and they felt real bad about that. Old Phoebe took a job cooking dinners for some rich family on the other side of town, towards Newark. She worked all day Sundays cooking and cleaning up, and she went after school whenever they needed her. Daddy talked his way into some part-time work with a cabinetmaker. He didn't know the first thing about that kind of work, but, as Aunt Lizzie always said, he could talk his way into most anything. I guess most people was done with sprucin' up their houses, 'cause Mama couldn't find anyone who wanted wallpapering done. She scrubbed our clothes and mended and cleaned twice as hard as she ever did.

Me, I became a great cake-maker. My German Chocolate cakes got better and better, and I had trouble keeping my pride down when Mr. Conners told us how much his customers raved about our baked goods. I started thinking how maybe we should open our own place where we could sell our pies and cakes. I would be the head baker, and I would be the person out front selling everything to all the people. I'd get to be famous, and I would make all kinds of money for my family.

When I told Mama and Grammy about my plans, they said that was a wonderful idea, but maybe I should wait until I was a little older and finished school. They pointed out that eleven-year-olds was usually not allowed to set up their own shops. When I reminded them that I was going to be twelve by the end of the month, they looked at each other like they was surprised or something. I asked if they remembered, and they said why sure, how could they forget a day like that?

Sure enough, my birthday came and went quick as a flash. Didn't get any presents. None of us ever did 'cause there was too many of us to buy for. The only gift was Aunt Lizzie and the beef and noodles she brought for supper.

I filled up my stomach and slept real good that night.

All of our extra work didn't amount to much, seein' as how our plates didn't take on any more food than usual. We went to bed earlier every night so we could cut back on lamp oil. Oh, we was careful, all right, but no matter what we did, we couldn't seem to get ahead.

Then one day Daddy announced to us at the supper table that he would be taking a little trip to visit his cousin in Zanesville the next day. The cousin worked at a factory there that was hiring extras to work on a temporary basis. He said he'd come home whenever he could between days off—if he got days off. He sounded excited about the new job he might be getting, but the rest of us couldn't muster up much to match it. He left the next morning. Left in our only wagon, with our only horse pullin' it.

He got home on a Saturday, exactly ten days after he left, and was his old self again, all happy and teasing us and giving Mama little hugs. He said he wouldn't tell us anything about his stay in Zanesville 'til we was all together, and he went back out with our buggy and Glory and picked up John and Phoebe and brought them home. But he still made us wait 'til after supper for the really good news he had, and I thought I'd pop, I was so excited.

"Well," he said, clearing his throat to make room for the rest of his words to come out, "While I was in Zanesville, I talked to my cousin who you've never met, except Mama and Grammy of course. Name is Thomas, on my Daddy's side."

Who cares about Cousin Thomas? I thought. *Just tell us the good news.*

"Well, Cousin Thomas knows someone who owns a big house in Thurston that's used as a kind of boarding house for railroaders. The owner has someone else live there and manage the place for him."

Daddy got a smile on his face and looked around at us all real slow, making us wait a little longer for his good news. I couldn't imagine what all this had to do with us.

"Well," he said, and he dragged out that word forever. "Guess what? The man who has been running the place is quitting. Actually, he's quit already, and the owner needs someone to take that man's place."

He paused so long I thought I'd split.

"And he asked me to take the job," he said.

"You're going to live somewhere else, Daddy?" It was George, and he sounded scared.

Daddy laughed. "No, son. I'm not going to live anywhere else again without all of you. Nope. We're all going. We're all going to move to that house in Thurston. All of us."

He was talking fast now and his arms spread themselves out toward us the way Preacher's sometimes did on Sunday mornings.

"We're going to move together and start a brand new life there. We'll have a wonderful time. We'll be able to buy new clothes. Grams will be able to start a new quilt for us, and Mama won't have to work. The school is right there in town so you won't all have to walk so far every morning, and Phoebe will be able to get to the church whenever she wants and take classes. You'll have lots of friends close by to play with. It will be so good for all of us."

I waited for Mama to say something, or Grammy, but they was busy looking at their hands. My heart got all tight in my chest, and I felt something like a wad of spit-up come up into my throat.

"What about our farm here, Daddy?" I asked. "Are we keeping our farm to come home to?"

His smile left his face, and he shook his head. No words came out.

"Yeah, Daddy, what about our farm here?" my big brother asked.

Daddy looked at Grams, and she took over for him. "We're giving up the farm, honey. Your daddy and mama and me have talked about doing it for some time now. Not that we want to, really. We all love it here, but it's just time to move on."

She got kind of stuck on the last words, and I knew it would be hard for her to get more out.

Now it was Mama's turn. "Just think how nice it will be to have all that extra room," she told us. "There are how many bedrooms, John?"

"Six, Mama, six bedrooms. Course, they won't all be for us. We'll rent some out, but we'll definitely have more room. There's a long front porch where we can all sit in the summers and look out onto the street and watch the people go by. There's a big kitchen, and the parlor is as big as all downstairs here. Why," he chuckled, "we'll have so much room we'll have to hunt for each other in there."

I'll admit that the porch and the extra bedrooms and all the other big spaces sounded real good. But...the farm? How could we leave our home?

"When do we leave, Mama?" It was brother Clyde.

"Well, there are a few things we need to take care of here, but probably real soon," she said. "We'll likely leave real soon." She didn't say nothin' else. No one in that room was feeling really happy-go-lucky at that particular time except Daddy, maybe, and we was all having trouble pretending we was.

"Is someone going to take our house?" Little Grace's lower lip was quivering.

"Honey," Daddy said, "a real nice family will move in. There's a little boy your age and a little girl about the age of Nellie, and...well, anyway, we got a good price for it, and we'll have the money to get a real good start on our new home. And here's the good part. Here's the really big surprise. Once we get ourselves settled, we're going to see about buying a truck."

Now that bit of information took the breath out of all of us. Even Mama and Grammy looked surprised. We was getting a truck. That perked us up.

"Yes indeed," he said, and I could see that he was real proud of himself. "We're going to have a great time in Thurston. In no time at all we'll forget this place and just think how fortunate we was to get this chance. You just wait and see."

We didn't go back to school. None of us. There wasn't no need. There was only a week left before we had to move and so we just stayed home and packed. Not that there was much to pack. Mama and Daddy sold almost every piece of furniture we had to neighbors or the new people moving in. Even our beds. The new house came with furniture.

Edith came over a lot those last weeks and helped me say goodbye to the farm. We walked every inch of the land. We trudged up to the top of our hill where the berry bushes was, and even though they was bare now and not pretty, I knew how they would look in the spring, and I touched each one so they'd remember me.

Me and the boys climbed our favorite trees and hung out on their branches as long as we could in the cold air, and I promised myself that I would never ever forget the way our farm looked from up there. Mama let us take our lunches out to the barn, and we sat on the bales of hay while we ate, but we didn't take much pleasure in it. We mostly stopped playing and hung around the house and waited for the day we was to move.

The day before we had to leave, I took Little Grace around with me to my special places. I reminded her how pretty Mama's garden always was and how good the vegetables tasted in the summers. I made myself go down to the swing at the end of the drive, and we swung double together like me and Edith used to do. I didn't want Little Grace to miss anything about the place just because of me and what happened out there. We didn't go real high because I didn't want her to be afraid, but I showed her how to lean backward so she could see the sky above.

She giggled and shrieked and said, "More, more, sissy," and we stayed there 'til she wanted to stop.

The last place I went to was our summer kitchen. I needed to go, but it was a long time before I could get my feet to take me in there. I made myself go real slow around the little room so every part of me would remember the place. I hummed a song I made up as I went along, and I made myself dance around the table. But it was a short dance, because my heart and spirit just wasn't in it. I tried real hard to think of myself as the princess I always imagined myself to be, but I couldn't get the picture to come into my head. I knew my dreamin' and pretendin' days was over.

I sat down in front of the window where there was no sun and I cried.

PART 2

We pulled into Thurston the final hours of a cold and gloomy day at the end of October, right before Halloween, and clunked slowly past a few houses with piles of pumpkins for sale in their front yards and corn stalks tied to their porches. The trees had pretty much dropped their leaves, and the rain had left the yards soggy and brown. There was only a couple of streets in town, and ours was the main one that went right through the center of it.

We saw a few people up and down the street lookin' at us, and I began to wave, thinkin' I should be friendly to my new neighbors.

But Old Phoebe pulled my hand down and said, "Quit it, Nellie, don't make a spectacle of yourself. Can't you ever learn how to behave?"

Everybody else in the wagon was lookin' straight ahead, and I followed their direction.

We pulled up at the end of the street to where Daddy said our new home was, and I told myself that it would look pretty, maybe, when the sun came out.

Daddy said, "Here we are, here we are. This is the place." He looked back at the piece of paper in his hand and then up again at the house facing us. The sign out front said "Welcome Railroaders."

"It looks all broken." Little Grace was still little enough to speak up and be honest.

The lump in my throat hurt.

The grownups led the way up the short distance to the front porch, and us kids followed and pointed out to each other how the railroad tracks was so close to our house that most of us could throw a soft ball twice as far. Daddy pulled himself up the stairs, and he was smiling, but his lips was pressed tight against his teeth.

"Well, boys, we'll have to get to these steps soon, won't we?" And as he walked across the porch to the door, he continued, "We'll have this fixed up in no time, and next spring we'll get a big old swing and a rocker to put out here. It will be real nice, won't it, Mama?"

She nodded in his direction.

Daddy couldn't get the door to open so he climbed back down the steps, and we all followed him to the yard, the side away from the tracks. There was a door there, but it was stuck, too. Out back, the tracks cut kitty-cornered, right through our yard over to the side where we had started. We was pretty much surrounded by tracks. Grammy took hold of Mama's hand. I wanted to get between them and grab onto them, too, but I didn't have the chance 'cause all of us was so bundled up together. We all felt the need to be close.

Daddy explained that the place was a perfect location for business. Townsfolk would come because of our good food and friendly hospitality, and the railroaders would be staying with us since the car switching house for the trains was right there just beyond our house on the right. There was already a restaurant at the depot across the street and down at the intersection where all the tracks came together, but we planned for our place to be better than that one.

Mama took Baby Faye from Phoebe and told everyone to be real careful walking over the broken glass and pieces of metal that was left here and there on the dirt leading up to the back door. She still had hold of Grammy's hand. The key worked this time, and after Daddy pushed against the frame several times with his shoulder, the door flew open.

He was real excited, talking a mile a minute about what this and that room would be used for and how, if we all pitched in, we'd have the place up and running and ready for business in no time. There was four bedrooms upstairs and three rooms that could be used for bedrooms for sure downstairs. The kitchen was big compared to our old one, and Grammy said that it was good that us girls would have plenty of room to move around while we was fixin' meals for everyone.

Off the kitchen was a nice little space for a dining room for our family, and up at the front of the house, facing the road, was the room where our customers would eat. There wasn't any tables there for the customers, just a counter-like thing with stools pulled up to it. We talked about how we'd have to walk from the kitchen through our dining room and then up front to get food to everybody. Our customers' space was separated from the family's part by a ply-board wall that needed painting.

"I didn't see a privy, Daddy." It was Clyde talkin'. "Where's the outhouse?"

Daddy laughed and said, "Good question, son. Let's go find it." And we all followed him out back again. "Looks like some kids or some drifters got to it, don't it?" he said. "Well, I guess this is the first thing we'd better tackle, right men?" And he ruffled Homer's hair with his big hands and jostled George's shoulders with his, like men do with each other, like he was expectin' it to be fun to build up an outhouse.

All I could think about was how anyone in town could watch us coming and going to do our business out there if they wanted to 'cause there wasn't any trees or bushes or nothing to hide us and keep it all private.

"Well, family," he said, clapping his hands together, "let's get that wagon of ours unloaded before it starts in raining again. We've got some work to do before the sun goes down. We'll get our beds and things set up before supper, and then we'll take the night off and really start in fixin' this place up first thing in the morning."

We no sooner got back inside before we heard a low rumble outside somewhere. We all stopped what we was about to do and looked in the direction of the back door. When the rumble turned into a steady high-pitched screeching sound, we all froze. The floor and the walls of the house we was standin' in rattled and shook, and I was sure we was all going to be flattened by whatever was outside. Daddy brought us into a tight little circle and shouted over the roar that there was no reason to be afraid, that it was just the train comin' by.

He ran outside with all of us right behind him, and we covered our ears as we stood and watched the cars marked Toledo and Ohio Central storm by. The hot air all around the huge black train blew into us and messed with our hair and clothes, and we had to shut our eyes to it. The engineer blew the train's whistle three long times somewhere past our house. When the last car rumbled past and the man standing against the rail of the caboose waved, we remembered to take our hands down from our ears, and Daddy said that we needed to get a sign up out there first thing to let the train people know we'd be open for business real soon.

We knew a lot of the train people before we opened for business 'cause each time we heard a train comin', we ran to the side yard and waved to the conductor and the brakeman. They was real friendly and sometimes threw us pieces of candy or gum out the windows and from the back of the caboose, and we got so the noise didn't matter so much.

The signal man's name was Jake, and he was the friendliest of all. Sometimes he let me and the boys stand in his shack that was right at the end of our side yard and showed us how he gave the signals. He was especially nice to me and was real happy to tell me all about how the trains worked. The boys got bored with going there pretty quick and so did I, but Jake was so nice to me I felt obliged to act interested.

We worked real hard to get the place ready for business—harder than we had ever worked before. Mama gave each of us older kids certain jobs to do that would fit in with our school schedules, once we started school. It was a couple of weeks before we had the place in order and could put the sign out that we was open for business.

Mama and Grammy cooked all the meals and did all the washing and ironing, and every day after the railroaders left, they cleaned up all the rooms. Mama had the extra job of taking care of all the finances. Me and Phoebe baked pies and cakes and bread at night so they'd be fresh in the mornings, and we helped the youngins get fed and put to bed. The boys had the worst jobs of all because they had to clean up the supper dishes, empty the chamber pots, keep the outhouse clean, and scrub down the kitchen floor every night.

We practically crawled to bed after the days' work, happy for the first time I could remember to put on our night clothes and wash up so we could get a good sleep. But we was real proud at what we made the place look like. Mama said we'd probably always have roach problems, and we'd just have to deal with it, so we was all careful not to walk around in our bare feet.

A few of the townspeople came in for breakfast and lunch from time to time, but it was pretty obvious that the railroaders was our real customers. Thurston folk was all farmers mostly, and Daddy said they just wasn't the kind to eat out much. People taking the trains didn't take the time to walk over to our place. They ate at the depot.

We fixed up our front steps, but before too long the rail men just came in the side door through our part of the house. Daddy said it didn't make much sense for them to be formal and come up to the front to get in. Grammy had always said the shortest way to a friend's house was through the back door, and those men was Daddy's friends.

Looking back, we shouldn't have been so friendly.

Us kids all went to the same school, but we was spread out in different rooms, and I didn't like that very much. The kids in town wasn't too friendly; at least, I didn't feel real comfortable around them. Mama said that because they came in from farms all over the county, they didn't have time to get to know me good. That was all right with me. I wanted to start out real good there in my new town, and I'd decided a long time ago to keep my friendliness down like our old preacher said I should. I sat in the back of the room so nobody would notice me, not even the teachers. Outside at recess, I stood at the side and watched everyone play. It wasn't a whole lot of fun, but I figured I wouldn't be misunderstood that way.

The boys made friends pretty quick, and whenever they had the time after school, they hung out with them in the field out back or out in front of the general store down the street and beside the bar where the men hung out Saturday nights. Phoebe was having the best time of all. Like Daddy had promised, she could get to the church often, and that made her real happy.

Me and Phoebe was stuck together a lot at night when we baked, and we got along better than I thought we would. She talked to me more there in that kitchen than ever before. One night she wanted to tell me a secret, something no one else knew, and she made me promise on the Bible that I would keep it to myself 'til she could tell the others. When I put my hand on her old beat up Bible and promised, she looked down at me real sweet and put her hands over her heart. She was so close to me I could smell her body, and it wasn't good.

Finally she got around to telling me what was on her mind and, whispering real important-like, she said that she had decided to "go into the ministry." That was how she put it. She said our new preacher had told her that it was her destiny to lead others and he would try to help get her into a preacher's school in Chicago when the time came. I had no idea where Chicago was, and I told her so. Then she got mad at me and said who cares where Chicago is. I don't think she knew where it was either, but I kept my mouth shut about that. The important thing, she said, was that she knew what her calling was.

I could tell she wanted me to be excited about her new job, but no preacher I ever knew ever appeared to be too happy doing what they did, so I couldn't think why she thought she'd like to be one. But I tried to act happy for her.

She reached over to me and took my hands in hers, and I thought she was going to slap me or something. But she looked at me real dreamy-like and whispered like she was sayin' a prayer, "God has called me. I'm going to save you, Nellie. I'm going to save the whole family."

The railroaders generally left after supper and came in late at night, usually filled up on whiskey. Daddy didn't mind it that they drank. He said it was just their way, and so long as they wasn't hurting anybody, we'd just have to put up with it.

But Mama didn't like it one bit.

Sometimes we was all still up when they came in that way, and I kind'a liked them after they had their liquor. They laughed a lot and sang and was real friendly. They had fun. But Mama rushed us kids into our own parts of the house those nights and told us how drinking whiskey changed people. Phoebe said how whiskey was the drink of the devil, and she offered to pray for their salvation.

Daddy wondered where they was getting it. From time to time he reminded Mama again that they could be makin' a little extra money on the side if she'd let him set up the still he needed to make the bootleg, and Mama would tell him again that she wouldn't have anything goin' on in our house that was against the law.

Daddy must have decided to check it all out anyway, because before too long, some nights after the chores was done for the evening, he'd give Mama a kiss on the cheek and tell her he'd be going out for some man-time and she shouldn't wait up for him. Sometimes I was awake when they all got home, and I'd peek out and see that Daddy was actin' pretty much the same as our boarders.

I had extra time after school since I didn't have anyone to play with like the boys did, so Daddy asked me if sometimes when he got real busy would I like to help out serving the railroaders their suppers? Well, that sounded like real fun, and the first chance I had, I did it. Before long I was helping him serve almost every night.

Phoebe didn't approve. She said that my friendliness was unbecoming and that my pride would surely lead me to misfortune. She was talking even stranger since she started spending more time at the church, trying to learn to be a preacher. Jake the signalman praised me when I served suppers, and I decided to listen to him and ignore Old Phoebe.

One night after everybody was all finished eating, Jake reached into his pocket and pulled out a nickel and said that that nickel was mine for doing such a good job. I looked at Daddy to see if it was all right to take it, and when I saw he was grinning and winking at everyone, I put it in my pocket, just as bold as brass. From then on, every time Jake came to visit us, he gave me a nickel. Me and him was good buddies. He reminded me that I was welcome to go on out to his little signal house whenever I wanted to so I could learn more about the trains, but I told him I was really so busy in the house now that I didn't have the time. I pretended I was sad about that so he wouldn't think that I wasn't appreciative or anything.

Sometimes the others followed what Jake did and gave me a few cents for my good work. Mama wasn't real happy about me taking money from strangers, and she told me I needed to put it to work for some good when I decided to spend it, and so I kept every single one of those coins and saved them for a present for Mama, or for a rainy day like Grammy did.

I thought hard about my waitress job, and I decided that until I could have my very own bakery, I was going to become the best waitress you'd ever find anywhere. To get to that point, I went over to the restaurant at the Depot whenever I could and watched how the waitresses there did things. I told the two girls working there, Maggie and Ann, that I was learning to be a waitress, same as them, and they said I was welcome to go in anytime and sit at the counter and watch them. That's how they became my after-school friends.

Things was going well there in Thurston, and I allowed myself to think that maybe things really was going to change for the better for me and my family.

Then one night my joyfulness came to an end.

We had just three rail men staying over with us that night, and all three of them, including Jake, went out after supper. It was late when me and Old Phoebe finished our baking. We got ourselves ready for bed, and she went back in the kitchen to read her Bible, and I grabbed a quilt and slipped outside to have a look at the stars and roam around in our yard a little. I jumped when the door opened, and I turned around fast to see who was there. It was Jake.

"Well, hi, Nellie," he said all cheerful-like. His words ran together and he was talking real slow. "What are you doing out here in the cold like this?"

I explained to him how sometimes I wasn't ready for bed at night and so I'd sometimes come outside to look at the stars. He said he understood exactly what I meant, because he liked to get out alone sometimes, too. We talked back and forth a little bit, but I have to tell you I didn't feel quite right bein' out there in the dark with Jake.

After a while, he looked across at me real hard and said, "You must be cold, honey." And he walked up close behind me and took his jacket off. When he put it around my shoulders, I could smell the whiskey on him. "There, now, that's better, isn't it?" he asked, and there was something about the way he said it that gave me goosebumps. I didn't like Jake's hands on my shoulders, and I didn't like having his coat on me. I felt closed in.

"I gotta' go," I said.

"Now, Nellie, honey, don't you rush off," he said, looking back at the door and holding my shoulders a little tighter. "Stay out here with me a while longer."

When he said, "I'll keep you warm, sugar," the words didn't come out too good, and when he pulled me up close to him the breath they was carried on smelled bad.

My skin prickled, and I prayed he wouldn't pick me up like the man in the woods did. I had allowed myself to be misunderstood again. It was all coming back, just the way the preacher said it would.

"I have to go," I said and I could feel the tears pushing out from my eyes. "Please, please let me go."

"Hey, honey, don't cry," he said against my cheek. "There's nothing to cry about, I..."

This time I could move. And I did, real quick, leaving his jacket there on the ground where it fell. When I was safe in my own room, Preacher's old words and Phoebe's new ones kept coming back to me, and I went over and over again everything I did when I was selling Mama's jars that day not so long ago on our farm. And then I went over and over again the things I had said to Jake, and I could see that both times I was too friendly and that everything that happened had all been my fault. Then I prayed to God that He would help me be a better person, more restrained, like our old preacher said I should be, and I promised myself that I would stop showing my joyfulness. That way I wouldn't be misunderstood ever again.

I asked Daddy the next day if I could take a little break from waitressing, and after that I stayed in our own part of the house.

Thanksgiving was right around the corner, and we decorated our room at school with pictures of Indians and turkeys and Pilgrims and drew pictures of the same things to take home with us so our mothers could decorate our houses with them. Mr. Arnsley, our teacher, told us to write two paragraphs about what we was most thankful for, and I made a list of everyone in my family, including Aunt Lizzie. It made me sad when I thought about how we'd left Aunt Lizzie behind us, and I went home and asked Mama if I'd ever see her again. She got a little smile on her face and said that you never know what might happen and maybe if I prayed real hard about it, Jesus would make it possible.

I prayed real hard then. Every day. I even bargained with Jesus, and I told Him that if only He'd let me see Aunt Lizzie and Little Edith again soon, I'd work harder and be a really, really good person.

It wasn't more than a week after I got into all that praying and just the day before Thanksgiving when we heard a knock on the door. When Mama and Grammy told me to go see who could be out there, I opened it a crack and peeked out, ready to tell whoever was there that we was closed, and don't you know, standing there, grinning from ear to ear was not only Aunt Lizzie, but Aunt Edith, Uncle Dean and Little Edith, come all that way to our new place to have Thanksgiving with us.

Bottled Butterfly

They brought supper for all of us, and we ate ourselves crazy on a big old turkey, lima beans, pickled beets, sweet potatoes, hot biscuits and jam, and pumpkin pie. And we never stopped talking. It was like we had never been away from each other, and that old house was a happy one again. I tried not to think about when they'd have to leave.

When it was time for us kids to go to bed, Mama asked Little Edith and me if we'd like to have one of the railroader rooms upstairs to sleep in that night. We sure felt special when we went upstairs all by ourselves, and we stood at the stair landing and blew kisses to everyone downstairs like we was real fine ladies saying goodbye to people who didn't want us to go.

I was ready to talk, and I did. I told Edith everything I knew about Thurston and school and railroaders, and she told me about school and her friends. But when I asked her about my old farm and the new people there, she didn't have much to say, and I thought maybe she was still sad that we was gone. Or maybe she didn't want to tell me how nice the new people was 'cause she didn't want me to feel jealous. I let it go, and we climbed into the two little beds, and I stretched out my legs and arms and remembered how good it was to wake up by myself in Aunt Lizzie's big old bed and reminded myself to buy me my own bed first thing when I opened up my bakery.

I told Edith about my bakery plans, even what the shop was going to look like, and finally I made myself stop talking to allow her to catch up or ask questions. But it was awful quiet over there on her side of the room, and I sat up and asked her if she was asleep. She was off in dreamland, but my brain wasn't ready for that yet, so I decided to go downstairs and see what the grownups was doing.

I wrapped the blanket from my bed around me 'cause it was so cold up there, and I stopped by the pee pot at the top of the stairs, just for good measure. The pot was ice cold, and I couldn't hardly go, and I thought about how my pee might just turn to ice. A picture came into my head of the boys trying to empty a pot of frozen pee in the morning, and I laughed right out loud. After I calmed myself down, I made my way downstairs and stopped just outside the kitchen door, wonderin' if anyone would be mad if I came in.

66

"Oh, my God almighty," I heard Daddy say.

"John," Mama said, "please don't use the Lord's name in vain."

"Well, my God, Rebecca, it could have been our little Nellie. Jesus Christ. What else do they know?"

I was surprised to hear Daddy cussin' so much, 'specially in front of our relatives.

Uncle Dean was telling the story. "Well, they don't know much. People all over the county are looking for the little girl. Only ten years old. I can't imagine what he did to her."

"Why do they think it was the same man?" Daddy was asking.

"Well, people seen a man fitting the description you gave. Big, bearded man, wearing overalls. In and out of the woods. Never caught him. Gosh, John, why wouldn't it be the same man? One attack followed by another one not more than two months apart? I'm telling you, it has to be the same man."

"He must have been watching the house." It was Aunt Lizzie talking now. "He must have been looking for... Thank God you moved. I mean, I'm stricken that another little girl was taken, but thank God it wasn't our Nellie. Lordy, Lordy, it's just too much to think about."

I didn't direct myself into the kitchen. Something just seemed to take me over and move me through the door and into the circle of family sitting there.

Daddy leaped out of his chair and came over to where I was standing.

"Nellie!" he said. "What are you doing up?"

"Who got taken away?" I felt my nose running and wondered if I was crying.

Mama got up and put her arm around me. "Honey, it's nothing that you need to worry about. Let me take you back upstairs to bed. Where's Edith?"

"*Who got taken?*" I yelled it out. "*Who got taken?* Tell me who got taken?"

"Shhh, Shhh," Daddy told me. "Okay, honey, try to quiet down. Just breathe deep and try to calm down. We'll talk, all right? We'll talk. Now, come on. We're going to sit down quiet and tell you everything we know. Come on, Nellie, let's just let me hold you here, big girl, and we'll have some hot tea and talk."

Grammy brought the tea, but I didn't take it. I sat stiff on the stool and stared out at the wall, trying to push thoughts away, trying to get back into myself and push away the fear like I always did, but I couldn't. I had to hear.

"Nellie," Daddy said. "The people who moved into our farm? Well, they have a little girl a little younger than you, and they have a little boy too. Remember? We talked about them a little bit while we was packing up?"

I didn't answer him. I waited to hear what I needed to know.

"Well, several weeks ago, the little girl came up missing," he said. "She must have wandered off and got lost. We just found out about it from Uncle Dean. He was telling us about it, and we was all just speculatin' about what might have happened to her and how she'll get back home and all."

"The man took her, didn't he?" I said, way too loud. "The man that grabbed me from the road. The one you chased into the woods. He has the little girl, doesn't he?"

"Well now, honey," Daddy said, rubbing my hair like he always did when I was upset, "that's a possibility, but no one knows for sure. People just don't know yet, but they'll find out, and she'll come home just fine. Don't worry, Nellie, she'll be just fine."

"He's going to hurt her."

I knew absolutely what that man would have done to me. He would have hurt me. Hurt me so bad. Used his privates on me. Put that hard part of him into me. Let that spit that was drooling down his face get all over me. And I knew that was the way he had hurt that other little girl. He couldn't hurt me, so he took that other little girl living in my house. He took her into the woods and he hurt her. He put his dirty hands all over her and he hurt her bad.

And it was all my fault.

The other dream started that night. All I saw was white, white brighter than I ever saw before.

There was no sound.

No one was there except for me. I was there but I didn't see myself because I was nothing. I felt like a giant thumb had reached out over everything, and it was pushing down slow and hard on that nothingness that was me.

It became pretty clear that things wasn't going to change much for us there in Thurston. We didn't get the truck Daddy said we would, and we didn't get any of the pretty things we thought we'd have by now. Some of the regulars who had been coming to stay with us didn't come any more, and I stopped askin' why because I could tell it made Daddy uncomfortable to talk about it. I thought we'd be smart to just go back to our farm and pick up from where we'd left off, but then I remembered that other people was living there, and I prayed to God and Jesus that now the little girl was there, too.

No one talked about the girl or our customers. No on talked about our hungry bellies. Nobody was makin' exciting plans for our future. We just worked, and us kids went to school.

Christmas time came, and we was drawing Christmas trees and coloring Santa Claus pictures and singing Christmas songs in school. Preacher talked about the birth of baby Jesus and what a gift He was to us all. Just in case preacher was right about all that, I thanked God for Jesus, and I prayed to Jesus to help make me a better person and to come into my heart and make me pure, just the way Preacher told us to. I threw in an extra prayer for me and my family, asking both God and Jesus to help us out if they wanted to. I figured I might as well give them a try since nothin' else seemed to be workin'.

The day before Christmas, Daddy and the boys went somewhere outside of town to look for a tree to cut down for our parlor, and us girls stayed back and threaded pinecones and pretty scraps of paper on string to decorate it. Grammy and Mama went into the kitchen, and it wasn't long 'til sugary and buttery smells came floatin' out to us.

They was still in there baking away when someone knocked on the front door, and we all ran to see who was out there on our porch. They started singing Christmas songs soon as we opened the door. Two ladies carrying baskets came up on the porch, and we could see there was presents for us in some of them and a big old roasted chicken in another. Mama thanked them, but Grammy went back inside without sayin' anything to them, and I figured I knew why.

Phoebe started delivering a sermon, asking God to bless them all, and it was terrible embarrassing. They backed away, wishing us a Merry Christmas and waved like we was all the best of friends. I'd never seen most of them before, and I was pretty certain I wouldn't see them again.

Mama made us wait 'til the men came back so's we could all open the presents together. There was something for each one of us kids, all wrapped up real pretty, and Mama let us open each one right there and then. I got a little pink flowered box to put things in, and I thought about how I would keep my pennies and nickels in it. I was happy when Little Grace got herself a tiny little brown teddy bear with a red bow around its neck. Old Phoebe's present was a round mirror with its own little handle. I have to admit that I would rather have had the mirror than the box, but I tried hard not to let that show. Mama and Daddy and Grammy didn't get anything. They said Christmas is for children and they got their happiness from watching us open our gifts.

There was food inside the baskets, and before we set it out on the table, we all held hands and thanked the Lord for all our blessings, and we asked Jesus to bless the townspeople for the wonderful feast we was about to have. We finished off our supper with the cookies and candy Grammy and Mama had made earlier for us.

The new year didn't start off so good.

My big brothers was bored there in that place, and they didn't mind who heard them say so. They started sneaking out Saturday nights. I know they did 'cause I saw them do it. They'd wait 'til they thought we was all asleep and then they'd tip-toe out in their stocking feet, carrying the clothes they put out earlier over in the corner where no one would see them. I followed them a couple of times and watched them get dressed out in the back yard, shivering and giggling and acting real silly—and I wished I could go with them.

They got away with it until late one Saturday night in the first part of February. We was woke up by somebody banging on the front door. Daddy told us all to stay right where we was, and we heard him go to the cabinet and get his shot gun. Mama was at our door before we had a chance to follow him, and we all waited huddled inside our room.

"Who's out there?" Daddy yelled, and we heard him open the door and go outside. "I'm sorry this has happened, gentlemen," we heard him say. "Thank you for bringing them home. I'll take care of this."

We decided it was all right to come out of our rooms to see what was going on then, and there was daddy with his hands on his hips and his legs spread, staring at my brothers who was studying the floor and looking pretty pitiful. I didn't know what they had gone and done, but I knew they was in a heap of trouble.

"Boys, I am so disappointed in you," Daddy said. "You have shamed your entire family. Family, I want you to take a real good look at these boys. The authorities brought them home. They was hiding out behind the school down the street with some ruffians from somewhere out of town. Drinking. Drinking and smoking. What have you got to say for yourselves?"

"We didn't hurt anything, Daddy." John spoke up. "We was just having some fun, is all. We get bored hanging out here. We need to get out with friends, same as you."

I could see Daddy had some trouble getting past that one.

"You're kids," he said. "You broke the law. You could have been put in jail."

"You could, too, if you're ever caught," John shot right back at him.

"That's enough," Daddy said, and some of the sureness went out of his voice. "That's two different things. When you're grown up and know what you're doing, you can make your own decisions. Right now you have to obey the law and follow your family's rules."

71

Daddy unbuckled his belt. "You know I don't like to take the leather to you. You know how I hate it. But I don't have no choice. You've caused trouble in town, and you've hurt your whole family with your bad behavior. You have to be punished."

"Family," he said to the rest of us, "I want you to go back into your rooms now. You don't need to see this." Then he told my brothers to pull down their pants and bend over."

We all hurried off to our beds, even Mama, and we stared out into the darkness and listened to the two loud whacks each of the boys got to their backsides. I cried for them, and I cried for Daddy because he didn't want to hurt them. I cried for all of us. Nothing was right in that house.

Seems like when bad stuff starts, it just doesn't stop, and bad stuff just kept happening at that place in Thurston. Things started to break, and we didn't have the money to fix them up. Grammy's eyesight got worse, and she could barely see at all, so Phoebe and me had to help Mama more with everything.

Us kids skipped school a lot because we was just so danged tired, and I just gave up trying to learn everything I was supposed to. I'd find Mama roaming around the place late at night, waitin' up for Daddy when he was out with his railroad friends, and John and him was always at each other.

I wanted my farm back, and I prayed to Jesus to see if He would find a way to get us back there. Then I thought about the evil man in the woods and the family living in our house, and I just didn't know what to ask for.

I needed to talk to someone besides Jesus about what was on my mind, so I decided to find a time to talk with Grammy. We bundled ourselves up against the cold and headed outside for a walk across town so we could have some privacy together. I held onto her tight, and she trusted me to guide her so she couldn't get hurt. When she asked me what was on my mind that needed talking about, I told her what I was feeling, and she said she understood. I asked her why, with all of us trying so hard to make things good, they just kept getting worse.

"Well," she said, "our boarders are going through some hard times, too, just like everyone else. Quite a few of them have been laid off. Some of the others have had cuts in pay."

She acted like she was done talkin', but I asked her to go on. "Well, over the past month or so, a lot of them haven't had the money to pay for their room and board. Your Daddy's been real kind-hearted, and he's told those railroaders that they could put off paying us for a while. Now most of them intend to pay us back, and I hope they do, but some of them never had any intention of paying us, and they just quit coming and there's no way we can get that money they owe us now. Your daddy keeps after the ones who still come, but they always have excuses for not paying up."

"Well, why don't we tell them not to come anymore if they won't pay us?"

"Well, truth is, if we tell them they can't come, there's no one else to take their place. Our business is the railroaders, plain and simple. Without them, we don't have a business."

We both thought about that for a while.

"What are we going to do, Grammy?" I said, holding onto her hand good and tight.

"Well, honey, I don't rightly know right now. I just don't know." She gave my hand a little squeeze and told me not to worry myself about it, that things would work out fine.

Sometime at the end of March, Daddy called a family meeting after supper. It was the middle of the week, and we had only one boarder.

"Family," he said, "I have something important to tell you, and I'm real sorry to have to say it, but... Well, business here isn't good as you know. It hasn't quite turned out the way we all wanted it to. We've all worked real hard. No one could have worked harder, and I'm proud of all of you. Real proud. But. Well, we can't stay here any longer. We have to move out."

"Yea!" Clyde yelled. "We're going back to the farm, right?"

"Well, no, son," he said, shaking his head. "We can't go back to the farm. It doesn't belong to us any more. I know that's what you would all like, but we just can't. We need to get that out of our heads."

I was wondering if maybe we was going to have to live with Aunt Edith or Aunt Lizzie, but there wasn't enough room for all of us at either of their places. I was scared because I knew we didn't have money and without money, I couldn't think of where we could all go, and I was worried about what happens to people who don't have nowhere to live.

"But we're going back close. We're moving to Newark," Daddy said. "I have a job there at Burke Golf Factory. We don't quite have a real house to live in there yet, but we will soon. The company is going to let all of us stay in a house where they store some things. We'll stay there 'til we get our feet on the ground and can get ourselves a real nice place of our own."

Mama spoke for the first time, and we all shifted towards her. "We're going to pack up over the next couple of days," she said, fiddling with the hem of her apron. "We think we have some more boarders coming this week, and then we're going to shut the place down. We'll move on to Newark and our new home as soon as we can. We'll be closer to our relatives there. And it will be a new adventure for us."

Mama was tryin' real hard to make it all sound good. I looked at Grammy to see if she was going to add anything, but her head was facin' the wall.

"What about school? What about Church?" It was Phoebe talking now. "How can we move? Pastor was going to help me." She stopped short and her face got all red.

"Help you with what, Phoebe?" Grammy asked.

"Nothing! Nevermind!" Phoebe said, and she raced out of the room crying.

"Oh, dear," Mama said, as she got up to go after her. She turned back to us, and I'd never seen so much worry on her face. "Everything is going to be just fine," she said—but her lips didn't show any happiness.

PART 3

Our first house in our new town wasn't a house at all. Like Daddy had said, it was part of a storage building that Burke Golf Company owned on Maple Avenue. We all lived in four rooms off the back of the place, and the only thing that kept us going was the hope that Daddy kept in us that soon we'd have a real home of our own. Mama said we needed to feel grateful to Daddy's new boss for putting a roof over our heads, and I was looking forward to meeting him and thanking him.

The company gave Daddy a grey uniform to wear to work, and he looked really handsome in it. I asked him what he was going to do there at the factory, and he said he was going to be a custodian, and he'd work different times of the day, depending what shift he was put on. He didn't talk much about his job because, like he said, there wasn't much to tell, but he did say the people he worked for was real nice people.

Mama made all of us older kids start back to school. It was the end of March already, and we all kind'a argued with her about going 'cause there was only a little over two months left of school, but Mama said that if we didn't finish out the year we'd probably be held back a year in the fall. I sure didn't want to go to school any more years than necessary, so I stopped whining about it.

We was only there maybe a month when Daddy was able to get an advance on his pay and we could move into our real home and a different school—the third one in a year. The thought of meeting a whole bunch of new kids and tryin' to figure out how to act around them sent me into a real tizzie. Mama said I'd just have to work through it.

I decided to keep myself invisible again.

Our new home was real nice and was pretty clean when we moved in. We had a parlor, a kitchen, and a living room downstairs. Upstairs was three bedrooms. As usual, Grammy had a bed in the front parlor. Our yard was big, with plenty of room out back to play ball.

There was a fence at the one side that separated us from our neighbor, and as soon as summer came, Mama put her vegetable and rose garden there. Later on she added some gladiolas and some sunflowers and hollyhocks. I liked the hollyhocks the best because Mama made flower dolls from their blossoms. Grammy roasted the seeds from the sunflowers when the flowers died and stored them to last all winter. All summer long, Mama put fresh-cut flowers in our used glass milk bottles and sat them at the window in the parlor so they could catch the sun and cheer the place up. They reminded me a little of the jars back home in our summer kitchen.

Beyond the garden, just behind the back door, was our outhouse, and just beyond that was where we put our chicken coop. We decided we couldn't get along without chickens, and we decided to sell their eggs out front to our neighbors. We put them on a table up close to the street and put out a sign "Eggs for Sale," and people took what they wanted and put their money in a glass jar we put out for that purpose. People liked our eggs, 'specially the brown ones. They was my favorite too. They tasted almost sweet.

Way back behind our yard was a train track. We could hear the trains go by when we was inside the house, but they sure wasn't as loud as the ones in Thurston. Us older kids liked to go back there and walk on the tracks and see if we could feel the trains coming before we heard them. We got down on our hands and knees and kept real still, and if there was a train coming from somewhere close and heading our way, we felt the tracks move inside and kind'a vibrate. We stayed there on the tracks long as we could and played "dare" to see who would be the last one off. Whenever we had a penny, we put it on the track right before the train came and let it be run over just to see how flat it got.

Hoboes hitched rides on the trains from town to town, and sometimes, if the trains was going slow enough, they jumped off close by our place and wandered into our yard and asked for something to eat. Mama always came up with something for them. She said that even bums had to eat and that we should pray for them. Sometimes at night we saw the glow of their fires down close to the tracks. Daddy said they was harmless, but we kept our distance.

At night when we was all in bed, I'd lay there and listen for the whistle of the last train to go by. It made me peaceful, and I'd wonder hard where those railroaders was headed. The songs of the doves just before sunset told me when it was time to be inside, ready to eat supper with my family, and the songs of the trains' whistles told me when to go to sleep, that everything was the way it should be out there, and it was all right to put the day aside.

At night, we burned oil lamps and carried them from room to room, wherever they was needed, but not to the kitchen. Nope. Our new kitchen had gaslights, and they was almost my favorite things in the house. Matter of fact, they *was* my favorite things 'cause they made the kitchen glow almost like my summer kitchen did in late afternoons.

Some nights when I couldn't stay asleep, I tip-toed downstairs, made my way past Grammy's bed, and sneaked in there. I'd find the little key Mama kept hidden, the one that let the gas come out, and I'd turn the lights on real soft. I'd just wander around in there, touching things and thinkin' about stuff, like how me and my family would have a house plenty big enough for all of us someday and have pretty dresses and suits and birthday presents and lots to eat. And I thought about how I'd help make it all possible when I had my own bakery.

I didn't dance anymore, and I didn't sing, but I had some dreams. The kitchen was cozy and quiet. It was my place to get back to myself.

There was a tiny back porch stuck onto the house, and that's where our ice box was. It was left there by the people who lived in our house before us. The ice man came three times a week down the street in his truck, and we put a card in our front window to let him know when to stop.

I always tried to be home when he came 'cause I liked to watch him pick up the heavy blocks of ice from his truck with his huge silver tongs. He'd hook that ice with those tongs, flip it high over his shoulders, and carry it on his back all the way to our icebox. I thought he was very strong, and I told him so. We became friends, him and me, and we talked together while he took the ice out to our porch. I was careful not to be over friendly so he wouldn't misunderstand me.

Mama's wash tub was out there on the porch too. She was always washing, as you can imagine, and when us kids wasn't working or going to school, we helped her bring the water from the pump out back to our wood-burning stove inside, and then carry it back out to the porch where she'd scrub our clothes clean. She'd have to do it all alone when we wasn't around.

You can just imagine the clothesline out back. Why, it stretched out forever, clear across our yard, and the clothes from all fourteen of us was lined up there straight out from the porch, baking in the warm sun, showing anyone who wanted to take notice what our state of affairs was. It was a pretty dull display, if you want to know. Mostly navy or brown pants, white or blue shirts, and pale print dresses of every size anyone could want. Mama didn't hang up our under things, thank heavens. That would have been just too much to share with everyone. Those things was kept private from outsiders, strung out all over the chairs and stove in the kitchen.

Across the street from us was a big pit that people called "the dump," even though no one ever really threw stuff in it. It was just a big hole in the ground that someone put there for some reason they forgot about pretty quick. That's where all the kids was playing the first day we moved in. They stood around the hole and counted to three and took a flying leap into it, one after another, and then they turned around and climbed out. The first one up was the winner. The hole was pretty deep, and just to jump down took a lot of nerve. Climbing up was hard, too, 'cause there wasn't nothing to hold onto to pull yourself up except the dirt itself.

We all just stood in our yard and watched everyone jump in and out of that pit for at least three days, and finally George and John said that, heck, they couldn't see what the big deal was, so they sauntered over and stood with their arms crossed over their chests, just watchin', 'til some other big kid asked them if they was from the house across the street. Seemed a pretty silly question to me since he had to have seen us standing there not more than three minutes ago, but I kept my mouth shut and tried not to laugh. I never was very good at what you call small talk.

The boy who talked first to my brothers was Dan Vickers. He looked them over real good and finally asked them if they wanted a chance at the hole. They said that sure, they'd give it a try. Well, once my brothers practiced a couple of times, they most always won, and that didn't sit too well with Dan. Up to when we moved in, he'd been the biggest and toughest kid in the neighborhood, I guess. Turns out, everybody agreed that he was just a pain in the ass—pardon my expression—but no one wanted to stand up to him. John and George was a threat to how he was seen in the neighborhood, and that meant me and the rest of my family was looked at that way too.

That spelled trouble down the road.

I got me a new best friend whose name was Sandy. She was the nicest to me at school, and we walked home together most days. She lived on a pretty street just a couple of blocks east of us. One day she invited me over to her house and Mama said I could go. It was wonderful there. There was lots of windows, and her mama had put up real pretty white curtains on every one of them. Everything was tidy, and things was put out real nice. There was pictures of gardens on the walls, and there was pictures of Sandy and her little sister in pretty frames sitting out on the tables in the parlor. It was quiet there, and we could hear each other good. Sandy's mama and daddy was real friendly and polite.

I talked to Grammy about Sandy's mother, and Grammy said she sounded "refined." I liked that word "refined," and I decided I wanted to be refined just like Mrs. Barry some day.

After the first time, whenever I went to visit, Mrs. Barry treated me real special. She met me and Sandy at the door when we came home from school, and after she hugged Sandy, she gave me a hug too and told me how glad she was to see me again. She always had milk and cookies ready for us, and we sat there at the kitchen table and took our time with them and chitchatted together. The glasses all matched, and the dishes was pale green see-through glass and looked real pretty out on the table. I hoped some day my family could have glasses and dishes like that.

I didn't mind it there on Magnolia. Actually, I kind'a liked it. For the first time ever, there was lots of other kids for us to play with, and I was learning how to make friends. Things was shaping up to be good for all us kids, but not for Mama.

Daddy came home late lots of afternoons, and sometimes he missed supper altogether, and that made her sad. She held supper as long as she could those days he was late, and she stood at the big window up front and watched for him to come down the street. One day she looked so sad I thought I'd try to cheer her up.

"Don't worry, Mama," I said. "Daddy will be comin' along any minute now."

"I know, honey." She had her arms crossed in front of her chest, and she didn't look at me. "He'll be coming along soon. I think I'll go out and meet him when he rounds the corner."

"Daddy works hard for us, doesn't he?" I said, trying to make her feel better.

"Yes. Yes, he does," she said, and she seemed a little flustered, like she was havin' trouble getting her thoughts around that.

Daddy came home soon after supper, all smiles and full of energy, like he'd just had a good walk around the block. He went right over to Mama to give her a big hug, but she turned away before he got to her and walked quickly out of the room. Him and John had a few words that I couldn't hear, and soon as they finished, John stalked out the door. I didn't understand what was going on, but I knew things wasn't right. Seems like there was always somethin' buzzin' right below the surface of things all the time, and it was hard to get a handle on it all.

Mama's belly was so big with the new baby she was carrying, I thought for sure she'd explode. It was past the time when the baby should have come, and she wasn't feeling real good. Her face didn't have any color and was usually wet with sweat from all that extra weight she was carrying. I wanted it to come soon even though the thought of a new baby in our house still wasn't something I liked. I didn't like seeing Mama sick like that.

One morning I woke up hearing something that sounded like moaning. The sun wasn't even up yet, and I got the willies, thinkin' maybe one of those hobos had come into the house and was hurting someone. I laid real still to see if I was just imagining things, but, sure enough, I heard the same sound again, and it was louder this time.

I was too scared to say anything, so I kicked Old Phoebe's rump. Little Grace woke up just then and asked right out loud what was makin' that sound. Both of us kicked hard at Phoebe again, and she finally woke up and told us to just quit it, in that loud sassy way she had. Right then Daddy came runnin' into our room with the lamp and Baby Don. He handed me my brother and told Old Phoebe to come with him right now.

Us girls ran into our brothers in the hall, just outside Mama and Daddy's room, and before he shut the door on us, Daddy told Clyde to go down and get Grammy. The rest of the morning me and him was running up and down the stairs for fresh water and pans and bowls and rags and tea, while the rest of the kids sat outside wide-eyed with their hands on their ears to block out the sound of Mama's moans and screams.

It was the middle of the day when the moaning and screaming stopped and we heard the sound of a baby crying. The door opened, and

Phoebe came out and rushed by us without sayin' a thing, which was pretty unusual, and then Daddy came out and told us that we didn't have just one new baby. No sirree. We had two.

That's right, we had us a set of twins, one boy and one girl.

Mama and Daddy made beds for our little babies in two drawers in the bureau in their room. They was so small they just fit perfect, and it was easy for all of us to get to them when they needed attention. They was the cutest little things. Polly was definitely the more lively one. Carl was real quiet and he was smaller too. I took real good care of him because I just knew he needed the extra attention. I made sure that he was always warm and that his little bottom was dry. Mama didn't know, but I put extra cloths down under him there in the drawer so his tiny body could snuggle in softer.

My favorite place to take him was out in Mama's garden. We'd sit and look at the flowers, and I'd rub the petals across his little hands to show him how soft they was. Then I told him what the name of each flower was and named him their colors. Mama said he couldn't see colors yet, but I didn't care. I wanted to give him a head start in the world by filling him in on things real early.

Phoebe, George, and Homer and John all got jobs around town cleaning houses, running errands for people, delivering papers— anything they could find to do—soon after the twins was born. I wanted to get a job too, and I put up a real hissy fit about it, but Mama and Daddy said I was too young to go to work; and, besides, Mama and Grammy needed me to help out at home. Now, you know how I hated to do dusting and washing and all the rest of it, so I wore my brain out trying to think of some way I could help bring some money to my family by workin' outside, just like my older brothers and sister was, and get out of the house some. Finally, I came up with a great idea.

Now, I need to tell you that one of my favorite things to do was to run errands downtown. I never went by myself, you understand. I'd always have to go with one or two of the boys, but that was all right 'cause they usually ran off and did some stuff on their own and let me wander around by myself. I didn't mind being alone because there was always people around.

See, Newark was a pretty big town. The downtown was built like a square. In fact, that's what they called it: The Square. You could walk clear around and see in every building and never have to get off the walkway. In the center of The Square was a huge stone building where all the people who took care of the city worked. It was square too. It was called the Licking County Courthouse, and people came from all over just to see that building. You could get into it from all four sides, and there was sixteen steps you had to climb to get up to each huge door. Way up on top was a beautiful golden clock tower that you could see from far away in any direction, and all around the clock was fancy statues of famous people. I don't know who those people was, but they had to have been famous or they wouldn't have been there in the first place.

Wandering around The Square by myself was a treat, and I never got tired of it. I peeked in the windows of Kuster's Restaurant, the tailor shop, the photograph gallery, the Auditorium movie theater, and the Haynes jewelry store and planned for the time when I could walk in and out as a real customer. I sneaked into the book store there on the North Side, next to the restaurant, and pretended like I was lookin' for somethin' important to buy. I looked at the ladies' fashion magazines and decided which dresses and hats I'd look good in. There was a ladies' dress shop at the North end of The Square that was my favorite place. There was beautiful clothes in the window, and the lady who worked there was real pretty and I just knew she was refined. I thought she could be on the cover of a fashion magazine. Sometimes she saw me looking in the window and she'd smile real nice. I decided I'd like to work there some day. The shop was called The Fashion. I thought that was a great name for it.

I allowed myself to go into the pharmacy. The sales clerks there was real nice to me, and I just walked up and down the aisles, looking inside the counters at all the stuff that was for sale. I got friendly with the people at the candy counter, and it wasn't long before I learned that if I hung out around there long enough and talked friendly with the sales clerk, she'd usually offer me a piece of gum or a lollipop or something. Me and her got to be real buddies. One day while I was waiting for John outside there, a great idea popped into my head.

Now, I have to tell you that a favorite thing of mine was to pack a sandwich and walk to Burke Golf to meet Daddy during his lunch break so I asked Mama if I could surprise him again and meet him at noon the day after I got my great idea.

I saw him before he saw me.

He was talking to some people just outside the factory door, and I couldn't help but compare him to his friends and see that he was a lot handsomer than they was, and that he was always the center of attention. I waited 'til everyone walked away, and just as I was about to yell and wave to him, a pretty lady walked up to him and started talking, and Daddy put his arm around her shoulder.

He looked up just then and saw me and moved away from her real quick and opened his arms like he always did so that I could run into them. And then he picked me up and swung me around and I gave him a big kiss and he gave me one right back. The lady just stood there smiling. She was older than me but younger than Mama, and I tried not to stare. Daddy told me that her name was Hanna, and she shook my hand and said that she had heard all about me.

I whispered to Daddy that I had something really important to tell him and so he put his hands on the pretty lady's shoulders again and said goodbye and a few other things I couldn't hear. Seeing them together, all friendly like, made me feel funny, but I determined to forget all about it like I'd done with other things I didn't like to think about.

Anyway, me and him walked over to our favorite tree and opened up our sandwiches, and I made myself stay calm 'til he finally asked me to tell him what my important news was. And I told him that when I was down at the pharmacy yesterday, down at The Square, I stopped by the candy counter like I always did, and one of the sales people came over with a huge carton that had small boxes of candy bars in it to put in the glass cases.

"Well," I said. "I asked him where the boxes of candy came from, and he said they pick them up right here in Newark, at some place a couple of times a week from someone he called a supplier, or something like that. He said he pays the supplier, and the customers pay him, and I thought, well, why can't we do the same thing 'cause it would be a good way to make some money for us."

By now Daddy had a big grin that he couldn't hide on his face and told me to go on and tell him how I could do that.

"Well, if you and me could go to that person I talked to and you was to ask him exactly where he gets that candy, we could get some too, and I could sell it to the people here at the factory during their lunch times," I said. "I could be out here when people take their lunch shifts. Then, just in case I didn't get to everyone when they was outside, I could walk up and down by those big windows over there and ask people inside if they'd like some of my candy. It would be easy to hand it to them through the windows. Then I could hurry on back home and get my chores done, and everyone would be happy. What do you think?" I stopped and took a deep breath 'cause I'd been goin' on talkin' so fast I was out of wind.

He waited so long to answer that I had time to think how I could argue at him after he told me no. He was very quiet, and just when I was about to start in again, he said, "You know what, Nellie, that is a very smart idea. Maybe it could just work."

I thought I'd pop.

"We'd have to think about how we could talk the company into letting us have the boxes of candy and how much they'd pay you to sell them, and we'd have to make sure it was all right with the bosses here, but…" and he nodded and smiled and shook my hand like he would a grownup's and said, "You're really a smart little gal, Nellie. Let's think about it, and when I get back home we'll talk some more."

Well, the way it worked out was that Daddy and me got the information we needed from the man at the pharmacy the first afternoon Daddy was off work, and the next day we hitched a ride with a neighbor going in that direction and went right over to that supplier. Daddy told the man inside there what my idea was, and he said that we could do it. The big bosses at the factory said it was all right with them, too, and within a week I had my business going.

First, the supplier let me have just one box with sixteen candy bars, but I sold those sixteen bars so fast he decided to let me have three or four boxes a week. I was at the factory when the whistle blew at twelve noon sharp three days a week, usually, when Mama didn't need me at home, and I held up those candy bars in one hand and yelled, "Candy for sale! Candy for sale!" and those factory workers rushed right over and gave me their money. Then I walked all along the side of the building where the windows all was, and I yelled the same thing real loud to the people still working inside, and they'd pass out their money to me and take the candy bars and that was all there was to it. Simple as could be.

At the end of each week, I counted up the money I made, took out what I needed to pay the supplier man, and gave the rest to Mama. I did it all by myself, and I never made a mistake. Me and Phoebe and my big brothers gave Mama the money we made all week just after supper every Sunday, and we all celebrated our "good fortune," as Mama said. I had that job all summer long, and I know it made a difference in our lives.

Things was going really good all right that first summer in our new home. Sunday afternoons in our back yard there was always softball games with the kids from our neighborhood. Mama's vegetables grew, our chickens laid us eggs, and I had a best friend.

Then on August 22nd, part of my family's world fell right in on it-self. It happened on a Saturday night at exactly six o'clock.

Phoebe and me was helping Mama finish up the dishes. I stopped what I was doing at exactly the same time Mama did, and we asked each other if we was hearing an alarm going off somewhere. The three of us went in to the parlor to listen and asked Grammy if she heard it, too. When she said she did, Mama started up the stairs and I was about ready to follow her, but Grammy grabbed me by the wrist and told me to sit down. She said that this wasn't my business and she looked scared.

Mama went up to her room to where her clock was and yelled down that the noise was coming from up in the attic. She called for John, and they both crawled up into the attic and went through some boxes of stuff until they found an old clock of Grammy's that was goin' off.

According to John, after they got themselves down from the attic, Mama stopped at her bedroom again to check on Polly and Carl. Polly was sleeping real nice and moved a little bit when Mama pulled the cover up over her. Then she looked down in the drawer below at Carl, and he didn't look just right. She felt his face and tummy to make sure he didn't have a fever or anything, and he didn't squirm at all or make any baby sounds.

John said she picked him up under his arms and held him, dangling there, and said his name again and again, and we could hear her fear all the way downstairs. Me and Grammy started up the stairs when Mama started to scream that something was wrong and that he wouldn't wake up. We found her holding Carl tight in her arms, rockin' him back and forth, whisperin' to him through her tears.

Homer was sent out to get the doctor, and when he came he told us that Carl had just died. He said his little body was still warm.

Grammy went around and opened all the doors and windows in our house so Carl's little soul could leave. When that was done, she went to all the steps outside and threw salt on them to keep evil spirits away.

The day after our baby died, Daddy and brother John went out and got a tiny casket for him, and we laid him out in the front window in the parlor so people could see him from outside if they didn't want to come in. For three days our friends and family from West Carlisle and Broomstick Valley and our brand new neighborhood came by to see our baby and to tell us how sorry they all was.

I kept right there at the foot of my brother's casket as much as I could so I could protect his little soul if I needed to in case it hadn't left yet, and if his soul was already in heaven, the way Mama said it was, well, then, he'd be able to look down and see how much I still loved him. We buried his body up on the hill at the Barns Cemetery in Wilkins Corners.

I asked Grammy about the alarm. She said that there are forces at work in the world that we just don't know about. She told me that sometimes spirits visit us from beyond. When I asked her to explain, she said that some things are best left alone.

I thought about Aunt Lizzie's rocker and her Ouija Board, and I wondered where Jesus fit into all this. If He was so good and loved all the little children, how could He let a little baby die the way He let Carl go? How could He allow so much hurt to come into our lives when we was all tryin' so hard? And I thought if God, His Father, allowed Him to do all of that, well, then, God wasn't too good either. Believe me, I was scared to have those thoughts, but I couldn't keep them from coming.

It was a sunny, crisp early afternoon in fall, the kind that is so perfect you just feel you want to run out and give yourself up to all the beauty around you. The air was clear, and the leaves on the trees was glimmering gold and red and purple. I was remembering this time of year down at our old home place and thinking how, if I was back there now, I'd have to climb up on one of my old trees even if I was too big to do it now. People said climbing trees was a child's game, but I figured that even though I wasn't a child anymore, climbing trees was still something I'd like to do. Seemed to me that if a person felt the need to climb a tree and they could still get up in one, well, then, why not do it? I never seen an adult climb a tree, though, so maybe when a person gets fully grown up, they lose that desire. I thought that was too bad. Tree-climbing was just too good a thing to give up.

Anyway, everybody was home that day, and the voices was loud and was interfering with the thoughts in my mind. I seen Daddy staring out the window at the sun same as me.

I walked over to him and whispered, "Daddy, would you like to go for a walk with me for a little bit?"

"Good idea," he whispered back, and he was grinning. "Let's not tell anybody. You go out first and I'll follow. We'll just sneak out by ourselves for a little while."

We headed out toward the tracks where we thought it might be pretty quiet and hoped nobody else on the street had the same idea before us. We wasn't in a hurry to break through the quiet, and we got almost to where we was headed before we was willing to interrupt the peace we was feeling by talking out loud.

Daddy and me understood each others' moods.

He asked me if there was anything particular on my mind when we reached the little tree grove we was headed for, and I told him that I was thinking about the Valley where we had lived and everything that had happened to us since we left there, and I wondered if he ever thought about going back.

"I think about it, sure," he told me when we was sitting comfortable under a big old Buckeye Tree. "That was our home for a lot of years. But I don't think I'd want to go back. It's hard to go back someplace and have it feel the same, I think. Would you want to go back?"

"Just to visit, I guess," I said. "You left, though, and you went back. You went to the mines. You went away to another country and fought in a war. I'd like to know more about that. I'd like to know a lot about you when you was young. I'd like to know about you and Mama when you first got together."

"How'd you know about that, about the war?" he asked me. "Mama tell you?"

I told him about me in the sheets at Aunt Lizzie's place, and it wasn't easy for him to stop laughing.

"What you did made me awful proud of you," I said.

He chuckled. "I was just a crazy kid. Hell, I didn't know nothin' about that war. I just wanted to get away and see something else besides the hills around Carlisle. Darned near killed myself out there in that God-forsaken jungle."

"So you're sorry you did it? Do you wish you hadn't gone?"

"Oh, no. I'm glad I went. I wasn't no hero or nothin'. I could have had a little more sense and tried something a little safer, that's for sure, but if I had the chance to do it all over again, I probably would."

He picked up a piece of grass to chew on and leaned back on his elbows.

"Sometimes a man just has to spread his wings and see what he's made of. Try something new. Meet different people. Have something to talk about."

I thought about that for a while. "Is that why you worked down there in the mines? Because you needed to be away, to see something more?"

He turned his head at me and looked at me thoughtful-like. He picked up another piece of grass and I knew he was considering things.

"I love your mama, Nellie. I love all of you. More than you could know. I could have found other things to do, I guess, but...I needed my own space. I needed just a little freedom to be my own man."

He couldn't look at me, and I understood that what he was about to say was goin' to be hard. "I always thought I'd find something somewhere that I could do that would be special. Or just find some place that was exactly what I was hoping it would be. It's hard to explain, honey. It's just something maybe men would understand. Mining was dangerous and dirty. But...I can't say I didn't enjoy it. It was exciting in some dumb way I can't explain."

"Maybe you was antsy."

"Yep, I was antsy alright." He sat up and rested his elbows on his knees. "You antsy, Nellie?"

We'd never had a talk quite like this one before, and I wasn't sure how much I should say. I decided to just dive right in with exactly how I was feeling. I knew I could trust him.

"Yes, I am. I have dreams about doing things," I told him. "Something inside makes me jittery and impatient, like there's something there that wants to jump out and be real. I dream about doing something important. I just can't wait to open my eyes up some morning and know what it is I should do and how I should do it."

"What is it you think you want to do, honey?"

"I don't know yet. I just don't know. I have some ideas, but... Do you have dreams, Daddy?"

"Used to," he said kind'a sad like. "Not any more."

"Maybe 'cause you grew up?"

"*Gave* up is more like it, Nellie," he said, laying back and looking up into the sky. "There was a time when I thought things was possible. Why, I'd wake up in the mornings and think hard about the places I'd see and what I'd do in those places, and just thinkin' about it all made me feel good and proud, like I'd already done it. Then I'd look around and see what needed to be done right then and there, and I'd put those exciting thoughts aside and think I'd do them later. And before I knew it, I forgot what those dreams was. They just went away like smoke in a leaf fire."

Daddy turned directly to me and had a look on his face that was so serious, more serious than I'd ever seen on him. I knew this moment was one I'd never forget.

"That don't mean you have to give up your dreams when you grow up, Nellie. I suppose most people do, but you don't have to. It's too late for mine, but it sure ain't too late for yours. The worst thing that can happen to someone is to wake up some day with no energy left and know that your dreamin' is done, that it's too late for you. Don't allow yourself to get side-tracked. Don't get trapped, honey."

None of us was ready for school to start so soon after Carl's passing, but Mama said nothing should stop us from getting ourselves educated, so we all went to sign up to go. I hate to tell you this, but I have to tell everything because that's my purpose. I was told that day we went in to sign up that I had to be held back a year. I don't know how I missed that when I got my final report in June. I don't know how Mama could have forgotten to tell me, but she did, and so I found out just days before I was supposed to start again. The shame hurt so bad. I couldn't look at nobody, especially Mama, knowing I'd let her down like that. And I couldn't stand looking at myself 'cause I was so dumb—and I knew my dreams would never come true.

Now I wouldn't be in the same class as Sandy, and I was sure she wouldn't be my best friend anymore. And to make matters worse, me and Clyde, my younger brother, would be in the same grade, and I knew he'd be just as embarrassed by that as me. I kept Aunt Lizzie's words in my head, and I practiced real hard to be strong and not let the hurt touch me too much.

Birthdays was real important in our new school. Whenever it was your special day, you got dressed up and brought cookies or candy to pass out to your friends. I always looked forward to other people's parties, but as my special day got closer, I got nervous and worried about what I'd put on and what I'd take. I'd grown out of my good dress from last year, and we never had cookies except at Christmas time and sometimes at Easter, so I didn't know what I could take to my friends for my school party. I finally got up the nerve to talk about it with Mama, and she told me to nevermind, that she had a little surprise that would be ready for me real soon.

Well, the days and nights passed and still there was no surprise, and I thought I'd die with not knowing what it was going to be. Then finally, just three days before my big day, Mama and Grammy told me to tell my teacher that I'd be bringing treats for everyone in my school room on Thursday. Well, what a relief that was. But I still didn't know what I'd wear, and that was a big worry. Well, don't you know, the night before the big day, Mama called me and Grammy out to the kitchen, and they made me close my eyes while they counted to five. I did, and when they told me I could look, there they was, both of them looking so proud, holding up a brand new dress.

My birthday dress was lavender with tiny white flowers on it, and it had a lace collar and a wide sash that sat low below my waist. Because it was real long, Mama tied it in a big bow in the back, which I knew was not in style, but Mama said it was perfect, so I didn't say anything. I rushed to the mirror in our parlor and stood on one of the chairs so I could see into it, and I stood there for a long time and turned this way and that to see the dress from all sides, and I fixed the sash and tucked the ends in, and I thought I looked real good.

Mama and Grammy was standing behind me, and they knew I was happy. "I can't see you in that dress real clear, honey," Grammy said, "but I know how pretty it is. Your mama worked real hard on it nights when everyone was sleeping."

I climbed down from the chair and ran to Mama and told her how beautiful her gift was, and I told her I couldn't hardly wait to wear it to school. Then she took me by the hand and led me back into the kitchen and told me to close my eyes again. This time when I opened them, there was the two of them again, holding up our best platter with a huge pile of sugar cookies on it, and I couldn't believe it. I asked them how they got cookies, and Mama told me to nevermind, that I was to just enjoy them and not forget to thank the Lord for taking care of us.

I couldn't hardly pay attention the whole morning there in school. I was thinking so much about my pretty new dress and those cookies up there on the teacher's desk, and I was thinking about how important I was that day and about how all the kids would like me more now because of my party.

We went outside for morning break because it was such a warm fall day. Me and my girlfriends walked around the yard, and I was real careful not to dirty my dress. I did everything right to take care of myself, but I hadn't planned on big old nasty Dan Vickers.

Dan bullied everyone in our neighborhood, and for some reason he bullied me more than he did anybody else. It was clear he hated my big brothers because they was stronger and smarter than him, but I couldn't figure out why he was nasty with me. He never came right out and said anything about me being held back a year, but he made fun of me being taller than the other girls and sometimes he talked funny and said he was talkin' like me.

He'd ask real loud, "How many brothers and sisters do you have, Nellie? How many was that?" And then his friends would laugh. Sometimes he'd yell, "Where you get those clothes, Nellie?" and then he'd tell everyone how we got them from the church, and I just ignored him like Mama said I should, but it hurt.

This day, though, out in the school yard, he came up to me and my friends and asked me, "Is that thing you have on new, Nellie? That's an ugly dress," he said. "Just about as ugly as you." He made it sound like "oogly" and he laughed.

My friends yelled at me to walk away and ignore him, but I just couldn't because all I could think of was Mama and Grammy and how hard Mama had worked on that dress, and I decided I didn't need to take any more of Dan Vickers' bad mouth. Makin' fun of me was one thing, but sayin' bad things about what my mama did was something else.

"You shut up your mouth, Dan Vickers," I said, "or I'll shut it for you."

"You're ugly and your dress is ugly and your Mama's ugly too," He shouted real loud so everyone could hear him. "What you gonna'do about that?"

A big knot-like thing came up into my throat, and I had to get that anger out somehow. I hurled myself right up to him and put my hand over his big mouth.

"You're nothing but a big bully," I shouted. "Everyone thinks so. You have no right to talk about me and my family like that. I'm warning you, if you ever do it again, you'll be in big trouble. Do you hear me?"

Dan was so mad he couldn't get whole words out. He was bright red with rage, and I felt myself cringe from him. That's when he shoved me.

I guess the fall kind'a stunned me 'cause when I got up, the madness in me was gone, and all I saw was the mud all over me and my new dress. Teacher rushed up to us and asked us what was going on, and I thought about telling her, but something stopped me. I had a problem, but I wasn't going to let no one else take care of it for me. I was going to be stronger than that. I told teacher that I fell down, and I asked her if I could go home and clean myself up.

I told Mama what had happened while she helped me wash up, except I left out what Dan had said about her being ugly. She kept real quiet, but I knew she was thinkin' hard same as she does whenever she has a real problem to tackle, and I gave her time to mull it all over.

When I asked her, finally, what to do, Mama told me to be a lady and go back to school and have my party and ignore Dan. She said there would always be people who don't know how to behave and who get pleasure out of hurting others. She said she feels bad for people like that because they're unhappy with themselves or they wouldn't be hateful, and she told me that those people always get their due in the end. Hitting and saying mean things to them wouldn't make things any better. I listened hard to what she had to say, but Aunt Lizzie's advice about how I shouldn't take anything off of anyone kept getting in the way.

"I hate Dan," I said. The words spit themselves out of me before I even knew they was coming. "And I hate being poor."

It was the first time in my whole life I had ever said those words. I didn't even know the feelings was there to put the words together. I looked up into Mama's face, and it was so full of hurt that my only thought was about her.

I flung myself over to her chair and hugged her hard as I could. "I'm sorry, Mama, I'm so sorry," I said, burying my face in her neck. "I didn't mean to make you feel bad. I don't know what made me say that. I didn't mean anything. I don't feel poor. Everything is just so mixed up sometimes that I don't know what I want or think."

She made me stand up in front of her, and she put her red, chapped hands on my shoulders and gripped them tight.

"Nellie," she said, speaking soft and determined, "there is no shame in being poor. Having things isn't what matters. What matters is what's inside each of us." She tapped at where my heart is. "What matters is family. What matters is..." She stopped. "It hurts me that you feel shame."

I started to tell her that she was wrong, that I didn't feel shame. I only felt mad about the way things was working out.

She put her finger up to my lips to keep me quiet. "Nellie, she said, "I want you to go back to that school with your head held high. I don't want you to ever let anyone make you feel ashamed again. You're as good as anyone, and don't you forget it. Promise me you'll walk back to that school tall and straight and proud. Promise me you'll never again let anyone make you feel what you're feeling now. You may not have a lot of pretty things, but you can still have your dignity. You carry yourself tall and behave like a lady, and people will treat you with respect."

Well, that sounded a lot like Aunt Lizzie talking, and it got me going. The mud on my dress had dried now so I brushed off as much as I could and told Mama not to worry. I was going to walk proud. On my way back to school I kept saying to myself that I was as good as anyone else, just like Mama told me to do, but I heard some of the kids whispering and giggling when I walked by, and I heard them say something about me having the same dress on. My dignity took a little dive down.

The last thing we did that day, after everyone sang happy birthday to me, was have Mama and Grammy's cookies. It didn't feel the way I had dreamed it would. I looked across the room at Clyde, hoping he'd smile at me or something and I'd feel better, but he wouldn't look up from his desk.

I couldn't wait to get away from that place that day, but teacher took so much time telling me happy birthday and how good the cookies was that I was one of the last ones to get out the door. I looked around for someone to walk home with, but everyone was already on their way. I hurried down the street to catch up, but Dan and his friends was waiting for me down the block.

"Why are you wearing a dirty dress, Nellie?" he said. "Oh, I know! You don't have another one to put on. Poor Nellie. Hey, want us to walk down to the church and get a new dress for you?" He looked around at his friends and asked them if they'd go with him and me to get some new clothes for me. "Oh, shit, that's right. They don't hand out clothes to poor people 'til Saturday."

I tried to walk away from him, but he put himself in front of me and got up real close in my face. "Your Mama's like a rabbit, Nellie. Keeps having babies just like a rabbit. And you and your big brother rabbits are all ugly."

That did it. Without thinking, I brought my hand up and hit him on the side of his head so hard it felt like my hand was broken.

"Don't you ever talk about us that way again or you'll pay!" I screamed at him. "And you'll pay big. You're the ugly one, Dan Vickers. And you're stupid. No one likes you. You're nothing but a stupid, idiotic bully."

Even as I was saying those awful things, I was wonderin' where the words was coming from, but they needed to be said, and I didn't even think about holding them back.

"You shut up your fuckin' face, you stupid girl." Dan shouted as he moved closer.

The other boys had formed a circle around me. I knew I was in big trouble, and I was so scared. I looked down the street to see if anyone was left there to help me. Then, right out of nowhere came my brother John with Clyde running behind him trying to keep up.

John was panting hard, and I couldn't tell if it was from runnin' or from being filled with the same hard stuff I was feeling. I guess I hadn't realized how big he was until he plowed right through the circle of Dan's friends and grabbed Dan's shirt at his shoulders and pushed him hard.

"You bother my sister again, you shithead, and me and my brothers will come after you and give you the beating of your goddamn life," he shouted. "Do you hear me?"

Dan didn't say a word. John's face was blotchy and red, and the veins in his neck pushed out against the skin there. He stood thrust forward, his body rigid, his hands balled up in fists, and I knew he wanted to lay into Dan hard. But he just stood looking down at him and said, "Do you understand me, shithead?" Then he turned around at the others and said, "All of you, do you hear me? Just give us an excuse. Any of you. Don't you mess with us."

John swore all the way home. The cuss words was hurled at someone or something I didn't know but was beginning to understand. Finally, he stopped and put his hands on my shoulders and told me that I never had to take that kind of treatment from anyone again. Not ever.

"It's time our family stands up proud. I'll take care of you, Nellie, and I'll take care of the rest of the family too. Don't you worry." He put his arm around Clyde. "We both will, won't we, little brother."

"You're just like Daddy, John," I gushed.

"No, I'm not."

Daddy came home late after supper one night in early January, and we was all waitin' for him in the parlor. Mama had been at the front window looking for him, as was her habit now, and when she finally saw him coming down the street, she let out a sigh and went back into the kitchen. Daddy didn't look so good when he came in and didn't say much to us in the way of a greeting or anything. When he went into the kitchen, he shut the door. The two of them was in there together for a long time, whispering, and after a while Daddy came out and put his coat back on and left. When I started to go to Mama, Grammy told me to hold on until her and John could find out what was going on.

The next day, John explained to us older kids that Daddy had lost his job and was going to look for another one at the Wehrle Factory. Eventually he got a job working half-shifts. George and Homer and John quit school so they could take on more work, and I begged Mama to let me quit, too, but she told me that was ridiculous.

Our new little baby brother Danny was born the first of June.

Right after the baby was born, Mama told me not to make any plans to see my friends that evening because her and Daddy wanted to have a little talk with me that night about something important. I was nervous at supper, and I looked around at everybody to see if they might give me a hint about what the big talk would be about, but they was all acting pretty normal. The whole time me and Phoebe worked on the dishes, I tried to think if I'd done something bad, somethin' I was going to get punished for, but when we settled back down at the table later, after we got all the little ones to bed, Mama and Daddy was smiling and so I relaxed a little.

The three of us just sat there at the table chitchatting for a while like there was nothing out of the way at all, except that Daddy kept fidgeting and taking quite an interest in the scratches on the table. When we kind'a ran out of little things to talk about and it got quiet in our little circle, Mama cleared her throat and got down to business.

"Nellie, you know how you've said before that you'd like to help out the family and bring in some money just like your older brothers? Well, you're going to have a chance to do that now. You're growing up real good, Nellie, and you're right, we could use your help. You can have a real job the rest of the summer and after school some days."

She paused like she was waiting for me to get excited about going to work, but I couldn't get my enthusiasm up right then. I had kind'a changed my mind about working now that I had all those friends and was enjoying myself. I waited to hear what Mama had in mind before I said anything out loud.

"My boss down at the factory could use some help," Daddy said, clearing his throat. "His wife, Mrs. Becker, just had a new baby, and she needs some help cleaning and helping with the other kids. Mama has been telling me how good you've become at cleaning and taking care of the little ones and all, and we thought you might just want to take on the job of helping Mrs. Becker. Why, I'll bet you she might even let you help take care of the baby from time to time. I told Mr. Becker how good you are with your little brothers and sisters." He was rambling.

I thought about how hard my own mama had to work. How she had thirteen kids to take care of. "How many kids does Mrs. Becker have?"

"Well, she has four now. Four, with the new baby."

"She can't take care of four kids? Is there something wrong with her?" I don't know what was making me ask these questions and acting so snotty.

Daddy shifted in his chair. "Well, Nellie, some people are not as fit or as able as others."

I looked over at Mama to see how she was taking all of this crazy talk about how a mother couldn't take care of just four kids and keep the house up, but she kept her eyes away from mine. I wouldn't like Mrs. Becker and I suspected Mama knew that.

"Maybe Phoebe would like to work there," I said. "She's better at that kind of stuff than I am."

"Well, honey," Mama said, "we thought about Phoebe, naturally, but she's taking on more work there at the church, and you always seemed to want to…"

I was feeling bad about how I was acting, and so I interrupted her and said that I'd go to the Beckers and do a real good job and make her proud. I smiled at Mama to let her know I was all right. But I didn't know how I felt about Daddy just then and so I didn't look at him.

So, everyday for the rest of the summer, I walked the two and a half miles to work. I left at eight in the morning when my older brothers did, and I got home usually by five. The Becker family was nice to me. I washed dishes and helped make beds and took care of the little kids while Mrs. Becker tended to the baby and ran errands. In a way I didn't work much harder than I would've if I'd stayed home, and everything was fine, especially at the end of the week when I brought home the money she gave me.

At home I helped with supper and cleaning up after. Then it was time to go to bed and start all over again.

I was tired, and I was scared I'd lose my friends because I didn't get to see them hardly at all. I never told them exactly what I was doing. I never told them I was working. I told them I was visiting my cousins or doing special things for Mama. I felt bad fibbing. I knew it wasn't right. But I didn't want to look different from them. So I lied.

At night when I was supposed to be saying my prayers, I wished Daddy could get another job, and I wished we had a bigger house and I could have my own bed room. I wished I could be a little more like my friends. But I didn't feel real confident that anyone up there was listening to me or, if they was, that they'd do anything about what I wanted, seein' as how none of my prayers had been answered so far.

My favorite time in school was physical education class. Our teacher was a real pretty lady named Miss Jackson, and me and my friends liked her a lot. She was tall and thin, but not skinny, and her hair was cut in the latest style and her clothes was real smart. All us girls kind'a looked up to her. She seemed always happy, and she complimented us all the time and never made us feel bad if we came in last in a game or something. We liked to stay and talk with her after class, and we all hoped we'd run into her after school just to have the chance to talk to her.

One day just before the end of class late that fall, she told us all to sit down in a circle right there on the gym floor 'cause she had something important to talk to us about. She told us that she was going to put together two girls' basketball teams so we could compete, and she would like to know if any of us would be interested in playing. We'd meet after school several times a week to practice and play. Well, everyone wanted to play, and we all raised our hands when she asked for a vote to put the teams together.

Now, one big problem I could see right away was the fact that Miss Jackson had to have our parents sign a piece of paper that said it was all right for us all to play. I just knew I'd have a problem with that one. Daddy would think it was a great idea for me to be on the team, but Mama would probably have a hissy-fit about it. Then there was my after-school job, but I figured I could work that one out.

That night I waited for all the other kids to get to sleep, and I sneaked down to the parlor where Mama and Daddy and Grammy was finishing up some things.

"Well, Nellie, honey." Mama was surprised to see me. "What are you doing up out of bed? Is something wrong?"

I picked out the spot to sit on the floor where I thought I might have the best chance to get all three of them involved in what I was about to say. I'd practiced my words very careful, but now that I was there with everyone lookin' at me, I wasn't so sure my speech was that good anymore. I just started in.

"How are all of you doin'? I'm not interrupting anything am I?" I said, figuring I had to get into this thing slow-like.

Daddy smiled and said that they was all just fine and that I wasn't interruptin' anything. I wanted him to go on and talk a little to kind of warm things up, but when he didn't say anything more I had to plunge right in.

"Well," I said, "I wanted to talk to you about something important at school. Nothin's wrong or anything like that, but I have to see if something would be all right for me to do." I took a deep breath and hurried on. "See, we was in gym class today with Miss Jackson, and she came up with a great idea. All my friends and me are really excited about it, and she said we all had to go back to our parents tonight and ask them if it was all right with them."

I had trouble getting the real crux of the matter out.

"Well, we've been playin' basketball in class and us girls really like

101

playing," I said, going real fast now, deciding it was best to get it all out there in a rush. "Miss Jackson said I was very good at it, actually, and so did my friends. Well, anyway, since we all like it so much and don't have a lot of time during class to really learn how to shoot and play and all, Miss Jackson thought maybe we'd like to put together two teams, and we'd all play after school and have real games. She said we'd play just like the boys do, competing and all, except of course, we'd play just between ourselves, not against other teams from other schools like the boys do. So, anyway, I'd like to play on one of the teams. It would only be once or twice a week, so I could still work for the Beckers and keep up with my chores here, and on weekends I could still work wherever I'm needed." I ran out of steam. "I'd really, really like to be on the team, Daddy."

I held my breath.

Daddy spoke up, "Well, Nellie, let's see now. Let me make sure I understand." And he went over everything I'd just said to make sure he had it right, and I told him that was it, in a nutshell, and he told me that I should go back to bed and let him and Mama talk about it, and they'd let me know soon as possible.

I couldn't sleep that night, and I prayed with all my heart that they'd say yes. Then I thought there was no use in praying 'cause Jesus was probably mad at me since I'd had those bad thoughts about Him from time to time, so I just kept my fingers crossed instead. The next morning no one said anything about it, and we was all so rushed that I just went on to school. Me and my friends talked about the teams all day long, whenever we had a chance, and every one of them said their moms and dads said it would be fine, that it was a good idea to get more exercise and learn to compete and all. I hoped my mama and daddy would say the same thing.

I worked hard on my chores after school and even volunteered to take sister Polly for a walk before supper. I acted real cheerful and gave Mama and Grammy big hugs and tried to put my best face forward, as they say. That night before bed, I went over to where Daddy was sitting and asked if him and Mama had decided yet about the team. He called for Mama to come in, and they told me together that it would be all right for me to be on the team so long as I could keep up my grades and do a good job at the Beckers.

I ran to school the next morning and found my group of friends outside waiting, and we all hugged each other when I told them that I could do it. As far as I was concerned, we was already a team. Miss Jackson had some forms all ready for our parents to sign, and she told us about our new uniforms that she was looking into. Uniforms. Oh, my gosh, we was getting uniforms! We couldn't believe it!

But then she showed us the catalogue pictures she'd been looking at, and I knew that I was going to be in a heap of trouble where Mama was concerned. The uniforms was shorts and a long shirt. I knew Mama would never let me wear shorts. And then there was the problem of how to pay for them.

Right then and there was when I started to be a little sneak. I gave my parents the form to sign, but I didn't give them Miss Jackson's letter about the uniform. I told Miss Jackson that I had to pay for the uniform myself, and I even asked her if I could give her a little bit of money here and there when I had it, and she said that was fine. She'd get everything for me, and I'd pay her back whenever I could. She told me not to worry about a thing.

I wasn't proud of what I was doing. Every time I put those shorts on, I felt the guilts come. I knew I was sinning, just like I knew I was going against the Lord when I skipped choir practice and wore my hair down at school. This was worse.

Well, I played basketball that whole year, two times a week after school. Miss Jackson had us play on the days when I didn't have to work, and I swear I will always love her for that. Sandy took my shorts to her own house ever so often so her mama would wash them for me, right along with hers, and I gave Miss Jackson a little here and there from my pay whenever I could. See, I was not being honest there either because I was telling Mama that I was making less than what I really was so I could pay Miss Jackson. Seems like once you begin to sneak and lie, it gets easier and easier each time.

It was a relief when the last game was held that spring and I could stop fibbing to everyone. I had to watch myself so careful all the time to make sure I didn't let the cat out of the bag that it really started to wear me down. I was anxious to get back to being honest with Mama. The last sneaky thing I did that spring was ask Sandy if she'd keep my uniform at her house for safekeeping.

Us kids was used to Daddy missing most suppers, but I could tell Mama felt really sad about it. One night she just stayed out on the porch and told us to go ahead and eat without her. Me and my brothers tried to entertain the little ones and act like everything was normal. After Phoebe and me and Grace got the dishes done and all, I decided to find Mama and try to cheer her up.

She was standing out by her garden with John, and when I came up behind them, I heard him say, "This has got to stop, Mama. It isn't right."

Well, I came to a halt and listened real careful. I'd never seen the two of them talk so serious together before. And I couldn't get over how grown up John appeared.

"Don't get yourself all riled up, John," Mama told him. "I know you care. I know you're concerned, but, really, it's all right. He's probably working late or had something important to do before he could get home."

"He doesn't have to work this late. You know what his hours are."

"Well, my guess is he stopped down by the pool hall to see some of his friends."

"He doesn't need to be down there. He needs to be home with his family, spend some good time with you."

"Your daddy needs some time to himself. Time to do some manly things. He..."

"You need some time to yourself, too, Mama," John interrupted her. "When do you ever have time to be with your women friends?"

"It's different for women."

"No, it ain't." John fidgeted and stood lookin' out at the street. "Mama, I'm going to go lookin' for him. Me and George will go out and find him, and we'll bring him home. I'm not going to stand this any more. I think I know where he is. George and me will be right back. Don't you worry."

My brother moved away from her before she could say anything and stopped in front of me, surprised to find me there. "You take care of Mama," he said. "George and me will be right back. You take care of her."

There was tears on Mama's cheeks, and the sight of her crying made a pain come into my heart. I took her hand and waited. When she was ready, we took a little walk across the back yard and out to the tracks. We tried to make small talk, but our hearts wasn't in it. The words came out awkward and unconnected.

When John and George came back to the house later that night, they was alone.

The last day of school I found out I was going to be held back another year, and my shame stuck out all over me for everyone to see. It didn't matter much to John and George and Homer. They quit before they had a chance to fail, and Daddy told me how hard school had always been for him, too, and said how me and him was alike in that respect. But he said I had to try harder for Mama's sake. Grammy didn't offer any excuses, and she didn't act any way in particular about my schoolin'. She just told me that everybody was going through changes right then and I was no exception, that things would get better eventually. Old Phoebe told me my failure was because I had turned my back on Jesus.

"Turn your back on Him, and He turns away from you," she said. "Come to the Lord, Nellie. Come be saved, and He will make all things possible."

By now I was way beyond trying to understand anything she said.

Sandy stayed my friend and helped me through my guilts. I visited her house every chance I had. We sang songs we heard on her radio. *Tea for Two; What'll I Do; and It Had To Be You* was our favorites. Sometimes

Mrs. Becker sang too. She let us dance in Sandy's room, and sometimes she showed us steps she knew. I decided that if I ever was a mama to someone, and I wasn't so sure I wanted to be, I'd be like Mrs. Becker. She let joy in her house.

Mrs. Becker liked her house to be filled with Sandy's friends. There was always room for us. We looked at magazines and cut out pictures of hairdos and make up and pretty clothes and our favorite singers and movie stars. 'Course, I'd never been to a movie. Actually, none of us had, but we still had our favorite stars. Clara Bow and Colleen Moore was beautiful. I wrapped my pictures up inside pieces of scrap paper and hid them in my drawer under my underwear.

I went back to school that fall, and I started out the same way I finished the year before: real frustrated. I couldn't keep my mind on what was going on. Seemed like no matter how hard I tried, I couldn't keep track of what teacher was saying, and all I could think about was getting out of that room. I felt closed in and fidgeted all the time. I know that 'cause teacher was always mad at me for movin' around so much. Why, I had to stay after school so often I just kind of expected it every day, and I got to thinking more and more how I'd be better off doing something else with my time.

The only thing that kept me going was basketball. Miss Jackson and the other girls was always telling me how good I was. All that dreamin' about flying and that tree climbing I used to do helped me. I could see right there in my head how I could jump up for a ball and throw it in the hoop. Miss Jackson said I was strong and coordinated, and I told her my Daddy was definitely the one to thank for that. Those softball games with him taught me how to never stop watching the ball, and those times he kept tellin' me to run faster taught me not to hold back. All in all, things was going pretty good. Then, right before Christmas vacation, I made a big mistake, and it changed everything.

Do you remember those basketball shorts that I kept hidden away from my mama over there at Sandy's house? Well, it just so happened that our last practice for basketball was two days before Christmas vacation and so we played just a little because Miss Jackson thought we'd all be too excited about the Christmas festivities that was going on, to keep our minds on basketball. But before she let us leave the gym, she sat us down in the middle of the floor and told us all to have a beautiful Christmas, and she gave each one of us a little candle, all wrapped up in bright red tissue paper and a green bow. Some of the girls had gifts for her too, and I felt bad that I didn't have anything to give her except the card I'd made. But when we all got up to leave, she took me off to the side and told me she liked my card gift a lot because I'd taken the time to make it all by myself.

Well, by the time her and me chitchatted and wished each other Merry Christmas again, the others was already started home, so I pulled off my shorts and top behind the gym door and stuffed them in my coat pocket when I was dressed. Well, don't you just know, by the time I caught up with everybody, we was so excited about things that I just forgot about the uniform. When I got home, I remembered how it was in my pocket, and I rushed upstairs to my room and folded everything up into a little ball and was just hiding it in the drawer where all my pictures was when in walked Old Phoebe.

I must 'a jumped when I saw her, and I definitely slammed the drawer shut in a hurry, so she asked me what I was up to. I said I wasn't up to nothin', and, to get her mind off me, I asked her if she wasn't supposed to be at church or something. But Old Phoebe wasn't about to be sidetracked.

"Well, let's just see what you have in there that you're so worried about," she said and pushed me out of her way.

"You can't just go pokin' around in my things, Phoebe," I told her. "You just can't do that. That's my stuff in there, and it's none of your damned business."

That stopped her right in her tracks.

"What did you say? What did you say? Now you're cussin' too, huh?"

I was just as surprised as she was about my cussin'.

She got up real close and said in a hateful way, "I know about the pictures, Nellie, and I know you're headed straight for Hell."

She opened my drawer and pulled out the shorts and top like she was afraid she'd get a disease from them, like they was the vilest things on earth. "What are these? Where are you wearing these shorts?"

"It's none of your business," I said confident as I could. I was having trouble breathing.

"Oh, all right, little miss high-and-mighty!" she said. "All right. Let's go down and have a talk with Mama."

"Mama knows I'm playing basketball after school and so does Daddy," I told her. "They told me I could do it a long time ago. So there. Now give me my shorts back and keep out of my drawer."

"I don't believe Mama gave you permission to play basketball and allowed you to flaunt yourself around half-dressed," she hissed.

"Well, she did," I said. "You don't know everything that's going on around here. How would you know? You're always over at that church, acting like miss goody-two-shoes. Maybe if you was around here more, you'd know more about what was goin' on."

I was afraid maybe I had gone a little too far. It was hard to get the upper hand with Old Phoebe. I grabbed for my uniform, but she was quicker than me.

She looked at me hard and turned around and walked out the door with my shorts dangling out in front of her.

Mama and Grammy was in the kitchen. "I found these shorts in Nellie's drawer just now," Phoebe said, "and she's told me that you and Daddy gave her permission to wear them and play basketball after school. Is she telling the truth? Have you permitted her to play a man's game and to wear shorts?"

Phoebe's voice was taking on the same sound it did when she was talking to me. I couldn't believe she was talking to Mama like that.

"Nellie, is that true?" Mama asked me. "Are you wearing shorts to play basketball in?"

I looked right at Mama and ignored Phoebe. I told her how everyone was wearing shorts and that their parents didn't care and the reason that I didn't tell her was because I just knew she wouldn't let me and I wanted to play so bad and not be different from everyone. I hadn't lied. I just didn't tell the whole story.

By the look on Mama's face and the fact that she didn't answer me back real quick, I thought maybe I had won this argument with Phoebe.

But she wouldn't have it.

"She has pictures upstairs of movie stars and women advertising skin creams and makeup," she said. "She's cussing too. She's using the word 'damn'. Mama, you have to do something right now about her or she's going to end up being a harlot. Who knows what else she's doing and what lies she's told you."

Grammy shifted in her chair. "Oh, my, oh, my," she said. I couldn't tell whose side she was on.

Phoebe threw the uniform down on the kitchen table. "We need to burn these shorts right here and now. We need to help her cast out the devil. Mama, we have to help Nellie. She is walking down the path of sin."

We all held our breaths while Mama thought about it. "Nellie, Nellie, I have no choice."

"Mama, please. We can't do that. I haven't even paid for them yet. I still owe Miss Jackson. Mama, all the girls wear shorts at school to play. I just wanted to be like them. Please don't burn my shorts, Mama, please."

"Nellie, you lied," she said. "You sneaked around behind your family's back."

Phoebe knew things was going in her favor. "And where are you getting the money to pay for these?"

I explained, and Mama's face took on a look so tired I was afraid I had made her really, truly sick.

"Nellie. I have no choice. The shorts have to go, and you have to be the one to put them in the fire."

"Oh, please, Mama, please. I'll do anything. Please don't make me do this."

Mama passed the shorts and top over to me and led me to the stove.

"I can't. I can't do this. Grammy, please, tell them they're wrong." Grammy didn't say nothin'. I held the shorts up and away from Mama. I cried out, "I won't do it. You have no right to make me. I'm not a bad girl. You can't make me."

Someone grabbed the shorts from my hands, and I looked up and stared at Grammy while she dropped them into the fire.

"There. It's done. The thing is done." No one spoke. "Each of us will have to find the truth of what has been said here in our own hearts in our own time. It's over."

I knew that I would never, ever forgive Phoebe. I was all mixed up about Mama. I lied to Miss Jackson and told her I'd lost those shorts. She asked me if I still wanted to play basketball and, Jesus help me, I said I did.

"I have an extra pair that will probably fit you," she told me. "And don't worry about paying me because they're used. I almost got rid of them a couple of times, but I held on to them. See, they were meant for you. Right?" She was trying to make me feel better. "And, Nellie, I hadn't told you, but you had paid off all you owed right before Christmas."

I played basketball for a few more weeks, but, truth is, my heart just couldn't get back into it. I felt guilty: guilty for going behind Mama's back again and guilty about Miss Jackson too. I knew I hadn't paid her what I owed her. That's one thing I could do right: I could add, and I knew I owed her fifty cents. It just plain hurt my pride to be beholdin' to someone, especially when it was someone I liked so much it felt like love. It was all just too hard. I quit basketball, and I lost a lot more than the chance to play a game.

Me and my basketball friends got together as often as we could, but it wasn't the same, and I figured it never would be. If you don't share things that are really important and spend special time with a friend, then something is lost between you. I could feel that hard place in my heart grow just a little bit each time I walked home from school alone on a basketball day.

Right before Easter, I told my family that I was quitting school and they didn't try to stop me. I was fourteen.

PART 4

I went to work full time as a housecleaner and babysitter at a rich family's house across town. Their name was Stone. Sometimes I'd have to stay on overnight if they needed me to clean up after their parties; or if they was going to be real late coming back from someone else's. I slept in a tiny room in the back of the house. I wasn't allowed to eat with the family, and I wasn't allowed to sit down in the main part of the house. When they had people over, they called me their maid.

I was able to swallow my pride up until one night after I'd worked for them for almost six months. The Stone's little girl Susie was eight, and she never liked me. I felt sorry for her at first because I wouldn't have liked it much either if my mama had been so busy with other people that she couldn't spend time with me when I was her age. The Stones drank a lot. I could tell that from the way they acted when they came home from being out with friends, and I wondered if that made Susie feel sad. Anyway, she bossed me around a lot and had me do things she should have done for herself, and I let her get away with it 'til this one night when I decided I couldn't take it any more.

After I tucked the kids in bed, I went into the little room where I slept when I was there and put on my night gown. I was just climbing into bed to look at the magazine and eat the bag of penny candies I had picked up on my way to work that morning when in walked Susie.

She asked me what I was reading in a mean way, and when I told her the name of the magazine, she asked me where I got the candy, and I said it was mine and asked her if she would like a piece. She said that she wasn't allowed to have it unless her mother gave it to her and that I wasn't allowed to read magazines or eat candy in her house.

Well, I wanted to tell her to mind her own business, and I wanted to sit her down and talk to her about how she should treat people. I didn't though. Instead, I put my things down and tucked her back in bed.

Don't you know, the next morning when I was washing up the breakfast dishes, Mrs. Stone poured herself a cup of coffee, sat down, and told me we had to have a conversation. She said that Susie had told her about the magazine and the candy. I didn't answer in any way 'cause I didn't know what to say. Then she asked me if I'd taken the candy from the cupboard. I felt my neck grow hot and knew my face was red. I asked her if she was saying that she thought I stole her candy.

"Well," she said. "Did you?"

Little Susie was standing at the door watching her mother and me, and she was smiling.

Why, you could have knocked me over with a feather. I couldn't hardly get words out. I told Mrs. Stone that I would never, ever steal anything from anyone, and I explained how I had bought the candy at the same time I bought the magazine. She said she thought she had made it clear that I was to bring nothing into the house for any reason. I told her I didn't think it would matter if I read when my work was done and I was in the room by myself. She said she needed to see everything, and she meant everything, I brought into her house.

What she said did more than embarrass me. It made me feel small. I had to fight with myself to stand tall.

"Mrs. Stone, I would never, ever steal from you. I would never steal from anyone. It hurts me real bad that you think that of me." I looked over at Susie. "I think Susie would rather have you here more so I wouldn't have to be. I think she wants me to leave, and this is her way to make it happen."

"Now you just wait a minute," Mrs. Stone said as she slammed down her coffee cup. "I won't have you telling me how to conduct things in my own house. My daughter is not a liar, and she is not unhappy."

"I don't lie either, Ma'am." I looked at the two of them and thought about that little room where I had to stay and how I was called a maid. The word "fortitude" popped into my head.

"Well, I'm real sorry that it's ending like this," I said, taking off my apron. "I hope you and your family will be well and happy. I'll get my things and say goodbye."

Mrs. Stone looked at me like I had just said the house was on fire or something worse. "Oh, no, no, no," she said. "We have things planned for the weekend. I can't possibly get other help in time. You come back just like you had planned, and we'll deal with this later."

I was surprised she still wanted me there when she thought I was a liar and a thief. I didn't want to help her out any more, but I didn't have the right words to explain how I was feeling, so I told her I'd be back like she wanted. I went into my little room and packed up my things, and all the time something inside told me that all of this stuff just wasn't right. I was polite when I told Mrs. Stone and Susie goodbye, but all the while I walked home, the shame spread out all over me and kept getting bigger. Aunt Lizzie's words kept coming up to me, and I thought hard about what she'd do in this predicament. Finally, I stopped right in the middle of the street, looked back in the direction I came from, and decided, right then and there, that I was going right back and speak my mind.

"Mrs. Stone," I said, "I've been thinking hard about what happened here today, and I came to tell you that I'm real sorry, but I can't work for you anymore. Seems to me if people can't trust each other and feel respect, well, then, they should just part company."

"Now, look here, Nellie," Mrs. Stone said, and it sounded like the words was getting stuck in her mouth. "We can work this out. We'll think of some kind of other arrangements we can make for you. Let's think this whole thing over and talk about it tomorrow right after the party."

"Mrs. Stone," I said, "you have trouble trusting me, and I have trouble respecting your family. Like I said, when there is no trust and no respect, there can't be much of a friendship. That's what my grammy always said. I'm sorry, but I have to leave."

My mama had told me to walk proud. I was tryin'.

After that, I went to work full time as a housecleaner and caregiver for an old woman who advertised in the church bulletin and didn't live too far away from us. She was real good to me, and I liked her a lot. I cleaned up around the house every day, washed out her clothes and ironed them, went to the grocery, fixed her meals, and stayed with her 'til her day was done, which was pretty early. Then I walked home and helped out there where I could. Mrs. Tildredge was always telling me how grateful she was that I was there. She said that I was the answer to her prayers.

I turned over most of the money I made to Mama just like always, but she told me to keep some of what I made for myself to buy things that I needed. She called it "mad money." I told her that was a funny name for it, and she laughed and said she thought so, too. Her and Grammy just got to calling it that a long time ago. It was a name they gave to what they put aside for a rainy day. She said every woman needed a little "mad money" set aside. I asked if she had some, and she said that she did have at one time, but she'd used it all and that she was going to start saving again soon as she could.

I only bought something when I really needed it so that mad money could grow. About once a month I counted those coins out on the kitchen table even when I hadn't added much: it was just something I got pleasure out of. Sometimes Mama helped me, and I think she got as much fun out of it as I did. I didn't have any plans on how to use it, but

114

looking at those coins there in that jar gave me the feeling that everything was going to be all right. It gave me confidence, and Grammy said that's what it was supposed to do. She said it was my security. I hoped that maybe I wouldn't need it for a rainy day at all, that maybe I could save enough to allow me to do something important. My old dream of a bakery popped back into my head from time to time, and I thought, well, why not?

John and George wasn't around much any more. They went out after work and often times came home pretty late. I know they drank because sometimes I'd be downstairs when they came in, and I could smell it on them. But they didn't act up. Them and Daddy had some nasty words at each other sometimes about it, but there wasn't much Daddy could do about how they was spending their time. I heard John remind him on more than one occasion about how they was no different than him. It hurt me to see how they went after each other that way, and I know that it must have broken Mama's heart. One night it all came crashing down on all of us.

I'd stayed up late with Mama, waiting for Daddy to come home, and finally I talked her into going on up to bed and get some sleep. She looked all run down and just wasn't herself lately. I laid down on the settee across from Grammy, thinking about how I'd have my own little "heart-to-heart" with Daddy and try to fix things up between him and Mama.

Long about dawn, I heard him come in the back door, and the boys came in after him. I was relieved that everybody was in safe and sound and, since they was in the kitchen talkin', I decided to go on up to bed and have a word with Daddy alone when the time was right.

The conversation in the kitchen started off real quiet, but things got louder real quick. I tip-toed over to the kitchen door to see what was happening. The arguing got worse, especially between John and Daddy. The bad words was going out all over the house, and soon the rest of my family was backed up there behind me. Poor Mama pushed her way through us to put a stop to the ugliness, but those three men was too riled up to even know she was there. John snarled something and Daddy shoved him and said something right back, and then I can't even tell you what happened, it came on so fast, but before we knew it, the two of them was on the floor pounding at each other.

I couldn't do nothing but stand there with my hands over my ears, and I watched my poor Mama pull at Daddy's shoulders, yelling for them both to please, please stop. George and Homer and Clyde finally broke the fight up and held our John and Daddy away from each other. John was still yelling about Daddy's being no damn good when he jerked the door open and staggered out.

The next day, before Daddy got home, John came back, his face all swollen and his eyes all bloodshot. I couldn't tell if they was like that from drinkin' or fightin' or cryin', and I decided it was probably from all three. He was in a terrible state. Mama sent us all outside so her and John could talk, but I stayed close by so I could hear what they was sayin'.

John got right to what was on his mind. "Mama," he said, "I'm real sorry about last night. I don't ever want to upset you, but it was all bound to happen. There's just been too much going on between me and Daddy."

"It wasn't your fault any more than Daddy's," she told him. "It was both of you. He feels real bad about what happened, too. It broke our hearts." Mama's voice broke, and I knew she was crying.

That was the second time I'd ever known her to cry, and both times was over Daddy.

"Mama, I want things to go better for you," John said, trying to comfort her. "I want to help, but I just don't know how. I can't stay in this house with him, Mama. I just can't. We both know what's going on. Things will never be the same with me and him. Never. I love him. He's my daddy. But I just can't tolerate what he's doing."

"Oh, John. Please. We'll work it out." She took a deep breath and put her hands up to her face. "Oh, dear God, I can't believe all this is happening to our family. Let's try real hard to fix it. Let's pray that things will change. If we put it all into God's hands, He'll find a way."

"God can't change how I feel, Mama. Maybe you can forgive, but I can't."

It got quiet again, and I thought maybe they would hug and somehow God would make things better right then and there, just like Mama wanted.

John went on. "I'm moving out today, Mama. I'm moving in with my friend Steve. You've met him. He's a good man. I should have done it before now anyway. I'm not a kid. I should be out on my own. The only reason I didn't do it sooner was because I didn't want to spend the money on a place of my own. Steve isn't charging me much to stay with him. I'll still be able to bring you money every Sunday, and I'll still have Sunday suppers together with the family. I don't want to give that up. I'm going to see if I can't take on some extra work somewhere nights. It will work out. I'm excited about it, and I want you to be excited for me."

"Oh, John." she whispered, and I knew she was in so much pain that it made my throat ache. "I'll miss you so very, very much. You are my rock."

I couldn't stand to hear any more. Besides, I knew I shouldn't. It didn't take long for John to pack up his things, and when he came downstairs with his bags of clothes, I couldn't speak. And I couldn't hold back the tears.

"I'm not sayin' goodbye, Nellie," he told me, holding out his arms for a hug. "And remember, you can always count on me, okay?"

As he walked out, I realized for the first time that he had been my rock, too, and that a big part of my childhood was walkin' out that door right with him.

Phoebe stayed on at the church and did some housekeeping for some people here and there. Her dream of going to Chicago and getting to be a preacher hadn't come true yet, and I could tell she was bitter about it. She was nastier than ever, and I just prayed that someone would find a way to get her out of our house and into that preacher school real soon.

Nobody but Mama could get along with her. Sometimes she just acted crazy, goin' on and on about Jesus and sinning and being damned and all. I don't know how Mama tolerated it, the way Phoebe preached to her about the rest of us. None of us wanted to mess with Old Phoebe.

George left home not long after John did, and the two of them found a bigger place to share with Steve. I prayed Homer wouldn't go, too. Our house seemed terrible lonesome without my two big brothers. But they kept their word and always came home for Sunday suppers, and we all acted like everything was normal.

Daddy looked smaller, and I figured it was because he wasn't standing so tall as before. He tried to be best pals with the littler kids, same as he had been with us older ones, but he didn't seem to have much zip to him those days. The laughter had gone out of him.

I went over to see John and George at their place as often as I could. We could be normal together there. They still played the big brother role with me, but we took on a new kind of friendship together. They teased me still, but it was all in good fun, and I teased them right back. I knew we had all grown up a lot over the past year, and even though the reasons for it was painful, the results was good in a lot of ways.

One time when I walked over after work, John was the only one there. I'd been thinkin' about Daddy a lot recently, and felt I just had to know the truth of what had happened between them. He'd come home straight from work for a while after the boys left, but recently he started showing up late again, and some nights he wasn't even home when I went to bed. Mama had stopped watching for him at the window, and she never walked down the street hoping to meet him now. I knew that whatever was going on back last summer was still going on now, and I had a pretty good idea what it was.

I asked John for the truth.

"Some things are better left alone, Nellie," he said. "You need to go on loving Daddy the way you always have. Me and George moving out was a good thing for all of us."

I wasn't about to let this go and didn't want to be protected from things by my big brother anymore. Something bad was goin' on, and I felt I was old enough and responsible enough to know what it was.

"It isn't a good thing and you know it," I told him. "Things aren't the same. We all miss you two like crazy."

"Well, I'm glad no one's forgetting us," he said and laughed.

It was a beautiful, but hot, afternoon, and when he asked me if I'd like to share a cold beer with him, I thought I'd pop. I told him it would be my first one and that I couldn't think of anyone I'd rather have it with than my big brother.

I can't say that it tasted good, but I was so happy to be treated like one of the boys, that I finished it the same time he did his. It went straight to my head and made me say things I wouldn't normally say. I told John I thought I knew what Daddy was doing.

When John didn't say anything, the beer let me go on.

"He's seein' a woman," I said. "A pretty woman with brown hair. He worked with her at Burke." John's silence told me it was the truth. "Mama knows about it, doesn't she?"

"She knows," John said. I could tell he didn't feel right sayin' more, but he must 'a decided I was ready to hear. "That woman you know about wasn't the first one or the last. There's others. It's been goin' on for a long time. People told her in their own ways. She doesn't want to believe it. Or maybe she just doesn't know what she can do about it. That's the reason he lost his job. I guess he just can't help himself. I don't know. Look, Nellie, you and me and George know. The others must never find out. I don't want the young ones to ever change how they feel about Daddy."

I promised him I'd always help take care of Mama, too, and I'd keep our secret. We clicked our glasses together to seal the promise, and I felt older than when I had walked up to my brother's porch.

On my way back home, I thought hard about how I felt about Daddy. I knew I shouldn't be able to forgive him and that maybe I shouldn't love him in the same way anymore, and it hurt me that he'd allowed himself to hurt Mama. But I knew by then that there is always more to somethin' than meets the eye. I thought about the way he used to be and how much life there'd been in him. I remembered about the dreams he said he used to have. And I thought about how it seemed Mama had set hers aside a long time ago, too, or maybe she never had any to begin with. Back on the farm, that night when they was sitting on the swing, they'd said how much they loved each other. I wondered how it could be that folks can fall out of love.

I knew that I loved Daddy so much that there was no way I wouldn't forgive him over time, and I worried if, by doing so, I would be disrespectful to Mama. No one could love her more than me, but did his hurting her mean that I had to love him less? I came to the conclusion that if Mama was able to forgive him for all the hurt, then it had to be all right for me to forgive him too.

I wasn't old enough yet to understand how complicated a marriage could be.

After a while, I got to be pretty tired working there at the house for Mrs. Tildredge. I liked her a lot, but I wanted to be around people my own age again and make new friends. I knew I could never go back to my old girlfriends because I wasn't the same person I was back in that part of my life.

I was honest with Mrs. Tildredge. I told her I was thinking that maybe I should get another job where I could meet some young people my age and see what else I could do in life. She said right away that she understood and that she'd been surprised I stayed on there with her as long as I did. We promised each other that we'd visit and stay in touch. I went over to the church to see if someone else would take care of her.

When it was time for me to leave on the last day I worked there, we hugged each other and cried a little. I told her I'd check in on her and make sure the new girl was doing a good job taking care of her. She said that no one could do as good a job as me and that she loved me just like a daughter. I felt like I was abandoning her. A good daughter wouldn't leave her like I was about to. She must 'a seen the guilt on my face 'cause she said real quick that the new girl was so very nice too and she was sure, absolutely sure, they'd get along famously.

She talked like that sometimes; used words like "famously," and "my dear," and "lovely," and "splendid," and "quite right." I liked how she talked, and I thought she was refined just like Sandy's mother. I tried to talk like her sometimes, but those words just didn't sound the same coming out of my mouth. I hoped that someday they might.

I walked around The Square every day looking in windows for "help wanted" signs. Finally, one showed up in a fine restaurant called The Sparta. I was so excited because that was one of the places I'd always peeked in at and imagined myself sitting there some day having lunch or supper.

I stood outside and looked out on the street, pretending I was looking for someone I knew while I was getting my nerve up to go in and see if I could have the job. I took a little walk part-way around The Square, talkin' to myself about how a fancy place like that wouldn't take on someone as young as me with no school certificate. But then I told myself that I was as good as anyone else, just like Aunt Lizzie had told me to, and if I didn't try, I'd never know if I could have got the job and I'd never get it out of my head. So in I walked.

The Sparta restaurant was one long narrow room. The front part, where I was standing, was the more relaxed part, if you know what I mean. There was a huge counter on the right with stools where people could sit if they was in a hurry to eat. I heard some people coming in saying they'd like to sit at the bar. Behind it, clear across the wall, was a huge mirror, and you could sit there on those stools and look at yourself and everyone else and know what everybody was doing and who they was talking to.

Just across from the bar was where people paid their bills, and right down from where the cashier stood was the candy counter that had at least forty different kinds of candy put out on their own shiny silver trays with a little white doilies underneath and a little white card in front that told what kind of candy it was. The glass in front was sparkly clean. The girl who customers paid the bills to was in charge of the candy, and I thought how I'd like that job.

Serious eaters sat on back in the room where the booths was. The walls there was covered in dark wood that someone kept waxed so good they shined. On the wall by each booth was mirrors that had gold lines running through them, and over each mirror was a little light that looked like a candle with a shade on it. The booths was made out of the same kind of wood that was on the walls so you can imagine with all those mirrors and that shiny wood, how that whole place just glowed. Well, I knew right away that if I could get that job working there at The Sparta, I would be so happy because anyone who would go there to eat would be real refined.

The girl at the cash register smiled nice at me and asked if she could help me.

"Well, yes," I said. "There's a sign out front in the window that says you need some help." And when she said yes, they needed a waitress, I said, "Well, that's good. I'm a waitress and I'd like to see if I could get the job, please." I knew right away how dumb I sounded and thought I might just make a dash out the door before I could say anything else to embarrass myself.

The girl smiled and gave me a piece of paper to fill out and told me to go over to the end of the bar to sit while I did it. It took me a while to get started because there was so much to look at with all the customers and the waitresses hurrying around in their white uniforms.

One of the questions was about how old I was. I wasn't sixteen yet, so I lied and said I was seventeen. After all, a girl's got to do what she's got to do. I handed the paper back to the cashier, and she told me to sit back down and she'd see if she could find Mr. Stenson. When she came back and told me that he could see me, I was so nervous that I had trouble thinking straight.

We went back past the booths and into a little hall and up some stairs to a little balcony that I hadn't seen before. There was a long table there with ten chairs around it, and the seats was covered in heavy green flowered material. I sat down and waited for Mr. Stenson and prayed that I'd get the waitress job and crossed my fingers on both my hands for good measure and wished I had put on a prettier dress.

"Nellie," I said to myself, "you can do it." And I kept saying in my brain, "Fortitude, Fortitude."

I smiled at Mr. Stenson. Boy, did I smile. I acted real happy and agreeable. And polite. My gosh, was I careful to be polite. I stood up when he came into the little balcony 'cause Mama taught us to stand up when an older person comes into a room where you are. I reached out and shook his hand and looked right in his eyes too, just like Daddy had taught my brothers to do. Daddy always said if you don't look a person direct into the eyes, they'll think you have something to hide.

I said "yes, sir" and "no, sir" when he asked me a question.

We must a' talked for ten or fifteen minutes, and then Mr. Stenson asked me if I had any questions, and when I said I didn't, he said, "Well, Miss Nellie, you're a little younger than most of the staff here, but I think we could give you a try. If you still want the job, it's yours."

I wanted to jump over the table to give him a big hug, but I held myself back. That was on a Saturday. I started my career at The Sparta the next Monday.

Finally, I had me a real job, one that I could just keep practicing on and keep getting better at. I was determined to be a great waitress. I wasn't paid much, but Mr. Stenson said the real money was in the tips. That made me think about the railroaders and how they gave me those nickels from time to time. That made me think about that night when Jake got too close to me and caused me to give up waitressing. I knew I'd have to be careful to keep my friendliness toned down.

I started my new job that Monday, and I knew it wasn't going to be easy. I followed the other waitresses around for a few days to see how they did things, and I thought I'd never be able to keep orders straight, and get them to the right people, and figure out the check and still have time to be friendly and all. Then, I was assigned to an older lady who was real good at taking care of customers, and she watched me to make sure I knew what I was doing. She said I was a "quick study." The cooks had some trouble reading my handwriting at first, but I learned some short cuts on how to list orders, and we did just fine. It wasn't very long 'til I was working on my own and getting to know the regulars real good. Pretty soon they all knew my name and said, "Hi, Nellie," when they came in. I was starting to feel important. It felt wonderful.

I thought hard about my job, and I decided to work twice as hard as I needed to because I wanted to be the best waitress in town. I wanted to matter to people. I listened hard to my customers and found out their names and memorized them best I could, because I knew it was important for people to feel special. I answered questions they had and tried to follow their "small talk." Pretty soon some of the customers was askin' to sit in my section.

Patty was the best waitress there, and I told her so. I asked her for advice from time to time, and she gave it. She took me under her wing, so to speak, and we became friends real quick. She was nineteen, a lot older than me, but that didn't matter at all. She always was rushin' off to somewhere after work each night and had the nicest way of wavin' and sayin', "Bye-bye, everyone, have a good evening." I thought how I'd like to have some place special to go and some special people to see outside of work.

Lo–and–behold, early on one week she asked me if I'd like to go with her after work on Friday to meet some people at Ritchey's, their favorite hangout, over on the south side of The Square. She said she'd like to introduce me to some other girls she thought I'd really like. She asked me if I'd ever been there, and I said no, but that I'd like to go.

Now, you see, I had to lie again to my mama. I knew she wouldn't approve of me going out after work with kids older than me to some hangout she'd never heard of before. But I really wanted to have me some friends. So, I hate to admit it, but I told my mama another fib and said I had to work late on Friday and that I was sure one of the older waitresses would see to it that I got home all right.

That decision to lie to mama and to go out with my new best friend was about to change my life.

Oh, my gosh, when I walked into Ritchey's that Friday night, I walked into a whole new world. Outside of church and school, I'd never seen so many young people under one roof in my whole life. And never had I ever seen so many just standing around laughing with each other and enjoyin' themselves like those people was doing there in that place on The Square. I would have been happy to just stand there and watch all of them. They reminded me of a flock of pretty noisy birds.

Patty knew everybody, and as soon as we walked in, she started in introducing me to all her friends. We went around from booth to booth where the girls sat 'til she had covered everyone, and then we finally squeezed into a booth where three of her best friends was saving seats for us. They said they was happy to meet me, and they all wanted to know everything about me. I told them some things the best I could, but I was real careful what I said and how I said it. I wanted to make sure they really wanted to know about me and wasn't just being polite. And I wanted to make sure they wasn't about to make fun of me. They was more up on things than me, if you know what I mean, and I felt a little unsure of myself around them.

We talked about work and dancing (I couldn't say much about that), and boys (couldn't say much about that either) and each others' figures. One of the girls, Carol, said how she wished she was tall and thin like me. They listened hard when I did talk, and they asked me where I was from. They was surprised that I was born just out a ways from Newark. I said something, I don't remember what it was, and I saw a couple of the girls smile at each other. I worried that I had said somethin' wrong.

When I told them I had to get on back home, they asked me if I was coming the next night. I told them that I probably wouldn't be able to see them again until next Friday, and they said they'd be lookin' for me. I guess you could say my new life began that night.

I met my new friends at Ritchey's about every Friday night after that. They all went out and danced later those nights or Saturday nights, but I knew I couldn't do that. There was no way I could stay out that late or get away on Saturdays. But I wanted to. They was so free and so happy-go-lucky and just so...well, they was just so *alive*.

I remembered the last assignment I had at school, the one where I had to write what kind of animal or insect I would want to be most like if I could, and I'd settled on wanting to be a butterfly. Well, every Friday night at Ritchey's, that's how I felt: just like a butterfly. Not a bird like them. Nope, I definitely wasn't a bird. I wouldn't ever have so much to say as they did or joke or be so quick to laugh like them. I wanted to be their friend, but I didn't know how to be exactly like them, and I wasn't sure I wanted to.

I had written in class that day that felt so long ago, that butterflies was special because they brought joy to everyone. There wasn't anyone I knew who didn't love watching butterflies. I pointed out that you'd often see flocks of birds together, but you hardly ever saw butterflies together in groups. Other creatures that flew was noisy. Butterflies never annoyed you with their sound. They keep their distance because their wings are fragile, but they are strong enough to travel far and hold up against the winds. You could trap birds and bees and ants and frogs and put them in bottles or cages, and they'd survive. But you couldn't put a butterfly in a bottle and expect it to live.

Butterflies had to be free.

I had my first real birthday party at The Sparta. Course, everyone there thought I was eighteen, not sixteen. I felt bad about that, but it was too late to tell the truth. I thought, shoot, how much difference could there be between a sixteen and an eighteen-year-old girl, anyway.

It was time to close up that day, my birthday, and I was getting things ready so I could help wash down the booths when Patty grabbed me and told me to put that stuff down and follow her up front. I argued with her, sayin' how I had to get everything done so we could all get out of there. She laughed and said to nevermind about that just now, that I needed to hush and do as she said. She pulled me up front and over to the counter and told me to sit down and close my eyes. I couldn't imagine what for, but I did what she told me to do. I heard a lot of people walkin' up close, and I called out for Patty to tell me what was goin' on, and she told me again to nevermind, and to just keep my eyes shut.

Then it got real quiet, and when she told me to open my eyes, there was everybody who worked there, even Mr. Stenson, smiling and yelling "Surprise!" They all sang Happy Birthday, Dear Nellie, and Patty came out of the kitchen carrying a pretty little birthday cake with eighteen candles on it that I was supposed to blow out. And when I did, everyone clapped and whistled and yelled, "Good job, Nellie."

Then up comes one of the other girls with a pretty little box covered in white paper and done up with a pink bow. She said that the present was from all of them and that I should open it. Inside was a pretty pin shaped like a heart with pink shiny stones all around it. My throat got all tight, and I couldn't say nothing. Patty said they picked it out 'cause all my customers liked me so much and so did all of them. They said I had a good heart.

Well, I have to tell you, when she said that, I started blubbering. And I could feel my face getting hot and red. But I wiped my eyes and got ahold of myself, and I told them how happy I was and how nice they all was and how no one had ever done something like that for me before. And then for some reason I just started giggling, and everyone else started doing the same thing, and right away it felt like a real party. Mr. Stenson said Cokes was on the house, and we cut up my cake and had a great time. I thought to myself that things just couldn't get any better than that.

It was pretty late by the time we finished up the party and got the place cleaned up for the next day, and so one of the older girls told me her husband and her would be happy to drive me home, it being so late and all. I accepted her offer.

Patty grabbed me right before I left and said, "Now listen here, Nellie. I'm not going to take a no from you any more. There's a big band coming out at The Lake this Saturday. Straight from Chicago. Everybody's going to go. The whole gang. You need to come with us. Say you'll come."

Well, I thought real fast. I'd been wanting to go out with her and her friends for months now, but I hadn't been able to figure how I could do it. I was thinking about how I'd explain that I was going out dancing to Mama. And I was thinking about where I'd get the money to go. Should I take all the money I'd saved up to go dancing? I told Patty I'd think about it and let her know, but she said I had to go because they always celebrated friends' birthdays out at The Lake so long as the ballroom was still open.

"Nellie," she said, "you won't believe how beautiful it is. Everybody will be there. We want to treat you. It's your birthday, for heaven's sake."

"You all don't have to treat me, Patty," I said, not wanting her to think I didn't have any money. "I can pay. It's not that."

"Silly," she said. "I know we don't have to. Now, remember Saturday night. You're going to put on your best dress and dancing shoes, and you are definitely going out."

And before I could say another word, she gave me a big hug and took off down the street.

Well, that night, as you can imagine, I couldn't sleep at all. I went from happiness about the party I'd just had to being so scared about what I was going to do about The Lake. Having all those people be so friendly was making things pretty complicated.

The next morning, a plan started to come into my head, and it grew all day long. I even came up with the exact words me and Mama would say to each other later. Course, it meant telling Mama another lie, but I was getting real good at that. When I got to work, I knew I was going to the Ballroom. By the time the lunch customers was mostly gone, I'd decided to tell Patty I couldn't go. Then by the time the early crowd came for supper, I had made the lie even better in my mind, and I was thinking about all the fun I was going to have dancing with all my new friends.

I told Mama I was going to have to work Saturday supper hour and help clean up and that it was likely to be late when I finished.

"That friend Patty I told you about?" I said. "Well, she has to work, too, and she invited me to stay over at her house that night. Her daddy will bring me home in time to go to church, if that's all right with you."

I tried to look and act real normal. I was glad she was mending one of the boy's shirts so I didn't have to look direct in her eyes.

"Are you sure you'll be all right there?"

Bless my mama. I was sixteen, and she still worried about me. "Sure. I'll be all right. Don't you worry. Patty is a good friend. A really nice girl. She already checked with her parents, and they said it was fine if it's fine with you."

I couldn't believe how easy it all was. I had gone and done all that worrying and lost a whole night's sleep for nothing. I walked out of the kitchen and turned around to thank her for letting me stay at Patty's, and I took a good look at her sitting there in the dim light, working late again on something for her family, and my love for her welled up inside me, and I wondered how long it had been since Mama had been able to go out and have fun and dance with friends. It hadn't happened in my lifetime. I felt so bad for her, and there I was lying to her again.

I walked back to the table and sat down and took the shirt and sewing needle away from her and told her to go on in the parlor with the rest of the family and relax a little bit. I'd finish the job. And so I sewed, but I thought about dancing.

Oh, my, how can I begin to describe that night and all of the other wonderful nights I spent dancin' there at The Crystal Ballroom at Buckeye Lake? Just thinkin' about it still makes me feel young again. Even after all these years, the place is just as vivid in my mind as it was that very first night.

We all got there in three different cars, all scrunched in, boys and girls together, tight as we could be so everybody would have a ride. We pulled into the huge parking lot and joined hundreds of other people of all ages who was either coming back from the amusement park there or going to the ballroom to hear the big band. I was excited and nervous at the same time about where I was going, and my heart took to beating so fast I could hardly get my voice out.

To get to the ballroom, you had to walk along a little gravel path along the lake, and as soon as I got on that path, I felt like I was in some kind of wonderland. There was soft lights everywhere, soft little white lights from the boats and the little cottages close by, and colored lights up ahead from the rides at the park. Everything twinkled. The moon was bright, and its beams spread out over the smooth lake, and it reminded me of words in love songs.

Music came out from the cottages and down from the Ferris Wheel ahead. Little waves came in and gently touched the shore, and the soft swish of them was one of the prettiest sounds I ever heard. Somewhere on one of the cottages, bells tinkled from a wind chime. Food cooking in the cottage kitchens, the fishiness coming up from the water, the earthiness of fresh-cut grass beside the path, and the cotton candy and taffy in the hands of the youngins all blended together to make its own delicious perfume.

I stepped off the path and stood by the lake and took a big breath and closed my eyes to hold it all in. A little breeze wrapped itself around my face and played with my hair, and I felt like I was living in one of my fairy dreams.

Patty put her arm through mine. "We're almost there," she said. "Wait 'til you see it." Then, at last, she told me to look up.

It took my breath away. The trees in front was all dressed up in tiny blue lights that twinkled in the breeze, and the huge white building was outlined the same way. It looked like a gigantic present all done up sparkly. Patty had to push me to get me to move to the open door.

Nothing I had ever imagined, even when I was little, had been as beautiful as the inside of that ballroom. There was a big round crystal ball hanging way, way up at the top of the ceiling, and it turned around real slow and made slivers of light that fell down onto the floor and the walls and the tables and all the people there, and it felt like we was all angels playing around the stars in our own part of the sky.

The men in the band came out all dressed up in white shirts and ties and beige suits. The lady singer had a long black dress on, and she wore sparkly earrings and bracelets like I seen in the magazines. Her hair was pale blond, and it was waved so that one side hung over her right eye. She was prettier than any picture I had ever seen.

I danced. Oh, my, did I dance. That big band was big alright, and the sounds coming from all those men playing all those instruments was the most beautiful music I ever heard. They played fast, and they played slow and dreamy-like, and I danced to every single song. I didn't think about what I was sayin' or worry about whether I was laughing too loud.

I felt that music. It seeped its way right into every single part of me and took me over. I was a different person out there on that dance floor. Remember that fairy princess I pretended to be back there on the farm in the summer kitchen? Well, that's the way I felt then.

Only better.

My girlfriends all smoked and I didn't care. For a long time I turned them down when they asked me if I wanted one of their cigarettes. I was already filled up with sin with all my lyin' and dancing. I was afraid to add one more thing Jesus could condemn me to hell for.

The devil got hold of me one night, though, and when one of the girls asked me at Ritchey's if I wanted a cigarette, I took it. And I darned near passed out there at the booth when Patty lit it up for me. I couldn't imagine what they all saw in those things. It made me dizzy, and my chest felt like it was on fire. They was all laughing, but I knew they was laughin' with me, not at me. They said I had to try another one, and this time they showed me the right way to light it on my own and how to puff on it and blow the smoke out. They showed me the right way to hold it too. I was so sick by the time I had to go home that I wanted to throw up to get all that stuff out of me. Even my brain felt smoky.

I kept on smoking because I thought everybody looked so grown up and sophisticated while they was puffin' away. I never did inhale, though. I just more or less held the cigarette in my hand and tried to look good, taking a couple of little puffs now and then and blowing them out real fast before I could really taste it. I had to smoke. I didn't want to be different.

Cigarettes was expensive so usually us girls went together to buy a pack, and we split it up between us. Sometimes the boys gave us some of theirs that they rolled themselves. I kept my extra ones hidden in my drawer in my room in a little purse I had. That was a mistake.

One afternoon when I came home from work, Little Grace and Pearl knocked on my door. "Nellie," Grace whispered. "Nellie, we need to tell you something. Me and Pearl know you smoke. We know because we saw Old Phoebe going through your drawer, and we saw her take out some cigarettes from your purse."

It was all too much to think about: I had set a bad example for my two littlest sisters, Old Phoebe was sure to tell Mama that I was smoking, Mama would be terrible disappointed in me, and I'd probably be punished. The first thing I did was try to come up with an excuse.

"Hush, Nellie. We don't care about that. It's just that you need to check them." She looked at the door and leaned in close to me. "Phoebe did something to your cigarettes. We saw her, didn't we, Pearl?"

Pearl nodded. "She took them apart and put something in them and then put them back together again. We saw her. Don't tell her we told you, okay?"

I put the three cigarettes in my pocket and went outside and out toward the tracks. When I was far enough away from the house, I got them out and tore them apart. Buckshot. That's what Phoebe had put in them: buckshot. A picture came in my mind of one of my friends lighting up one of my cigarettes and having it blow up in her face. A chill ran through me. My sister wasn't just mean. She was crazy as a loon.

I made up excuses to go dancing every Saturday 'til the end of October, right before the ballroom closed for the winter season. That Monday before the last show, Mama and Daddy told me we had to have a big talk after supper. I knew what was coming, and I was almost glad that I would have to tell the truth about what I was doing. All that lying was making me feel real bad.

Daddy got right to the point. "Nellie, your mama and me don't want to feel that we can't trust you to be tellin' us the truth, but, frankly, we've had trouble believing that you're always working so late every Saturday." He took a deep breath and crossed his arms on the table and looked right at me. "I went down to The Sparta last Saturday night at eight-thirty, and the place was shut up tight." He waited a little for that to sink in. "Where was you last Saturday night?"

There it was. I knew the question was coming, but it still took me a while to get out the answer. It came out in a whisper. "I went out to Buckeye Lake with my friends." I looked up at both of them, and we all three waited to see what was coming next.

"What do you do out at Buckeye Lake every Saturday?" Mama asked quietly. She didn't look at me.

"Me and all my friends, we go to the Crystal Ballroom." It was dead silent. Mama and Daddy waited for me to take the big plunge. "We dance."

My Mama looked sad. "Oh, Nellie," she said. "How *could* you?"

I wanted her to understand, to say that what I was doing was all right. I thought maybe if I'd finally explain things, she'd be happy for me and I could quit living the lie.

"I'm a good dancer. My friends are all so nice. You'd like them a lot. I know you would. Oh, Mama, it's so beautiful there, and I have such a good time with everyone. We don't do nothin' wrong. We just have fun together. We don't do nothin' wrong."

Daddy interrupted. "Nellie, you know how your Mama feels about that. You've disappointed her terrible."

"But didn't you ever dance, Mama? Didn't you ever have friends you wanted to feel part of? Didn't you ever just want to laugh and feel free and joyful?"

Mama turned her eyes away from me.

"You're smoking too," she said.

Why would I think Phoebe would keep me smoking to herself? "Yes, Ma'am."

"Smoking and dancing. Are you drinking too, Nellie?"

"No, Mama. We don't drink. None of us."

"This is all wrong, Nellie. It's all wrong." She sounded so tired. "I want you to promise me you'll stop."

I decided I wasn't going to deceive my mama or my daddy anymore. I prayed I was making the right decision.

"I can't, Mama." The words came out like I had a big sore in my throat. "I don't want to stop havin' fun. I don't want to give up my friends. I can't do it again. I just can't. I just wish you would understand."

Mama got up slow from the table and didn't say a word as she walked out the door. Me and Daddy sat there real quiet, looking at nothin', and finally he reached over and patted my hand and just said, "Oh, my little Nellie," and walked out, leaving me there by myself.

The next evening when I got home I felt different and so did everything around me. Mama and Daddy and me had trouble looking at each other and sort'a skated around each other, polite, but distant. I wondered how long this would go on.

When I went to bed that night, Old Phoebe was already there, and I was careful not to wake her up. I turned off the lantern and found my spot in my part of the bed and kept myself from moving.

"You're a harlot, Nellie," Old Phoebe hissed. "A harlot. You've broken Mama's heart, and you're going straight to hell. No one can help you now. It's too late."

All I had thought about that whole summer was being independent and grown up and never gave it a thought about what risks there was in that and how hurtful it could be. Now, a part of me wanted to go back to the way things was, but too much had happened over the summer, and I wasn't the same person as before. The worst thing was havin' Mama feelin' the way she did about me. It hurt real bad. I needed someone to treat me like a little girl again and tell me what to do and help fix things. I was sure Grammy could do all of that.

"I know what's been happening, honey," she said, "and I know how much you must be hurtin', but you have to understand that this is just a part of growing up. It's painful sometimes. Your Mama loves you very, very much. Always has. Always will. You'll make your peace eventually, but you're right, Nellie, things can't go back the way they was, and you wouldn't want them to anyway. It's all right to try to figure out just who you are and what you're made of. Just take your time and know that you'll make mistakes along the way.

"I can't tell you what to do about all of this. Nobody can. You'll figure it all out on your own, and I have faith that whatever decisions you come up with will be good ones. Your mama has raised you right, and you have a good head on your shoulders, Nellie. I have faith in you."

Grammy said she couldn't fix things, but her understanding of the situation and her confidence in me helped get the fixin' started. She said exactly what I needed to hear.

That fall Patty and her good friend Louise decided to move out of their families' houses and get their own place to live. They said they felt it was time. They asked me if I would like to join up with them and be their third roomie, and I told them I would.

It's hard to explain how I felt about leaving my family that first time: sad, excited, guilty, worried, grown up. Mama said she understood why I felt it was time, and she helped me move, and so did John and Clyde and George. Little Grace cried and wouldn't go to my new place. Old Phoebe said "good riddance." Mama said for me to be happy, and she said that I could always move back whenever I wanted to, that the family home would always be mine, too. Grammy told me that I was all grown up and congratulated me on finding a place on my own. Daddy found it hard to say anything.

My new place was a one bedroom flat over a store on Main Street, about a block off The Square. We had a real bathroom. Soon as I saw it, I had to try it out. My, oh my, did I enjoy sitting down in that warm little room and peeing to my heart's content. It was the first time that whole winter I didn't rush to do my business. Patty and Louise came in and watched me, and it was a long time before we could stop ourselves from laughing. I slept on a small cot in the main room off the kitchen, and being alone in that room at night felt wonderful. I had never had so much privacy.

The three of us laughed out loud whenever we felt like it, and we sang our favorite songs, and we looked through magazines and shared each others' clothes. We got our groceries and cleaned our little home together. We was best friends, and we was free to do as we pleased.

And we talked. Boy, did we talk.

From the minute we woke up in the mornings 'til we put our tired selves down in bed at night, we talked and shared our dreams. And each night before I closed my eyes to sleep I thanked God and Jesus for bringing me to that place.

My nightmares stopped.

The three of us splurged ever so often and bought ourselves some good strong coffee. Our favorite snack at night was Saltine crackers in a bowl with coffee and sugar poured over them. Lizzie had made it for me, and now I made it for my best friends. Sometimes I made sugar cookies for us too, and sometimes I rolled the dough out flat and covered it with cinnamon and sugar and rolled the dough up and baked it that way. We fixed our meals together and shared in the cost of them. Suppers was happy times.

I paid my share of the rent for our new place, and I took most of the rest of my pay every Sunday to Mama when I went back home for family suppers. The few dollars I had left didn't go too far, and I knew if I was going to stay with Patty and Louise and put aside some "mad money," I'd have to make more. I started looking around for more work.

The fancy lady's shop I told you about a while ago, the one called The Fashion? Well, don't you know, just a few weeks after I started looking, there was a sign in the window there that said: "Help Wanted." I remembered how pretty and how nice the lady there looked when I used to peek in the window and how I had thought how great it would be to work there sometime. Well, I thought, maybe that time is now.

I took a deep breath and marched right in to that shop without giving myself time to think about it. The lady owner was sitting at a pretty little desk at the back of the room. She was beautiful, and I felt drab and young and dumb beside her. She smiled and asked me if she could help me with anything. My confidence left me at the door, but finally I blurted out that I was interested in applying for the job.

Bea was her name: Bea Taylor. She said she needed a sales clerk and asked me to sit down with her at her pretty little desk so we could talk. She was good at small talk and chatted away comfortable-like about this and that and gave me time to get relaxed. She asked me what my work experience was. I told her about my job at the Sparta and with Mrs. Tildredge before that. I didn't tell her about Mrs. Becker. For some reason I didn't want her to know I had been a house maid.

She asked me what I liked to do outside of work: what hobbies or interests did I have. I was warming up to the conversation, and I told her about my friends and Ritchey's and Buckeye Lake and big bands and dancing, and, don't you know, she had been to The Lake, too, and liked to listen to music. I was beginning to feel like we was almost friends. Finally, we got back to my purpose for being there, and she told me she thought I'd be perfect for the job and she'd enjoy having me work for her, but she needed someone there full time. The pay was good, better than what I was making at The Sparta.

I took the job with Bea.

Outside of my mama and Grammy and Lizzie, Bea was the best lady I had ever known, and working there at The Fashion was the best job I could ever have had. It didn't feel like work. She taught me what length a lady's skirt should be, how to add jewelry to make clothes look better, and what colors look good together. She taught me all of that so I could help my customers, but it helped me, too. I didn't know it, but I slouched, and Bea got me to pull my shoulders back, to hold my tummy in, and to stand tall and be proud of my height. She said that I could be real attractive if I only had a little more confidence. That's what she said, and I believed her, because I believed everything she told me. "Poised" was a new word I'd learned from her. I knew it all had to do with being "refined."

After a while, when new clothes came into her shop, Bea had me try them on if she thought they was young-enough looking for me, and, if they looked good, she had me wear them so the customers could see them on a real live person. She said that I was being her model. I started saving my money with another purpose in mind. I wanted to buy myself some of those clothes.

I couldn't guess Bea's age. I had the feeling she could have been born about the time my mama was because she often talked about her daughters who seemed close to my age. She looked so much younger than Mama, though, and I wished Mama could have had someone like Bea in her life.

Sometimes after work, Bea and me went out together for a cup of tea and talked about our days there at the shop. We talked about our customers and laughed about one or two who put on airs when they came in, and we talked about others who couldn't look good no matter what you put on them. Some of our ladies told us everything about themselves and their families—more than Bea and me wanted to hear sometimes—and we sat and drank our tea and tried to figure them out.

Those times together havin' tea, I watched her real careful. Why, she even looked good pouring the cream into her cup, and she held her hand so pretty when she took the sugar out of the sugar bowl with the little spoon. Bea didn't cross her legs. Oh, no. She crossed her ankles. I asked her about that, and she said that's what ladies do. She walked tall and straight, and I noticed that when she went into a place people turned to look back at her. Oh, she was a stylish lady, all right, and I wanted to be just like her. She was like Sandy's mother, only better.

I was feeling better about myself in lots of ways, but there was still one big thing about myself that bothered me bad, and I worked up my nerve to ask Bea about it because I knew I could trust her to tell me the truth about things. So one day, after we closed and was settling up the money and all, I took a deep breath and decided to tell her what was on my mind.

"Bea, I was wonderin' if I could talk to you about somethin' important."

She told me that I could talk to her about anything, anytime, because that was what friends was for. I had some trouble getting started, but finally I just blurted it out.

"I don't talk right," I said. "I know that. I don't say things the way smart people do. Sometimes people laugh when I say things, and I think it's more because of how I say them, not what I say."

It felt good to finally get out what I'd been thinkin' so long. Once I got started, it was easier to go on.

"I want to be able to talk like you," I told her. "I want to talk like a lady. I want to be a real lady, Bea. See, someday I'd like to have a shop of my own, maybe a little bakery or a restaurant-like place. But people would have to have respect for me to be my customers, and I don't think I can get a lot of respect until I can talk like a lady." I couldn't look at her direct. "Would you teach me to talk like you?"

"Oh, my dear Nellie, I wasn't expecting that. You are full of surprises. Honey, you don't talk funny. Why, you're like a breath of fresh air. I like how you talk. You are so expressive, so honest. Why would you think you talk funny?"

I told her about the kids in school and especially about Dan Vickers and how they'd teased me, and she listened and shook her head and said how cruel children are to each other.

"It makes me afraid to talk out. I don't want to be laughed at behind my back, don't want to be embarrassed about myself. I want to be confident when I say things. I want to be refined and poised."

"Oh, my dear Nellie, you are a gift. You have nothing to be embarrassed about. Your accent is a reflection of where you're from, what your roots are. It's a part of you."

I thought about that, and I told her I could see what she was saying. "But, Bea," I said, "an accent is one thing. Being wrong about how you say things is different."

"Well, maybe there are a few things we might change. If you want me to, I can make a few suggestions, but know that it's only you who has any kind of problem with the way you speak, Nellie. Your way of talking is a part of who you are. And you're lovely."

Well, Bea and me went to the bookstore there on The Square, and she picked out two books we was going to read together. Actually, she said I was going to read to her, and if I had any trouble saying the words right, she'd help me with that. Then a couple of days later she gave me a pretty little notebook where she wrote down words and then underlined the nouns and the verbs they was supposed to agree with. She said that I'd learn how to make my nouns and verbs agree in no time at all. I felt I was kind'a like back in school, but I had me a real purpose, and workin' with Bea wasn't scary. I tried real hard to copy how she said words.

I carried that notebook everywhere I went, and I studied. I really did. But the more I thought about all those verbs and the nouns that came before them and how they was supposed to agree, the more my tongue got tangled up. After a while, I couldn't say anything. The more I tried to speak better, the more confused I got. I was listening to everybody so close, to hear how they said their words, that sometimes they'd be waitin' forever for me to answer something they said, and they'd have to ask me what in the world was I thinking about.

I told Bea how it was, and she said that she understood how hard it was to re-learn things, but if I would be patient, it would all sort its way out for me. She told me that the correct sound of things would come to me little by little and that I shouldn't worry so much about it, and that maybe I was just trying too hard. But I remembered Mama saying from time to time that if somethin' was worth doin', it was worth taking the time to do it right.

This was definitely worth doing.

I never felt that way about any of the boys I went out with. Course, I daydreamed sometimes about how it would be to have a steady fella and how nice it would be to love someone in that special way. I liked to go out with boys, but when they put their arms around me or held my hand or wanted to give me a kiss good night, well, I just got a little panicky, and we usually ended up shaking hands with a promise to get together again real soon, which usually didn't happen.

Some of my girlfriends was going out with boys. Actually, all my friends was dating. One girl was even engaged, but she was almost four years older than me. Sometimes me and one of the boys from our gang would go out together and hang out with other friends. Sometimes one would take me to a movie or we'd go out for supper, but there was nothing more to it than that. Patty and Louise talked and talked about their dates and what good kissers they was and so on. Louise started to date one boy pretty steady, and she said she just might be in love. I was surprised at how quick it happened with her.

Patty and Louise just didn't understand, and they told me I was just too quick to pass judgment. They said I had to give relationships time, that you couldn't know right away if someone was "Mr. Right" or not. So I decided to be a little more patient and went out with a couple of the guys for several dates, but when they started acting all lovey-dovey, I stopped going out with them.

Finally, Patty insisted that I go out with her and her friend Johnny on a double date with a friend of his. It would be one of those blind dates I'd heard about. She said he was a knockout, and she guaranteed me that I'd have a real good time.

Gerry was his name, and he was real good looking, just like she'd said, and a whole lot older than me. He must 'a been around twenty or twenty-five. Anyway, the four of us went to a nice place outside of town and had sandwiches for supper and came back and walked around The Square and ducked into Ritchey's for a while. I didn't say much. I felt young and silly around him, and I figured I was probably boring him. They all wanted to keep going, but I was tired and told them that, if they didn't mind, I thought I'd just go on back to the house. Gerry said he'd take me home and maybe meet Patty and her boyfriend later. We walked the few blocks back to my place, and he held my hand.

I was saying goodbye to him at the door, trying to be real polite and all, when he just reached right over and started kissing me. I'll have to admit, it felt real good. So good that I wanted to relax a little and just enjoy it. At first he kissed me light and nice and held me gentle like and rubbed my back real soft. Then the kisses got longer and harder and wetter, and before I knew it he was flitting his tongue around my lips. Now, me and Mama never talked about anything like that, but I knew myself that this kiss was turning into something else.

I have to tell you, I didn't pull away. No, I didn't. So I guess I gave him the wrong impression 'cause before I knew it he was holding me real tight, and I could tell he was getting worked up. Then I felt the hardness of him coming through his clothes, and he pushed up against me and moved around me down there, and the warm feelings I was having turned cold. The face of the man in the woods came up in my mind, and I felt dirty. I pulled away and turned my back, breathing hard.

He didn't understand and came to me from behind and pressed himself up against me there, and I told him to stop. But he just said that he was sorry if he'd gone too fast for me and went on about me being so pretty and all and smelling so sweet, and all the time he kept pressing against me.

"Stop!" I cried out. "You need to stop. You just don't understand. I want you to leave."

The softness disappeared from him, and he seemed to grow even more and he told me that I was a cold fish alright, just like some of the other guys had been saying.

"To hell with it," he said. "You don't know what you're missing."

After that, I told Patty and Louise that I was going to give up this dating altogether for a while. Patty let me know she knew what had happened with Gerry.

"Maybe you really need to get some help, honey."

Bea was my very best friend. She kept working with me on my talking, and she never embarrassed me by pointing out mistakes I made. She gave me confidence that I could wear clothes good and had me model in her shop a lot. She introduced me to her friends when we went out for dinner together, and they treated me respectful-like. But as close as we were, she never brought up her family, and she didn't ask me questions about mine.

I was curious, and I just knew for sure that her children was real special. One day when we was sitting at her desk, finishing up the day, I came right out and asked her about them. Her body kind'a slumped, and her face almost changed shape somehow. I thought I had made a terrible mistake.

"I have three beautiful children. Three," she said. "But it's been a while since I've seen them. We talk sometimes. Not often. They're spread out in three different cities. They're doing well, but... Well you see, Nellie, it's like this... I left my husband. We're divorced now. I wear this gold band to make it easier for me to live here. It's easier to live another lie than to fight the stigma of being a divorced woman. Mark and I had been living a lie for years. He was a good man in so many ways, and he was always a good father. Our children love him deeply. I've never told them the truth about him.

"I stayed with him all those years to protect them, to make sure their futures were safe. That's what I told myself. In many ways it was easier for me too. Divorcees aren't welcome in most circles. But finally, well, I just couldn't live like that any longer. I thought the children were old enough to understand. I never anticipated their hurt, their anger towards me. When I left him, I lost them."

I knew, but I had to ask. "What did he do?"

It was hard for her to go on. "From the very beginning he had other women," she said. "For years I blamed myself, tried to make things perfect for him, willed him to give them up. But then I just got angry. At him. At myself for letting him humiliate me. Once the children were grown, I thought no one would be hurt by my leaving. I had to do it for my own self-respect. I got myself back, but in the process I lost them. It's a bitter price to pay."

I felt such deep sadness. How could children turn their backs to their mothers? How could a mother walk away?

I was beginning to understand that everybody has some unhappiness inside them, that even though a person seems to have everything, if you look deep, you'll find suffering there somewhere. And I was realizin' that nothing or nobody is perfect, and that we all just have to keep plodding along and help each other the best we can.

Too many good things was happening to me all at once, and I just knew it couldn't last. I sometimes think each person is allowed to have just so many good times and then God figures out another way to test us to see what we're really made of.

I was so happy back then that I kept knocking on wood for good luck to stay if I found myself talking about my good fortune. Grammy had always said to throw salt over your shoulder when you sit down to eat to keep the evil spirits away. I did that. I didn't pick up coins I found on the sidewalk 'til I saw for sure whether they was face up or not. Aunt Lizzie said that if they was face up, that meant good luck, but if they was lying the other way, you shouldn't touch 'em.

I worried about what could go wrong in my life to make all these good things come tumbling down. Patty said that I had a real mental condition and there was probably a name for it, but she couldn't think of what it was.

Sure enough, on July 3rd, the reasons for me being afraid was made clear. I was at The Fashion by myself, looking after the shop while Bea was out for lunch. I was all dressed up in one of our new suits we got in the day before, and I was putting price tags on things when the door flew open and Old Phoebe strode in, all sweaty and red in the face and breathin' hard. She stood tall with her hands on her big hips and took her time lookin' around the shop. I knew she'd never been in a place like The Fashion.

She looked at me hateful and hissed, "Well, look at you, Miss Fancy Britches. All dolled up in other peoples' clothes, livin' in a world of make-believe. This isn't going to change who you are, Miss Nellie. You're probably not interested in what's going on back home, but Mama made me come tell you that something's wrong with Daddy."

When she stopped, her sneer bore right into me. And I knew she never would have come if something awful hadn't happened.

"What's wrong with him?" I asked her. I was choked up with fear, and I knew she was enjoying it.

"He was out playing pitch with the boys, and he just keeled over. Mama and me and some of the little ones helped get him in the house, but he isn't sayin' anything. His eyes are open, but I know he isn't seeing anything. Mama was using our neighbor's phone to call the doctor. She told me to come get you. George is out hunting down John."

I felt sick. I wrote Bea a note and put another note on the door that we was closed, and I rushed outside with Old Phoebe. We didn't say another word to each other, and we raced home.

Daddy was layin' on his stomach on the floor in the middle of the parlor. I knelt down beside him along with Mama. I spoke his name and saw that his eyes was open. I could see that he was breathin' because the vein on the side of his neck was going in and out.

John and the boys said they should get him in a car somehow and take him to the hospital, but we was all afraid to move him without the doctor saying so. Finally, the boys got him up in his favorite chair and put a blanket around him, and we rubbed his back and his feet and his hands. We said his name, and once I thought I saw his eyes move. We prayed. We prayed so hard for Daddy.

It took forever for the doctor to come, and when he finally did, John told us all to go out and wait on the porch while he looked at Daddy. We tried to talk calm-like and say things to make us all feel better, but finally we just gave up and sat there, each of us thinkin' our own thoughts. John came out pretty soon with his eyes full of tears. Daddy had had a heart attack. A big one. And the doctor said there wasn't nothing he could do about it.

We moved Daddy over to Grammy's cot and tried to make him comfortable. We all kept thinking that there must be something we should be doing, but the doctor had said that there was nothing we could do but try to keep him comfortable. Mama never left his side. She talked to him and rubbed his hands and forehead and kept the quilt up around his neck so he'd be warm. She told all of us that Daddy was in God's care, that He would protect him.

God let us down.

Daddy just stopped breathing while he was lying there. Just went to sleep without saying goodbye. Mama said that he was in heaven, all safe and peaceful. She said that we must be happy for Daddy because he would never suffer again, that he'd been taken home. She didn't cry, and so the rest of us kept our tears inside, too, and tried to be real brave like Mama.

I looked down at him and wondered why we hadn't taken his rough trousers and shirt off and put something soft on him to make him feel better while he was lyin' there feeling so bad. And I wished I would have whispered in his ear how much I loved him and what all he meant to me. I wondered if I had ever told him that. I hoped so. I wished I had told him what a good ball player he was and how proud we was that he was called Coach by all the kids in our neighborhood. I wish I'd told him how much I liked our walks alone together, and especially that last one when we talked about our dreams. And I wished I'd told him how much he helped me when he told me how good I was at running and playing ball, and how I knew he didn't really want me to quit playing basketball with my friends. I wish I'd just laid down beside him and kept him warm and told him how good it felt when he held my hand in his. I wanted to tell him that I still loved him so much, even though I had moved out away from him. And I wanted to tell him that I forgave him for being untrue to Mama.

It was too late to say all those things to him so I thought them to myself real hard, and I prayed that if he had passed on to God and was living with Him right then, that he could hear my thoughts like God could. The tears wanted to come out of my chest, and since I couldn't let them, there was a big hurtful thing that grew right there, and I was sure it would never go away. I sat down next to Grammy and told her how I hurt. She said that time would heal. She told me, too, that it would be okay to let all that hurt out, to go ahead and cry. But I wanted so bad to be strong like Mama that I wouldn't allow it.

The boys put Daddy up on the table there in the parlor and left the room while Mama bathed him real good. She put his suit on him, and she sat with him all night. I sat on the stairs real quiet and watched her while she watched him. I wanted to be there with her, but I knew she needed to be by herself.

Friends visited us and said their goodbyes to Daddy there in the parlor. Some just walked by the big window and stood outside and paid their respects that way. After two days, the men came with the coffin and put him on their truck, and we drove out to the cemetery and put him in the hard dark ground next to Little Carl.

I knew my life was about to change again, and I dreaded it.

PART 5

Phoebe was still living with Mama, and so was eight of my little brothers and sisters, so I moved back in for a little while after Daddy left in order to help Mama. My big brothers and Clyde stopped by every day after work, and we all tried real hard to get ourselves back to normal. At about the second week, us older kids all met at John and George's place to talk about how we were going to take care of Mama and the little ones. We had all been giving most of what we made from our jobs to Mama and Daddy right along, and the family was barely getting by. Somehow we had to make up for the loss of money Daddy had been bringing in.

The boys all said they'd look for some extra work somewhere. Phoebe didn't think she could get any more money at the church, but she'd try to be home as much as she could to help Mama more. Somehow we didn't seem to be making any great progress in our talk except making promises to do better. I knew something more needed to be done, and I knew what it was, but I wasn't ready yet to talk about it. I willed myself not to be weak and selfish.

I met Patty and Louise after work one night and talked about our living arrangements. I asked them how much it would hurt them if I moved out and went back home to live.

"Why would you want to do that, Nellie?" Louise said. "We're having so much fun. We love having you as a roomie. It just wouldn't be the same without you."

Patty reached across the table and put her hands on mine.

"Don't go, Nellie," she said. "Let's see if we can't think of some other way. All those brothers and sisters of yours...surely you can all figure out some way you can all share in sacrifices that need to be made."

"I don't want to move either," I told them, "but you just don't understand. It isn't just the money. See, Mama has all the little ones to take care of all by herself now. I could help her with them; help get them fed and off to school and everything. I could help her in lots of ways if I was there more. I don't want her to have to depend any more than she already does on Phoebe. The money would help too. If I didn't pay rent here, I could give that money to the family."

Over the months we'd lived together, I hadn't tried to hide so much from Patty and Louise about my family's situation. I was learning that sharing feelings and problems with good friends was helpful. It allowed everybody to sort things out together.

"You'll still let me come and visit, won't you?" They both told me that there was no way they'd let me get away for too long. "I'll still be able to meet you at Ritchey's sometimes, and this summer we'll still go to the lake. We'll still be best friends. Let's swear we'll always be best friends."

We put our hands together in a circle in the middle of the table and swore we'd be best friends forever. I told them I'd be at the apartment that weekend to clear out my things. On my way home I prayed they wouldn't forget me the way those other old friends had.

I got me a cot and set it up in my old bedroom and went back to living with no privacy or freedom. Whenever I got angry or frustrated, I reminded myself that Mama had been living like this her whole adult life—I could put up with it a little longer.

John and Homer and Clyde took over Daddy's job of teaching the youngins how to play ball and skate and do boys' kinds of things. Homer became the one to talk sense to them. He had a calm way of explaining why some behavior couldn't be tolerated. Old Phoebe wanted the disciplining job, and sometimes she'd step in before Homer got home, but Mama stopped her in a nice way and reminded her that disciplining was best done by a man. She kept preachin' at them just the same and had them worrying about whether or not they'd get to heaven eventually and spend time with Daddy up there if they didn't follow her rules. I knew how her words could hurt and how she could strike fear into you. I was afraid she'd take away the joy in the little ones' hearts. Saving their joyfulness would be a battle between her and me.

I read them stories best I could and told them Daddy's spooky tales so they'd be a part of our family forever. When it was nice out, we played hide and seek or blind man's bluff or red rover or any of those fun games we had all played with him.

I taught my sisters how to behave like ladies too, and we pretended we was models. I made them walk around with books on their heads so they'd have good posture, and I told them to hold their tummies in too so the muscles there would grow tight and they'd look good in clothes later on. Sometimes we pretended we was having tea parties, and I made them laugh by sticking my pinkie up in the air when I was drinking from the cup. Oh, we had great times learning all the stuff Bea was teaching me. I was having fun, too, and didn't mind being back home nearly as much as I thought I would, because I had a purpose for being there. I was especially glad that I was keeping Old Phoebe from getting too close to them.

For once, Mama seemed to be on my side. When Old Phoebe complained to her that I was putting high-falutin' ideas into their heads and heading them into lives full of sin and that they'd grow up wild just like me if Mama didn't put an end to the pretending right then and there, Mama said in a nice way that she didn't think all that fun and good advice could hurt the girls in any way.

Sometimes Grammy joined in and told us about girls she knew when she was young and what was special about them. And she talked about Mama and how pretty she was and how she carried herself tall and proud and how she was always a lady, but was fun to be around, too. Oh, how we loved those stories. We couldn't get enough, and we began to see our mother in a brand new way.

There was a joy spreading throughout our house. We was all talking together more and laughing. I hate to say it, but Mama and Grammy was different, in a good way, since Daddy left, and I couldn't quite figure it out. I mentioned the change to Grammy to see if she saw it too.

"Maybe it's not so much the passing of your daddy that's brought change in this old place," Grammy said. "Maybe it's more that something new has brought in fun and hope. Sometimes the answer to things is right in front of your own nose, Nellie. If you looked closer, you might just see."

About that time, Old Phoebe's strangeness took an upward turn. She took to pacing around from one end of the house to the other, all the time mumbling to herself, getting all riled up about things the rest of us couldn't imagine. It was all in her head. Sometimes right in the middle of her conversations with herself, she'd drop to her knees and shout out, "Praise God," like she'd finally found out the answer to somethin', and it darned near scared the living daylights out of anyone who happened to be close by at the time. Other times, she'd stand back in the shadows with her hand over her heart and watch us girls play our games, and when she had had enough lookin', she'd walk away, shaking her head, mumblin' something to herself. Her prayers at suppertime got longer and longer, and they wasn't about thankfulness for the good food or about blessing us or nothing like that. They was all about forgiving us and driving out the sin from our hearts.

The little ones was careful to step around her, to stay clear of whatever had hold of her. I worried that she would get so strange that maybe even the church wouldn't tolerate her and she'd never be sent to that preacher school. The thought of having her around us forever was just too much to think about.

The boys was doing fine. John got himself a real good job as a brakeman on the railroad. He came home for supper one night with a sack full of groceries for all of us and told us the good news. Of course, it meant that he wouldn't be around all the time because he'd have to travel now, but we all agreed the good outweighed the bad, and we was mighty proud of him.

George got a job with the milk company and started delivering all around town in their white and green milk truck. He wore a crisp white uniform and looked very handsome. He had himself a real nice girlfriend, too. He brought her over for supper one night to meet all of us, and the next day he told us she really liked our family. John asked him if she was going to become part of us, and George got all red in the face and stammered and never did answer.

We took that for a yes.

I laid in bed at night and listened to the last train go by and wondered when it would be my turn to have adventure and find a man to love me in a good way.

The good things coming around at home helped take some of the sting out of what was going on in the world outside. It was hard to believe that all those problems in the big cities could filter on down to us there in Newark, but they did.

A lot of my friends was laid off from work or wasn't getting paid like they thought they was going to be. We didn't go out to the lake much and didn't order up much at Ritchey's either when we met there. We all felt bad taking up space and not ordering much except soft drinks, but no one was standing in line to get into the place, and we figured if we wasn't welcome, Ritchey would let us know. It seemed like me and my family didn't hurt as much from the Depression as most other people around, and I figured it was because we'd never had much to begin with. I guess the more you have, the more you have to lose.

Me and Bea cut back on our orders because a lot of women in town was making do with what they had. We got some stuff done around the place we'd been wanting to get to all year, and that kept us busy for a while, but we finally ran out of things to do. Bea worked a lot on her books, trying to figure out how to cut back here and there as much as she could, and I spent a lot of time looking through magazines and standing at the door, watching people out on The Square. Some of our customers came up to the window sometimes and looked at the clothes laid out there, but fewer and fewer actually came inside to look, and those who did kind'a acted embarrassed when they didn't buy anything. Bea was just as nice as she could be to those old customers, and you'd never know she was worried about her shop. But I knew, and I was worried too.

She didn't need me anymore. I knew I should talk to her about it so she wouldn't have to bring it up herself, but I didn't know where I would go if I left there. I crossed my fingers and, for good measure, said a prayer to whatever was out there listening, that we could just hang on somehow 'til things started getting better for everyone.

Didn't do any good. Several months went by, and I could tell that things wasn't getting any better at all, and I felt real bad for Bea. One night when I was getting ready to leave, I asked her if she'd like to go out with me and have a cup of tea. I was surprised when she turned me down. She said she needed to stay there a little longer and finish up a few things, and then she had to scoot on home to get some work done there.

It was a pretty fall evening, and I didn't want to go back home yet so I decided to take a little walk around The Square and enjoy the last few rays of sun. I put my face up to the sky and let the cool breeze wrap around it, and I took a deep breath and took in the dark earthy smells of the fallen leaves. Someone had a leaf fire going, and the smoke curled its way out to me and brought memories of falls on the farm along with it.

I cut back across the little park and crossed the street over toward where our shop was and saw that a light was still on. I peeked in the window and saw Bea still sitting at her desk in the near-dark, her head in her hand, and I knew right then that it was time to do what I had to do. I tapped at the window so as not to startle her and went right in and sat down right across from her.

"Bea," I said real soft, "Bea, is it all right if we talk just a little bit? I know things are really hard right now. I wish I could help, but I just don't know how."

She took out her hanky and wiped her eyes, and I let her take her time while I looked around the place that I had learned to love as much as if it was my own: all those pretty clothes we had unpacked and hung up together; the little pictures of French ladies Bea had hung just outside the changing room not too long ago to make the room seem cozier; the white curtains we had just washed and hung back up at the little window that opened up to the square; the tidy stack of new pink bags we picked out from the catalogue last summer; her little desk where we began and ended each day with news of our families and talks of our customers and dreams about a bigger shop someday.

"It's just everything," she said, trying to smile. "The shop. Everything. But things will get better. I know they will. I just hope it happens sooner than later."

I couldn't hardly stand to see her so sad.

"Bea, I just know things will get better. They will." I pushed myself to go on. "You've been so good to keep me on this whole time. I know you don't need me. I've known it for some time, but I've been selfish. I've held on here way too long. It's time I move on to somewhere else."

She tried to stop me from talkin', but I knew what was right. "I can find someplace else to go," I said. "Don't you worry. We'll still have tea together and we'll be friends forever. And when things get better, if you ever need help here, you just let me know."

She covered her face with her hands, and all she could say was my name.

"My Aunt Lizzie, who you remember really isn't my aunt?" I said, cheerful as I could. "Well, she taught me all about fortitude. Remember me talking about that? She said when things get tough—and things always do get tough sometimes—you just have to have fortitude. You just have to dig real deep down inside yourself and bring up your strength and not give up. That's what both of us need right now, right now, Bea. Fortitude."

"Oh, my dear Nellie," she said. "What a gift you are. Yes, my dear, I will try to have some fortitude."

We stood up together and gave each other a big hug. She told me she needed me at least a week more to give her time to get some other things arranged. I knew it wasn't true, but I agreed to stay for just one more week. I had six days to find me a new job.

No one needed waitresses. I tried everywhere. Homer checked at the dairy to see if they needed anyone to help out there, but they didn't need nobody. Burke Golf Company was layin' people off, but I applied for a job anyway. My six days was up. I had to say goodbye to Bea, and I had to tell Mama and Grammy and my big brothers that we was going to have to cut back for a while.

I was in a real pickle and didn't have anybody really to turn to without upsetting a whole bunch of people. I decided to ask my God to help me out one more time.

"God, I know You're out there somewhere and can see me. Well, I know You can hear me anyways. I'm askin' You for another favor, and I hope You'll agree to it. Please, just let me find a job real quick 'cause my family needs me to. I need to for my own self, too. So if You're not too mad at me, I hope You'll help us. Thank You."

Clyde lost his job soon after I did, and I figured we was really in a heap of trouble. Mama tried to get jobs wallpapering again, but no one had the money to have paper hung, and I admit I was glad because I didn't want her to have to do that. I prayed nothing would happen to John and Homer's jobs. If anything happened to them, well, I couldn't think about that.

I missed working. Missed it more than I ever dreamed possible. I found myself looking outside a lot, wondering what people down on The Square was doing. I thought about those beautiful clothes at Bea's and our old customers. I thought about the bustle and noise at The

Sparta and all of those people I wasn't getting to meet. I missed the freedom of being with Patty and Louise. Before long, it felt like my house was closing in on me.

I was all bottled up.

Mama and me worked as a team. We washed all the family's clothes and hung them up out on the line soon as the youngins left for school. Clothes was hanging everywhere, all over the kitchen, all day long, and there was nowhere to get away from the clutter. We cleaned, sewed, cooked, played with the little ones and started all over again with the same things every single day. My hands got all chapped and broken like hers, and I forgot to think about how I looked. That's the way it had always been for Mama, and I looked at her in a new way. I wondered how she tolerated her life the way she did.

One cold day when I was deep into feeling sorry for myself, Grammy called me over to her and handed me a small wooden box. She asked me to open it for her and find a piece of folded paper with Mama's name on the front. And she told me to take it somewhere where it was quiet and read it.

"Maybe it will help you understand your mama a little more and help you get through these times," she said. "She wrote it many years ago. I found it all scrunched up in the trash one morning. That's what she does. She writes poems and throws them all away. You know, Nellie, you and your mama are more alike than you know."

I had no idea my mama wrote poems!

Later that day, I put on my coat and stuffed the piece of paper into my pocket and headed out to the tracks. I leaned against a bare tree and read:

> I will sing when my way is lonely
> And nobody seems to care;
> I will sing when the cross is heavy
> And life is so hard to bear.
>
> I will sing when my heart is broken
> And nobody understands;

I will sing when the tears are falling,
And bow to the Father's plans.

I will sing when the storms are raging
And nobody takes my part;
I will sing 'til I enter Heaven
For Jesus is in my heart.

I will sing of a Father's mercy
I will sing of a Savior's love
And tell of a home in glory
Which He has prepared above.

The big hurt around my heart got bigger. When I gave the poem back to Grammy, she told me it was mine to keep.

"Sometimes, Nellie, people get all wrapped up in Jesus because they feel that they have nowhere else to go," she told me. "Religion is a lifeline when a hurt is just too big to bear. Sometimes having the right people around brings about a balance."

I wasn't sure what I should say to that.

"You just think about it, honey," she said. "Just think about it and you'll know what I mean."

Late one night I woke up, thinkin' I heard voices downstairs in the kitchen. For a while, I laid real quiet and tried to get back to sleep, but finally curiosity got the best of me. I got up and wrapped the blanket around me and tip-toed real quiet down the stairs to see who was there with something important enough to talk about at that hour.

Grammy's bed in the parlor was empty, and the door to the kitchen was almost closed, but I could see the glow from the lamp on the wall. I held my breath and listened hard and heard Mama and Grammy askin' questions to somebody, but I couldn't hear any answering. I moved a little closer and stepped on one of the loose boards on the floor.

The creak made them stop their talking, and they said, "Who's there?"

I didn't have a choice then. I had to go in.

There was my mama and my grammy, sitting at the table, and right in the middle of the table between them was a Ouija Board. A Ouija Board, just like Aunt Lizzie's!

"What are you doing?" I said. "What are you doing with a Ouija Board?" You could 'a knocked me over with a feather.

I could see that Mama wasn't sure what to say. "Well, we're just trying to find out some things, that's all." Then she looked up at me surprised and asked, "How do you know what this is?"

"Well, I've seen one before."

"Where did you ever see a board?"

"Well, I don't think I should say. I promised I wouldn't tell."

"Lizzie showed you, didn't she?" Grammy chuckled. "That Lizzie. She's the one, all right. That old gal. I should've known. Damn, she beat me to it. Good for her. Come on over here, Nellie, and join us."

Mama started to make a fuss, but Grammy shushed her.

"Oh, Rebecca, for heaven's sake. It's high time we stop keeping things from her. She's all grown up, and we need to treat her like the adult she is. I just wish I'd beat Lizzie to it."

Well, we got that board going real good that night. Grammy couldn't see the marker move, of course, couldn't see most things now, but we told her what it said. We asked questions about Homer and whether he'd marry his girl, whether Phoebe would go to that preacher school, and if I would find a job soon. It answered yes to all those questions. Then we turned to the question of money and how we could get more. It had trouble giving us good answers about that one.

The last question Grammy asked was if I was going to find a real beau soon. The marker started makin' circles around and looked like it was heading over to "yes," but then it circled around and headed on over to "no," but didn't stop there either. Grammy asked the same question again, and the danged thing just stopped altogether. I asked her what that meant, and she said that it meant that we had been given enough information already, and the Ouija was tired out.

Mama and Grammy was serious about using the Ouija, just like they was about almost everything. I wasn't sure how I felt about it, but I'll tell you one thing: I just couldn't believe I was sitting there with my mama who trusted in the Lord for all things, and there she was askin' spirits to come in and give her answers.

I loved all the new parts of her I was learning about. She wrote poems and she used the Ouija. I wondered what else there was to know about my mama.

Right after the time with the Ouija, I decided to walk down to see how my Bea was doing. I wanted to tell her about how good me and Mama was getting along and what I was learnin' about her and Grammy, and I wanted to get her advice on how to deal with Old Phoebe. I was hoping, too, that maybe we could start our lessons back up so I could start working on being a lady again. And I wanted to explain why I hadn't stopped by for so long.

It was one of those days when you felt like spring was right around the corner. It had been a long, hard Ohio winter that year, and I needed it to be gone. Seemed everyone was on edge, antsy to be outside on a regular basis. The cool winds was changing to warm breezes, and robins' songs was waking us up in the mornings. Daffodils and tulips was popping up in patches all over our yard, and that old sun's warmth took hold of me, and I felt lighter, felt like things was going to look up for all of us.

I walked to The Square the very day the warmth broke in and decided to stay, and I looked up at the big old sun shining down and said right out loud, "Hi, God. Thank You for all this beauty You put here for us. I promise I'll start thinkin' positive again and look out beyond just me."

I knew He heard. I told myself that I would never doubt the changes of seasons again, and I would learn patience.

Those same old feelings I used to have down on the farm at this time of year took hold of me, and I wished that I could climb one of those trees right there beside me right then and there; wished I could see the earth and feel the breeze perched right up there in the highest branches. I wished I wasn't all grown up and could be free to do what my head and body wanted me to do. Just like every spring, I felt that something real good was going to happen and that somethin' was just waiting for me around the corner. Maybe I could fly today, I thought, and I smiled at myself, remembering how, when I was little, I believed everything was possible.

I hadn't been down to The Square for a long time, and I didn't know when I would be back, so I took my time. I sat down on one of the benches in the park and made sure my ankles was crossed just right and that I was sitting up straight like Bea taught me, and I watched everyone hurrying around with their important business to attend to. I noticed that a couple of the store fronts had been painted, and they looked real good

I decided to splurge and get Bea and me chocolate ice cream sodas, our favorite, to celebrate seeing each other again, and I stopped and looked inside other shops on my way to the ice cream parlor and waved at the people I knew. I felt real good when they recognized me and waved back. Armed with the sodas, I made my way back to the north side and The Fashion. I managed to get my purse, the ice cream, and the magazine I had just bought in one arm and grabbed the door knob and pushed. And pushed again. It wasn't until I pushed a third time that I noticed the small sign posted on the inside of the window that said "For Lease" and a number to call.

I couldn't make myself believe it. I banged on the door and yelled out Bea's name. I twisted the knob again and again and peered in the windows, sure I would see her sitting there at her little desk. But the room was empty. The desk, pictures, curtains, clothes racks, everything was gone. Just a few open boxes here and there was all that was left.

I dropped everything at the door and ran to The Sparta and had one of the girls there dial the number that was on the sign. The lady who answered was with the company that was handling the lease and, no, she said, she couldn't give me the owner's phone number or address. We had the operator look up Bea's number, and she told us the phone was disconnected. She was gone. I'd lost her.

Several weeks later, I got a letter from her.

My Dear Nellie,

I gave much thought to the wise advice you gave me the day we talked about my family, and I realized, finally, that you were so right to urge me to try to win back my life with my wonderful children. It's not good to live a lie, to pretend you aren't who you are. I need to accept and forgive myself. Hopefully, those I love will do the same. I have gone back home. I am showing fortitude. I hope that you will be proud of me.

Please forgive me for leaving without telling you. It tore my heart apart to say goodbye each time to my three children. I couldn't stand to do it again with the fourth. You are like another daughter to me.

You feel such a need to change. I pray that you never do. You are so very special, and you have much to give to this tired and ever-exciting old world. Be yourself and be all that you are capable of. You are most definitely a Lady in the best sense of the word. Age will bring deeper wisdom.

I love you so. I am blessed to have had you in my life.

Your friend forever.
Bea

Along about July I got a job cleaning the "Newark Advocate" office just down off The Square on Main Street. I went to work right after supper every night but Sunday and stayed on 'til I was finished. My cleaning partner was an old man who had no teeth and smelled bad. I couldn't understand most of what he said, and I kept as far away from him as I could to keep his body odor from getting on me, but we got along fine. We started on opposite ends of the offices and cleaned our way to the middle. We didn't get to know each other very good.

One day that following fall, I walked over to Ritchey's to see the gang, and Patty and Louise grabbed me and told me they was so glad to see me 'cause they had something important to tell me. They sat me down in the booth and said that they needed a new cashier at The Sparta. The old one had been carrying off money from the cash register from time to time over the past year and had finally got caught. They said they thought I should apply.

I told them that I didn't know the first thing about being a cashier, but it seemed to me that it must be a pretty hard job, figuring up what people owe and making change, and selling candy and all. I got nervous just thinking about it, and I was sure Mr. Stenson would never hire me on.

"The pay is great, Nellie," Patty said, ignoring everything I'd just said. "The cashier is paid better than us girls. You could do it. You'd be great up front. Real classy."

I knew right then and there I wanted that job. "But if the pay's so good, why don't one of you do it? You've both been there a long time. You deserve it."

But they told me that they weren't good at figures and, besides, they didn't want all that pressure. They was happy doin' exactly what they was doin'.

Well, I told them I'd think about it, but I knew before they ever got across the street I was going to try to get that job. I remembered how pretty that candy counter was, and I thought about how I'd get to know every customer 'cause they'd all have to stop at me before they could leave.

This could be my big chance to be important.

I was going to apply, but I wasn't going to tell anybody just in case Mr. Stenson turned me down. I didn't want to embarrass myself. For the next two days I practiced how I was going to talk to my old boss and how I was going to convince him that I was the right girl for him.

I planned to sneak in and see Mr. Stenson without Patty and Louise seein' me, but, wouldn't you know, the day I went in they was both working the counter up front. Patty raised her eyebrows when she saw me and said, with no sound, "The job?" I nodded yes, and she mouthed "good luck," and gave me a great big smile and went over to Louise and pointed in my direction. *Great*, I thought. Now I'm going to be real embarrassed when I don't get it.

Well, hallelujah, I'll tell you right out, I got the job. Mr. Stenson said how glad he was to have me back and told me I could start Monday if I wanted to. I told him I would, and I told him that I wouldn't disappoint him, that I was going to be the best cashier he ever had.

I had me a new, real important job, and I made a promise to myself that I would never ever let The Sparta down. I practically ran home, thinking all the time about how I was going to keep that candy counter looking so good that people wouldn't be able to walk out the door without first buying themselves some candy. I was going to make everybody so happy as they was leaving the place that they would want to come back real quick. I was going to save The Sparta from going down with the Depression.

That Sunday when my family sat down for dinner, Mama and Grammy announced to everybody that I had a real important job and asked me to tell everyone what it was. When I was finished, they all clapped and said, "Good, Nellie" and "Yea, Nellie."

John, who was home from his job that week, came around to where I was sitting and mussed up my hair and said, "Congratulations, Nellie. You're doing a great job. My little sister is all grown up." And I thought about how much like Daddy he really was.

He told me to stand up, and when I did, he put his arm around my shoulders and said, "Do you know what today is, Nellie?" No good answer came into my head. "You silly girl. Today's your birthday. Did you forget?"

I guess I was just too busy and too excited about things that I just plain forgot what day it was. Course, normally it wouldn't matter much anyway.

John had Homer and George and Clyde come up next to me then, and he handed me a box all wrapped up real pretty with a big bow and told me to open it. They stood beside me while I pulled the paper off and helped me pull the gift out. I had to look real hard at it to make my mind register what it was I was seeing. They had bought me a doll, the prettiest doll I had ever seen.

"You've never had a doll, Nellie," John said, and his voice cracked a little, "but you helped make it possible for each of your younger sisters to have theirs. You've given us all a lot, sis, so, anyway, we just thought that you're never too old for something like this, and so, well, we just hope you don't think we're bein' silly."

He gave me a quick hug and him and the others rushed back to their seats. Everybody clapped, every single person in my family except Old Phoebe, and then they sang Happy Birthday Dear Nellie.

I held up my very first doll and had a real good look at her. She had reddish-brown hair and blue eyes just like mine, and her dress was a soft yellow, one of my favorite colors. No words would come up to tell my brothers what was in my heart so I just hugged my doll tight and managed to say, "Thank you," and told everyone it was time to dig in and eat.

After things was all cleaned up, I went upstairs and put my doll down on my pillow there on the cot beside my old bed. I'd never really missed having a doll to play with, and yet I'd always known it was important for my little sisters to have one. All of a sudden I sensed how it must feel to have a child of your own, and I smiled at myself and thought, well, maybe I did have some inclinations toward being a mother after all, that maybe the pain of having one would be forgotten when you held it in your arms and knew how much it needed you.

The next morning I started my new job.

I was scared at first, but I found that I picked up everything I was supposed to real quick. Adding all those numbers together was easy as could be. I couldn't spell a lot of words and my handwriting was something most people couldn't read, but I could do figures. Some of my old customers congratulated me and told me they was real glad to see me back, and I met some other real nice people besides. Well, I have to tell you, I felt pretty wonderful walking home that night, felt like my feet was barely touching the ground. I tilted my head up to the heavens and said thank you to my God and decided He must not be so mad at me after all.

Mama had supper waiting for me when I came home, and after the dishes was done and the youngins was tucked in for the night, me and her sat and talked about our day together. We asked Phoebe to join us, but she said she had studyin' to do, and she walked silent around the house carrying her Bible next to her big bosoms. We didn't pay much attention to her.

It was late when we finished our talk, and we kissed each other good night and went up the stairs to our rooms. I put my nightie on in the dark so I wouldn't wake my sisters up, and I lowered myself quietly onto my cot and snuggled under my quilt. Something didn't feel right. There was pieces of something stringy and soft spread out all under me. My foot touched something hard. It scared me. I jumped up fast and turned the lantern on low and brought it up close under the blankets to see what I was feeling. And there was my new doll, its hair all cut off and its face slashed. Her pretty yellow dress was torn and pieces of it was scattered everywhere.

I couldn't touch the pieces of her even though I knew her body wasn't real. The sight of that doll ripped to pieces sent chills up me, and I backed away from it. I knew Phoebe was watching and taking pleasure in my hurt and fear, so I went over to my old bed where she still slept.

"You are evil, sister," I hissed at her. "You are an abomination. My God is not in you, and you will never ever know what His real love feels like because you are too full of hate. You use religion to work your hate. You can't hurt me and you can't take away my happiness because I will not let you."

The next morning when I told Mama and Grammy what had happened, they said they didn't know what to do about Old Phoebe. I think they was afraid of her, just like the rest of us was. The three of us said that we'd have to think real hard about the whole situation and talk it all over after some time had passed and we could think straight about it. We agreed to watch her close. It was impossible to know what she might do next.

But in the end, the problem with her was solved for us. About a month after she cut up my doll, she started to change. She smiled more and was gentler with the youngins. She moved out of the shadows and joined us for stories and family conversations. Grace came right out and asked her one Thursday at supper if something had happened to her to make her so different. Phoebe seemed pleased by the question and told Grace that, yes, something was about to happen, something wonderful, but we'd have to wait to find out what it was that Sunday when everyone, including John, would be there.

The whole house was abuzz all that day because we was all so anxious to know what the surprise was that Phoebe had for us. When we got ourselves settled in our seats around the table that afternoon, we let Phoebe say grace, and she actually thanked God for His blessings this time and asked Him to bless and protect our family for all our days here on earth. We all looked up at each other with puzzled looks on our faces while she was saying her "Amens," wondering about her kindness and concern for us.

Then she stood up and told us that she was ready to make her important announcement to us.

"Family," she said, with the biggest smile I'd ever seen on her face, "I have some wonderful news. Not too long ago, Pastor Scott heard about an Evangelical group out in West Virginia that has decided to begin holding tent revivals down there in the hills this summer to save lost souls and bring them to God. Those disciples of God need more strong Christians who are devoted to the word of the Lord to help them with their monumental task of bringing those unbelievers to their senses and helping them find the way. Of course, not all are unbelievers down there, but some have been allowed to stray or are confused by the wicked ways of the world."

She looked at me when she said that, and I knew she thought I belonged in that category.

"Well, the thing is, I told the Pastor that I would be grateful to serve with that blessed group of evangelists. I told him I believe I have a calling. He agreed that I definitely do, and he contacted the leader of the congregation down there and told him that he had a disciple right here in Newark who was willing to make the sacrifice and head down to the hills of West Virginia to help out. He got a letter back just Thursday, saying that they would be delighted and honored to have me."

Me and my family waited to hear the final words that would set our own family free.

"I know how hard it will be on you all," she continued, " but I have to leave you and serve God down there in the hills." She smiled out at us and waited for our praise.

I said my own little prayer to God, thanking Him for taking her off our hands and asking Him to please protect those poor people down there in the hills from her crazy ways. I threw in a little request that He would take care of her and protect her and not allow her to do anything down there in those hills that would embarrass her or get her thrown out.

Grammy was the first one to find her voice. "Well, well, Phoebe," she said. "I'm so happy for you. We all are. This is what you've been wanting to do for as long as I can remember: to offer yourself up to God and to serve others in His name. Congratulations, honey, congratulations." She clapped, and the rest of us followed her example.

Phoebe just kept standing there with her hand over her heart, beaming out at all of us looking up at her, waiting for something more. Mama came to our rescue with her own prayer of thanks to God for giving Phoebe this wonderful opportunity. We all said our "Amens," and Phoebe finally sat down.

In no time at all, she was set to head out. Me and the boys bought her a pretty bag to pack her things in, and we sat in our room and watched her fill it up. There was nothing left to do but say goodbye.

When we was all gathered in the parlor to wait for the pastor to pick up our sister, Mama led us in prayer and asked God to protect Phoebe. And then Phoebe asked Him to protect us. And I asked Him to make sure the preacher wouldn't change his mind about picking her up. When we finally heard the pastor's horn out front, we all walked out with her to send her off to those poor unsuspecting people down south.

She had something to whisper to all of us, and she turned to me last. She told me that I should mend my sinful ways and give over pride or I would surely suffer the fires of hell. She put her hands on my shoulders and told me she was very worried about me and my salvation, and she assured me that she'd pray for me. And I told her to get herself on down there where those poor people in the hills was, and not to worry one little bit about me 'cause I didn't need any saving and could take care of myself.

I watched as the pastor's car disappeared down our street, headed for someplace I only knew the name of, and even though I sure didn't want to go down to the hills of West Virginia, I kind'a envied Old Phoebe. At least she was going somewhere.

PART 6

The gang was meeting at Ritchey's that night after work, and I made arrangements to meet them there. I was late and rushed in and found my girlfriends in the big booth by the window. They was all worked up.

"Nellie, wait 'til you see what's new in town," Annie said. "Don't look yet. He's over at the counter talking with some of our guys. Okay, you can look now. Turn around and check out the blond guy standing with Jimmie."

I couldn't help laughing. She was in such a twit.

"Just turn around," Dolly whispered. "It's the new guy who's working over at the shoe store. He waited on Pam yesterday, and she almost fainted on the spot, he was soooo good. Everyone's talking about him. He watched you come in. Couldn't take his eyes off you. Turn around and see what you think."

I turned around and saw Jimmie standing at the counter. The blond boy next to him was facing out towards the room, leaning against the counter, smoking a cigarette. He had one foot crossed casually in front of the other, and he looked more relaxed and at ease than any of the other guys there. You would have thought he knew everyone and had just dropped by to say hello. He was tall, taller than the others, and lanky.

"What do you think?" All six of my friends asked at the same time.

"Well, I think he's very good looking, but—"

"Oh, my gosh," Dolly said, "I think they're coming over."

Jimmie and a couple of the other guys brought the newcomer over to our booth and introduced him to us. "Everybody," he said, "this is Curtis. Curtis James, from Connersville, Indiana. He's moved to our lovely town, and he's working over at the shoe store."

I took a long sip of cola from my straw and kept my head down while everybody introduced themselves.

"I'm sorry," Curtis said, and I knew he was looking at me. "I don't think I got your name."

"She's Nellie," Pam said.

"Hi, Nellie," the new boy said with his big, beautiful smile.

"Hello," was all I could get out, and I could feel how red my face was. I kicked Patty under the table, and she got the conversation going away from me.

The fellas asked us to ride out with them to a dance hall out beyond Granville. Everyone decided to go, but I told Louise that I couldn't.

Louise looked at me like I had two heads. "Why in the world not?" she demanded. "What do you have to do?"

Just like that, all the attention was back to me.

"I just need to get back home," I said. "I have some things to do."

Louise stared at me hard and whispered, "What in the world is wrong with you?"

"Oh, Nellie, come on," Patty said. "Come with us. Do your stuff another time." Even Patty was talkin' at me.

I could see Curtis out of the corner of my eye. I pretended to look at the clock over the counter. "Uh, oh, I'm late already." I jumped up so fast I knocked over a glass and ran right into Joey. "Oh, my, I'm so sorry, I—"

"Never mind, Nellie. I'll take care of it. Go on. I'll see you soon, hon." It was Patty talking. I wanted a big hole to open up in the floor

169

and suck me down to China.

I glanced over at Curtis as I was leaving, and he was still smiling. "Bye, Nellie, see you later."

I couldn't concentrate on nothin' that whole weekend. I could not get Curtis out of my mind. I spoke just one word to him and barely looked at him, but, there it was, his face and every single word he said kept coming into my head no matter how hard I tried to stop it.

He came to The Sparta for lunch that Monday and talked to Patty and Louise and everyone else at the counter, and in no time at all he had everybody laughin' and actin' like he was a real good friend of theirs. For some unknown reason, it made me mad. Now, why in the world, I asked myself, should I be upset because he makes friends so easy?

When he came over to me to pay his check, I felt myself turning red again, and I willed the flush to stop, but, of course, I couldn't control it.

"Hi, Nellie. I was hoping I'd run into you here," he said.

I couldn't think of anything to say to that so I wiped the counter off like it was the most important thing in the world to do right then.

"We missed you when we all went out dancing. Had a great time. Too bad you couldn't have gone with us. We're going out again this Friday. Patty and Louise are going. Think you could go along with us?"

"I'm not sure," I blurted out. "I might be busy. I'm really not sure."

Dang, I thought, I wish I could think of something clever to say and relax a little bit.

"Well, I sure hope you'll be able to go." He stood there, acting like he was waiting for something, and I glanced at the people in line behind him. He leaned over the counter towards me and whispered, "You didn't give me my change yet."

I was mortified.

Curtis came in for lunch almost every day and sat at his favorite spot at the counter. By now he was best friends with all the staff and all our regulars. I had never met anyone so sure of himself as he was. Me? I was a wreck. I needed to talk to Grammy.

"Well, some people are just born with a gift of gab," she explained after I told her what was bothering me. "They just know how to say the right things. The easy talkers are usually the good-looking ones too. 'Course not always. They have self-confidence. Then too, new people always seem more special than the ones that have been around forever. People will get used to him, and the magic will wear off a little, I'm sure. Wonder what brought him all the way here from Indiana. Did he ever say? Well, no matter. I'd say, though, by the way you're feeling and all, you're maybe a little moonstruck."

I started to disagree with her, but she shushed me.

"You go on out with your friends and have a good time," she said. "You're a good judge of people. Just take your time and get to know him. Be sure to look at him with your eyes wide open, and you'll be able to see him for what he really is. See if there's anything to him to earn your respect."

Grammy was right, I thought. No sense in me being all worked up about him. He was probably no different than anybody else and just seemed special because he wasn't sayin' much about himself. Actually, none of us knew too much about him except that he was really, really handsome and different and mysterious. I'd just take my time, like Grammy said, and look him over real good and see how he proved out as time went on.

That Friday was the season's opening night for the Crystal Ballroom, and nobody could talk about anything all week but that. About Midweek Curtis told me, while he was paying his bill at The Square, that he couldn't wait to go. I hoped he wouldn't be disappointed. Friday night, we all met in the middle of the Square and piled ourselves tight into cars and drove to the lake.

Do you have any recollections of nights late in the spring when it's almost summer but not quite; when the air is still a little cool, but the breeze is coming in warm around you; when the trees are in full bloom and still smelling of newness, and everything is fresh and full and promising? Well, that Friday was that kind of night, and all of us was full of life and all its possibilities. We treated Buckeye Lake and The Crystal Ballroom like it was our gift to Curtis. We wanted him to enjoy it as much as we did.

Well, he took to it like a duck to water. He walked right in there with his arms around the shoulders of two of my girlfriends and stood right in the middle of the floor and looked around at all of it—and didn't miss a thing. When the music started, he snapped his fingers to the rhythm, and you could feel the need in him to dance. Oh, my, could he dance. I watched him as he twirled and dipped one girl after another around the floor. And I wasn't the only one who was watching. He stood out.

Then it was my turn. I knew it would happen sooner or later, and my palms was so wet from nervousness that I just knew he'd hate holding them in his hands. He was tall, a lot taller than me, and he was thin, but his hand across my back was firm and strong. I felt enclosed by him, and it felt good. He led real confident, and I followed easy, and when he whispered into my hair how good a dancer I was, I felt I had been given the best compliment a girl could ever get.

He didn't dance with anyone else the rest of the night. It was just him and me, and I forgot to be nervous. In his arms, I felt pretty and delicate.

We floated together.

After that night, we saw each other 'most every day and two or three nights a week, but we didn't get together on weekends. He caught rides from some buddy of his back to Connersville every Friday night and didn't get back 'til late Sundays. His mother was having some health problems, he said, and he felt he needed to be home with his family until she got better. Well, I sure couldn't argue with that. I'd do the same thing if I was in his shoes, and I told him so. Weekends was when everybody else went out, though, and I missed him a lot.

One Thursday night before he had to leave to visit his family, he

borrowed a friend's car, and just the two of us went out to the lake together. It was the day before the Fourth of July weekend. Buckeye Lake
was going to have a fireworks show that night, and he wanted us to see
it together. We drove out with the windows rolled down, and we let the
wind blow in at us. It was dusk, just when the sun was real low, and the
earth smelled beautiful. We held hands the whole way, and I put my
head on his shoulder. We didn't need to say much; we knew what we
was both feeling.

When we got out, he made me close my eyes while he pulled something out of the hatch, and when I opened them, there he was, standing
there with a basket of chicken, and some apples, a bottle of wine, and a
blanket. We had a picnic down by the lake just across from the amusement park.

We talked, and I couldn't get over how easy it always was to be with
him. He asked me all about my family, and I told him about the old
farm and how I grew up, and he told me what life was like for him when
he was young. His family was almost rich. He had finished school and
had started college. He came to Newark for a little break. We talked
about what kind of life we wanted for ourselves, and we agreed families
was important. He wanted at least three children, one less than his family had, and I told him I wasn't sure if I wanted any children at all since
I'd been kind of like a mother all my life to my little brothers and sisters. He said he understood how I could feel that way.

He wanted to make something of himself, just like me, and he told
me his dream of having a big house someday and a job that people respected. I told him how I wanted my own ladies' shop or bakery and how
I wanted pretty dishes, a huge bed with new sheets, and flowers in glass
vases everywhere. We talked about religion, and I told him how I didn't
think I'd go to church when I moved away from my family because I
hadn't met anyone who was church-going besides Mama who had the
same ideas about God as me. I told him I felt God all around me in the
great outdoors, and I didn't think I needed a church. He felt the same
way. His family wasn't church-goers.

We watched the fireworks, and when it was all quiet and the fire-
flies came out and the music from the Merry-Go-Round started up, he

reached over and touched my face, and there was tears in his eyes, and he said he was in love with me.

"I've never felt this way about anyone, Nellie. I can't believe I've found you. All day long, all night long, all I can think about is you. I'm crazy about you, Nellie. Crazy about you."

He kissed my eyes and my neck, and he ran his hands through my hair and said it was like silk. He kissed my lips soft and then hard and we laid down together, and he whispered the sweetest things to me. He looked deep into my eyes while he ran his hands across my shoulders and my neck and down to my breasts, and his touch took my breath away. I wanted to push myself against him and feel him all over me, but I couldn't. Something held me back.

"I can't do this," I said. "Not yet. I'm sorry, but I just can't. Please don't be mad."

"You've never been with a man, have you?" His voice was gentle.

I told him I hadn't. I told him some things had happened, things I couldn't talk about yet, and I couldn't get past them. The look on his face was so full of kindness and concern that I wanted him to know, to understand everything, and his patience and gentleness allowed me to bring out the words I had never been able to say to anyone before.

I told him about the man in the woods and about Gerry and finally about Luke, the railroader. I told him how they had made me feel dirty, how I was always misunderstood. I told him what Preacher had said to my Daddy and how it hurt me to think that I was seen as over-friendly, as someone who might give people the idea that I wanted to be with men in a dark way.

He held me real tender, like he would a little child, and I knew from his voice that he understood.

"My poor Nellie," he said. "It's okay. The fact that you could tell me all this makes me love you even more. Don't you worry. We'll take it slow. I want to take care of you. I swear I'll never let anyone hurt you again. And I will never, ever hurt you. I promise."

I believed him.

The next week I invited Curtis over to meet Mama and Grammy and my whole family, and we had a great time. He stayed longer than any of us thought he would and seemed to be really sad to say goodbye. He thanked Mama and Grammy and shook all my big brothers' hands. The little ones followed him out to the porch. He told me he'd like to take me to Connersville to meet his folks some weekend, but he wanted to give his mother more time to recover.

I had never known such happiness as I did then. I wanted more than anything to be Mrs. Curtis James. The places I had always wanted to go, the freedom I was always waiting for, my feelings of not really belonging had disappeared with the arrival of this wonderful man.

Several weeks later, Patty stopped by my counter and asked me to go on over to her house after work. She said she had something she needed to talk to me about.

"Nellie, honey, I hope I'm doing the right thing telling you this," she said when we was in her kitchen. "Lord knows I've gone back and forth on it, but, well, I think you need to know." She got up and poured our coffee from the pot on the stove and put mine down on the table in front of me.

I knew she was stallin' for time. I'd never seen her so serious, and I knew that whatever she was about to tell me would hurt real bad.

"There's no easy way to tell you this so I'll just say it." She looked me right in the eye. "David ran into an old friend of Curtis' down at the pool hall early this week. This friend is the one who takes Curtis back to their home town every weekend. They're both from there. He's the one who got Curtis the job at the shoe store. Well, anyway, honey, Curtis isn't going home to see his mother or any of his family. He's going home to see a girl. Her name is Darlene. Oh, Nellie, they're engaged. Have been for over a year now. He's seeing her on the weekends, and he's seeing you during the week."

That hurting place in my chest that I thought was gone forever popped its way up again and spread out all over my body.

I was shamed. The one person I had put all my trust in shamed me. I was a fool to believe someone could love me the way Curtis said he did.

He had used me for some reason I couldn't begin to understand, and now everyone knew it. I dug way down deep to figure out why this was happening. I dug for fortitude, but there was mighty little left in me.

Curtis came into The Sparta on Monday just like he always did. I watched him wave to the crowd at the counter and tell them he'd be right over. His blond hair was ruffled from the breeze, and his cheeks was red from the heat.

He wore the most precious smile, and he winked at me as he said, "Hi, honey. Boy, I missed you."

My heart was beating so hard in my chest that I felt light-headed. "I know about Darlene," I said, and tried hard to stand tall. "How could you do that? I believed in you, believed *everything* you said, and now..." I couldn't believe it was me sayin' these things. It felt like I was out of myself, like I was looking down at someone else who was talking to him.

He looked like someone had punched him hard in the stomach. He started to say something, but he must a' thought better of it. "We'll talk later, Nellie, when we have some time. I should have told you sooner, but I was working on breaking it off with her, I..."

He looked so pitiful I wanted him to tell me that it was all a big mistake, that he didn't love nobody but me, but he'd lied to me, and nothin' would make it right.

"No. Please don't say anything more," I said. "Don't you see? You're engaged to someone else. You know I can't ever see you again." And I turned my back on him so he couldn't see my tears.

He came back every single day for two weeks, and when it was clear that I wasn't going to talk to him, he left notes in front of me on the counter. I threw them out. Every time his name or his face came into my brain, I forced it out. I made myself empty.

Patty gave me more advice. "What if he's promised to change, Nellie? What if he's writing to tell you he broke it off with that girl? My God, anyone can see you're crazy about him. And look at him. Anyone can see he's hurting. He can't be faking it. Not even he could be that good. Maybe you should give him another chance."

Curtis came back the next day and waited in line behind the customers paying their bills until he was finally standing in front of my counter.

"Nellie," he said, "just listen to me, all right? I want to tell you that I'm going back to Connersville this Friday. Hold on. Don't walk away. Let me finish. Please."

I turned around and faced him, and it was so hard to look into his eyes.

"I'm going back to tell Darlene the truth," he said. "I'm breaking up with her, Nellie, because I'm in love with you. Darlene and I have known each other since we were little. I don't think I was ever in love with her. We've just been together through everything. But I knew the minute I saw you I wasn't meant to be with her."

I wanted so much to believe him. We had been good for each other. Why, we had the same dreams and knew that we could reach them if we worked together. He understood me, and I felt so safe when I was with him. In spite of it all, I still believed he was a good person.

"Please, Nellie, promise you'll see me Monday after work. I'll tell you everything. I promise. I swear to you I will never hurt you again. I can't explain why I did what I did. I can just tell you how sorry I am. Please forgive me. At least give me another chance. I've lost everything if I lose you."

I wanted to reach over across the counter and tell him I'd do anything for him, but I knew it would be better for us both if we went careful just now.

"I'll think about it," I told him. "That's all I can promise right now. You need to make absolutely sure you're doing what you want to do. We'll see when you get back. Now, I have work to do."

He came back to me Monday after work and told me that if I'd take him back, he'd be mine for the rest of his life. He had broken off the engagement with Darlene. It had been hard to hurt her, but it had to be done. Then he held me close and told me over and over how much he loved me.

I needed to believe him, and so I did.

Bottled Butterfly

Grammy was failing. We could all see that. She pretended to be fine and never complained, but she was just plain tired. One day late August, she asked if we could take a little trip back out to the farm to see Lizzie and the rest of our family out there, and to walk the land. Her and Mama and me squeezed ourselves into Homer's car, and we drove out that Saturday. The ride wore her out, and I thought that maybe we was wrong to take her, but once she was out there, she perked up a little bit and seemed to get some of her strength back.

We went to our old home place first, and the sight of it hurt so deep that I was glad Grammy was too blind to see it. Weeds grew so free and thick they seemed to have sapped the strength out of the grass and the very foundation of the old house. The steps and front door was losing their paint, and the screen door was loose at the top and looked like it was trying to get away from all the neglect goin' on. My swing was splintered and sad, rocking on its own in the little breeze. A painted "for sale" sign done in black was layin' on its back in front of our beautiful pine tree at the end of the lane. We stood there quiet for several moments, and I think everyone was remembering picnics and sing-alongs, and children's games from long ago. Mama put her finger to her lips and shook her head at me. We weren't going to let Grammy know how bad our old place was looking now.

We took Grammy by her arms and led her around real slow and told her how things hadn't changed much.

"Take me to the country kitchen and your garden," she said to Mama.

We couldn't tell her they was gone: the little building where my dreams was stored once was just a pile of rubble now.

"It's quiet," she said. "Nobody lives here any more, do they?"

We told her it appeared that way, and a sadness creeped in and circled around us. Seemed to me the horrible thing that had happened to that poor little girl all those years ago had put a curse on our old home.

When we got to Aunt Lizzie's, she took us out back to a big old maple tree, and there was Aunt Edith, Little Edith and her little baby boy waiting for us. She had piled up pillows for us to sit on, and spread out on her big quilt was enough fried chicken and potato salad to feed the whole county. We took our turns holding little Matt, and I watched with pride how good my old friend was in taking care of him. The way she glowed, told me her husband was a good man.

We all listened to Grammy and Aunt Lizzie tell stories on each other from when they was young, and when I heard the way they laughed, I knew we had done the right thing to take Grammy back. Places change, but good friends never do. It was like no time had passed at all. They just took up where they had left off more than five years ago.

Saying goodbye was hard for all of us because we knew great changes was about to happen. Grammy and Aunt Lizzie had little time left on this earth, but at least they had this chance to say things that needed to be said. I didn't know enough when Daddy was dyin' to say what I needed to say to him. Now I understood how important it is to tell people you love what's on your mind each and every day, just in case tomorrow doesn't come.

Mid September Grammy started making appointments with all her grandchildren for a little heart-to-heart there on her cot in the parlor. She started with John and worked her way down to me.

She got right to the point. "Are you happy, honey?" she asked, and when I told her how happy I was with Curtis and all, she took my hand and said, "All right, sweet girl. Now I'm going to give you my last bit of advice, and you can take it or leave it. Nellie, you're a good girl. I don't like to have favorites, but sometimes a person just can't help singling out one child over another. Your Mama was always my favorite. And you are, too. I've told you before how the two of you are so much alike."

She took a deep breath and pointed her face out to her memories.

"Your Mama could have done anything with her life. Anything. She was pretty and smart and sassy. Just like you. And just like you, she fell head over heels in love with a stranger. You can do anything you want to do, too, honey. You have dreams, and you could make them come true. You have it in you."

She put her arms around me and pulled me to her the way she did when I was a little girl.

"I know you and Curtis have talked about getting married, and, if you do, I pray you'll be happy. Just never forget who you are, honey. Don't forget your own self worth. Curtis is bigger than life, and I can see why you fell head over heels for him. I can see why."

I didn't understand what Grammy was tryin' to get at, but somehow what she was sayin' didn't ring real happy.

"And there's this, Nellie. He's going to be a handful, honey. My advice to you is to just make sure you don't give up any of yourself by lovin' him too much. You pull in the reins on him now and then when you need to, and he'll stay put. A man like that can't have too much freedom 'cause he'll take advantage of it. Understand?"

To tell the truth, I didn't understand totally, but a lot of it rang true. I thought about Mama and Daddy and the sadness that had been there.

When Grammy was done talking to me, she handed me a little paper bag and told me to open it. Inside was a locket with a picture of her and Grandpa when they was married. She said I could look at it every now and then so I didn't forget about her. There was also several old pieces of paper tied up by a piece of string.

"Read these when you want to, Nellie," she said. "They're those poems and thoughts your mama wrote down from time to time over the years. These are the only ones I could save from the trash. You can tell her you have them if you want. It's up to you. I don't think she knows I saved them. They're yours to do with what you want."

Grammy talked to every single one of us, and none of us spoke about it to each other. Those conversations was almost sacred-like, and to repeat them would have taken the richness of them away. When she was all done, she went to sleep happy...and never woke up again.

There was empty parts in all our lives with Grammy gone, spaces cut out all over the place that nothing or nobody else could fill up. She had brought fun into our house, and wisdom too, and I worried about who would keep the balance in our lives now that she was gone. Everywhere I went, memories of her came into my head, and they was all good. I always knew Grammy was smart, but when she was gone I understood for the first time how really wise she was. I felt sometimes like I could just reach out and touch her, and I understood she was stayin' real close to us to make sure we was all going to be all right without her.

When I was a little girl, Mama had told me that the stars was the doors to heaven for spirits climbing up to meet God. Each night when the sky was clear and I could see the stars, I picked out the brightest one, and in my head I tapped on it and said hi to Grammy.

I told Curtis that he'd have to ask my brother John and Mama for my hand in marriage, because I knew that was the proper thing to do. And I told him to wear his suit and tie when he did it because that was respectful. The day of his askin', the four of us sat ourselves down at Mama's kitchen table. I heard some giggling and whispering on the other side of the wall, and I knew Grace and the other youngins' had their ears to the door same as I would have done. It made me smile inside.

"Mrs. Ruthford, John, you know why I'm here," Curtis said. "Plain and simple, I'm in love with Nellie. She means the world to me, and I want to spend the rest of my life taking care of her. We want to get married. I want to join your family and be like a son and a brother to you, so I am asking you if I can marry your daughter and have your blessings."

I was so proud of him. I held my breath to see what Mama and John would say.

Mama was the first to speak. "If Nellie wants to be your wife, and if you promise to take good care of her and honor her the rest of your life, then, well, I see no reason why you can't get married."

It wasn't quite what I had hoped she would say, but I figured it was a lot for Mama to think about so soon after Grammy's passing and all.

Then it was John's turn to say something. "Is this what you want, Nellie?" he asked. "Are you absolutely sure? Because if you are, and it's all right with Mama, I'm not going to say no."

We all got up from the table and hugged each other, and my future husband and John slapped each other on the back, the way men do, and shook hands. I called out to Grace behind the door that she could come in now, and her and most of the other kids came bursting into the room, and it became like a party.

At one point later on, John and Curtis walked outside together. I asked Curtis afterwards what him and John had talked about.

Curtis grinned. "He told me if I ever hurt you or mistreated you in any way, he'd beat the shit out of me. He said they all would."

PART 7

I became Mrs. Curtis James on May 30, 1939, in the Courthouse down on The Square. John and Patty was our witnesses. I wore a brown suit me and Mama ordered out of the Sears Catalogue, and Curtis bought me a pretty white corsage made of gardenias that he pinned to my jacket. He looked very handsome in the beige suit, white shirt, and brown tie he borrowed from his friend at the shoe store. My whole family stood around us and smiled big and clapped when the Justice of the Peace declared we was man and wife. We thought everything was perfect except for the fact that Curtis' family couldn't be there.

After the wedding, we went back to Mama's house and had a family celebration. Mama had made a marble cake with thick chocolate icing for us, and Homer was churnin' ice cream by the time we got there. Little Grace and Faye had put a big "congratulations" sign out on the front door and had strung pieces of colored paper across the ceilings and around the doors for decoration.

We had our cake and ice cream, and then everyone made us sit down in front of them to open their presents to us. Aunt Lizzie gave us two dishes, two cups, and two sets of stainless steel. My big brothers had chipped in together and bought us a coffee pot and a set of towels and wash cloths and a table cloth and a pretty pillow for decoration in our new place. Old Phoebe gave us a Bible, which didn't come as a surprise. Patty and Louise gave us their gifts: two pans and a lacy yellow nightgown for me to wear that night. I was mortified that my family saw it, but it didn't bother Curtis at all. He grinned and winked to everyone in the room, and I thought I'd melt from the heat on my face. I didn't dare look at Mama.

Her and me had just had a heart-to-heart the night before, and she had explained that it was a natural thing for a man and a woman to be together in "that way" after they was married and that it wasn't as bad as I might be thinking it would be. She said that it was important for the woman to try to be as relaxed as possible and trust the man to do what was right. Mama went on to say that after a while "the act" would get easier and more pleasurable for everyone concerned, and then she asked me if I had any questions, and I decided that it would be just too hard to talk about what was on my mind with her or anyone else, for that matter, and so I said that I didn't think so.

I was hopin' that maybe Curtis and me could just kind of stay around for a little bit and keep on visiting after the presents was opened, but it was clear that that wasn't going to happen when Patty and Louise went around to everybody and gave them each a handful of rice to throw at us when we left. Right then and there, Curtis put his arm around me and thanked everybody for everything, and before I could even give Mama a hug, everybody was racing to the front yard to get in position to send us off. I could have strangled those two friends of mine right on the spot, but I smiled and waved and allowed Curtis to put me in the back seat of my brothers' car to be driven to my new home.

Our first home was a one-room flat above Smith's grocery store on Main Street. We signed the lease for it a couple of days before the wedding and fixed it all up real nice in the evenings after work. We had a chest of drawers, a small side table, and a rocker Mama didn't need. We had bought a bed at a thrift shop and splurged and got ourselves a mattress and a hot plate at Sears & Roebuck. The room had one window that looked out onto the street, and me and Mama had made some curtains out of some pretty flowered material we bought at Woolworth's and had Curtis nail them up to the wall. We thought our place was perfect.

John and George said goodbye to us out on the street. I asked them to come in for a while, but they acted all awkward and said they had to get on back to the house and help Mama out. They each gave me a quick hug and rushed away. Curtis took my hand and we walked up the two flights of steps to our room. Just outside our door, he picked me up and carried me in just like I had imagined he would. It was still daylight, and there wasn't anything more to fix up in our little room and nothin' came to mind to do so I suggested to my new husband, casual as I could, that it might be nice to take a little walk and talk about the day. He grinned and asked if that was really what I wanted to do.

Now, I knew that taking a walk right after your own wedding party wasn't something that was supposed to happen, but I was feelin' penned in. I looked at Curtis and realized that he was the man I was more than likely going to spend the rest of my entire life with, and, God help me, I prayed I had done the right thing. All kinds of thoughts was goin' through my head: Is he the man I thought he was? Was he pretendin' all that time about how much alike we was? Should I be afraid of him? I was breathin' a little too hard and I saw that I was sweating.

I thought that maybe some fresh air and exercise just might fix things. But when I saw that look on Curtis' face, I knew we wasn't going for a walk, and I decided to be grown up and take Mama's advice and let him take the lead.

He talked gentle and told me not to be afraid, that he loved me more than he thought it was possible to love anyone. He had us look at each other and took his time while he took off my clothes, and each time I tried to close my eyes and look away, he told me again and again that I could trust him never to hurt me and that this was natural and was being done out of love. I laid there and let it happen. It was done.

He held me in his arms and fell into a soft sleep, and I was careful not to let my crying wake him. He had told me that we would be the happiest couple in the whole entire world, and I made up my mind right then and there to make that happen, and I promised myself that I would learn to enjoy what was required of me.

We got Monday off work so we could visit Curtis' family, and we borrowed Homer's car and drove all the way to Connersville. Curtis warned me that his parents might not be real friendly. He told me that his daddy was a heavy drinker and his mama disapproved of everything his father did. They was a complete mismatch according to Curtis. I realized that we hadn't ever really talked about his family at all, and I saw how hard it was for him even now.

Well, I can tell you that from the very beginning I was real uncomfortable there. I couldn't think of anything to say to them, and when I did say something, it was pretty much ignored. I felt awkward and unsure of myself, and I stopped talking because I was afraid I'd say something to embarrass myself or Curtis.

Mr. James talked a little, but Mrs. James was real quiet. The strange thing was, no one smiled. Somethin' bad seemed to be churnin' around under everybody. It was about as different from being at my house as anything could be, with all our laughing and talking at once and all the horse-play going on, and I understood why Curtis had been so happy the very first time he had visited with us. He needed a real family.

The house was big and clean and had fine things in it, and I was real surprised at how rich the James family was. Curtis and me hadn't talked much about that, either. I looked around and thought about my family's house and decided that I wouldn't have traded houses with Curtis for anything. His house was grand, but it was cold.

I knew Mrs. James played the piano and read a lot of books and went to see plays and all. I guess she was a lady. But she was a different kind of lady than what I dreamed of being. All those fine things she did didn't seem to make her very wise or kind. She wasn't nothing like Bea or Mrs. Tildredge or Sandy's mother.

The second day we was there, Mr. James took us on a tour of the town. He made me sit up front with him, and I could smell whiskey on him. He was over-friendly and Curtis was too quiet. Things wasn't right.

But Connersville was pretty. At least the parts he showed me was. We drove around a little, and he pointed out this and that place and talked about some of the people in town while Curtis sat in the back seat, real quiet. We was almost back to their house when we stopped at a stop sign in front of a big old brick building set back on a huge lawn. It was grand, but dark and scary looking. The windows was all closed, and there was bars over them. I asked what the building was.

"Oh, well, that's the place where we lock up all the crazy people," he said like it was something funny. "We call it a sanitarium. That's just a polite word for a nut house." He laughed and put his hand on my knee. "That's where you might just end up someday, girlie, now that you're married to my son."

I asked him what he meant by that, and he said, "Being married to Curtis will be no picnic, believe me, little girl. He'd tell you the same thing if he was honest. He manages to mess up everything he does. You just wait; you'll see. You seem like such a nice girl." He smiled mean. "I feel sorry for you, honey."

I couldn't find anything to say. I was embarrassed for all of us. Curtis swore real bad and told his father to get us back home so we could get the hell away from him.

We packed up quick, Curtis cussin' under his breath about his father the whole time. We could hear his mother and father arguing back and forth at each other downstairs, and we packed faster. We loaded up the car, and I started to give his mother a hug and say something nice, but she backed away and barely said goodbye.

Mr. James had one last thing to say. "I'll bet Curtis told you he finished school and went off to college, too. Yep, I can see from your face that he did." He laughed. "Some things never change. Better not believe a thing he says, honey." He put his hand on my shoulder, and the smell of alcohol was strong. "I'll give him credit for one thing. He sure knows how to pick 'em. You're a real looker."

We drove for a long time without talking. Finally, I asked Curtis why his father had said those horrible things about him. And I asked him about school.

We pulled off to the side of the road, and he turned the motor off.

"I haven't been real honest with you," he said. "You deserve the truth so I'm going to give it to you straight. Truth is, I left school when I was fifteen. Ran away from home and sold knives door-to-door. Then it was stationery. I did real good. Daddy was embarrassed by what I was doing and had trouble explaining it to the folks in town. You know how it is; everybody knows everybody's business in a small town. You can see what I had to put up with."

I was having trouble keeping track of all he was sayin', all the new things I was learnin' about him. It was all just too confusing. And so disappointing. I hoped there wasn't anything else.

"I left because I wanted to get away from him and my mother," he went on. "They were always on my back about something. Of course, I went back home from time to time. Tried to work at a job Daddy got for me in a factory. There was an accident. Wasn't my fault. Some people was hurt. I've gone back and forth over the years. Last time I stayed was almost two years ago. That's when I got involved with Darlene. Daddy was all for that because he knew her father. God, was he pissed off when I called that off. Anyway, I moved to Newark to get away from my family. That's the long and short of it."

It was strange and unsettling to find out that a lot of what I thought was parts of him wasn't there at all. He gave me a long gentle kiss.

"I've got you, Nellie," he said. "You're the best thing that's happened in my life. You and me, we're going to make a new life for ourselves. You just put all this out of your head."

I wanted to. I wanted to forget everything that had just happened, everything that was just said. I wanted to be happy again, and so I put off askin' the questions in my head. After a while, it felt too late to talk about any of it, so I just set it aside and pretended it wasn't real.

We had great dreams. We was going to have our own business, our own car, and a big house. We took walks around The Square and watched people come and go and guessed what their lives might be like. We said how we was going to be happier than any of them. We held hands when we walked, and Curtis told me how proud he was to be with me. He said men turned around and looked at my legs when they walked by, and he liked that. We leaned against cars parked in front of the movie theater and talked about who we thought was fashionable and who wasn't. He told me he wanted to buy me beautiful clothes and jewelry and that I'd always be his princess. Curtis was a passionate man full of dreams, and he had me believing I was the only person in the world who could help make them all come true.

We packed our lunches and arranged every day to meet at The Square and eat together. It was a short walk for both of us. When he ran late for lunch or late at the end of the day, I walked over to the store to wait for him and watch him work.

Kettering's Shoe Store was the biggest in Newark, and I just knew that sales in women's shoes had grown since my husband started working there. Women's shoes was his specialty. He'd go up to those lady customers and take his time chitchatting about this and that, and then he'd finally get around to asking how he could help them. When they told him what they had in mind, he'd go to the display and bring back several shoes he knew would be just perfect on their feet, and then he'd go to work.

He'd hold those shoes up to those ladies like they was the prizes of a lifetime, and he'd run those long fingers of his over the straps or the heels or the soles like he was touching the neck of a beautiful woman, while he explained all the good things those shoes could do for them. If a lady showed interest, and practically every one of them did, he'd measure her feet and touch parts of them to see if there was anything special he needed to know about them, and then he'd go to the back room and get the perfect size and bring them out to her and present them to her like treasures. Finally, he'd bend down on his right knee and put his hand on her calf and place them on her feet and announce that they was perfect. Why, those women didn't stand a chance. With all that touchin' and praisin' and all, there was nothing left to do but buy those shoes. Then he'd put his hand on the woman's shoulder and walk her to the door, sometimes clear out to the sidewalk, and he'd tell her to be sure to come back and he'd give her his special attention. Even the oldest of 'em would set off down the street gigglin' like school girls.

You're probably wondering if I ever got jealous with his way with women. There was times I got close, I admit, but I talked myself out of it. I refused to let myself feel that way. I told myself how lucky I was that he chose me when he probably could have had any of dozens of pretty women in town. I was proud of him, and, after all, he kept tellin' me he was proud of me, too. We was a team, and teammates wasn't supposed to be jealous or cheat on each other.

I got called up to Mr. Stenson's office later that summer, and he told me what a fine job I was doing there at the check-out counter. I told him how much I liked being there and gave him a few ideas I'd been wanting to mention to him for some time.

"Nellie," he said, smilin' big, "your ideas are great, and I think we should let you try them out. But the reason I called you up here was first to tell you that I've decided to increase your pay a little each week if you'll take on a little extra work for me here."

I told him I'd like to do anything he had in mind. "Well, then, how would you like to start scheduling our girls? It's a big job and takes some time, but I could give you a little time off the counter to do it."

Well, I was so happy I thought I'd never get the grin off my face. I had myself an important job, alright, and I just couldn't wait to tell Curtis and Mama. That night me and Curtis went over to the house with some chocolates from the store and a bouquet of flowers for my family. We all had a great old time, and, as I was sayin' goodbye, Grace came up to me and told me how proud she was of me.

"I want to be just like you, Nellie," she said.

Those few little words comin' from my little sister meant more to me than I can begin to say. To think that I was setting an example for someone so dear, why, it just made me puff all up and made me want to do even better things for her. I vowed right then and there that I would never let her down, and, later on, I thought that that's probably how a mother would feel for her daughter.

Several months later, Curtis came into The Sparta in the middle of the morning, looking like a balloon that someone just stuck a pin in. He said he had to talk to me right then and there. I found someone to cover for me, and we went to a back booth.

"I've lost my job, Nellie," he said. "I went in to work like always, and my boss took me back in the stock room and fired me. Just like that. I can't understand it. Well, we never did get along. Not really. But I worked hard at that job. I brought sales up. He just came in this morning and said he didn't need me anymore and that was that. No explanation. Nothing."

It didn't make no sense to me. Curtis was the best salesman ever, and he was smart about the business. How could he get fired?

"He has to have a reason. He had to give you a reason. Why, you was doing so good. He wouldn't just up and fire you for no reason."

"I'm telling you, I don't know, Nellie," Curtis insisted. "Look, I'm feeling bad here. Is that all you can say? I don't know why. I'm upset. I've got to go out and look for something else now."

I apologized, and I told him I was mad at his boss, too. I told him not to worry, that he was the best salesman in Newark, and he could have any sales job he wanted. "Don't you worry," I said. "You take your time and find a job you'll like just as much as you did at the shoe store. Don't you worry at all." And I gave him a big kiss and told him how much I loved him.

My job was the only one we could really count on. Curtis lost one right after another, and there was never any good explanation for it except that him and his boss couldn't see eye to eye. I was so afraid that maybe he wouldn't be able to get new jobs with all the times he'd been let go, but he had such a gift of gab that he was able to talk his way into interviews and wind people around his little finger. Our friends called him a real "schmoozer," and I knew all too well that that was true.

Even as short as we was, I kept putting back a dime here, a nickel there, certain that a rainy day was coming soon.

Bottled Butterfly

A friend of Curtis from back in Indiana came for a visit and told us about a huge new shoe store that was going up in Lima, Ohio, and how they was hiring new people. He said the management was advertising that people who came in on the ground floor would have a good chance for quick advancement and good money. Right away Curtis wanted the job. He just knew he'd be able to make a good career there. He asked me if I'd move.

Now, I didn't know where Lima was, and I didn't know what kind of job I could get there, and I sure didn't want to leave Newark. I couldn't stand thinkin' about not being close to Mama. And what about my friends? And my job? I didn't want to leave The Sparta, seeing as how it was the only sure thing we had going for us. But Curtis told me what a pretty little town Lima was and how exciting it would be to start something new, and how we would probably make more money there, and he just went on and on, and, well, he made it sound so good that I couldn't think of any more reasons why we shouldn't go. He was so excited just thinking about all the prospects we was going to have that I got excited right along with him.

And so we moved, and I was happy on one hand and real sad on the other. I'd heard in songs how a heart could be torn apart, and now I knew how that felt. Mama acted brave, but she couldn't hide her feeling of loss, and I couldn't help but feel that I was abandoning her. It was a bad time.

We found a one-room apartment on the second floor of an old building several blocks down from the center of town in an area that most people wouldn't want to live in. It had a two-burner hot plate and a small cupboard. The bathroom was down the hall. There wasn't a closet of any kind so we hung a rope from one side of the room to the other to hang our clothes on. We kept our food in a window box outside in the winter to keep it fresh, and that summer we rented an icebox. It cost us fifty cents a month. We thought that was too much and gave it up and shopped for food every day.

I couldn't find a restaurant job and ended up going to work cleaning for a Mrs. Clapper. Felt like I was going backwards, but I had to take it 'cause we needed the money. Just when I thought I couldn't stand it anymore, Curtis came over to the house one day and told me to quit right then and there 'cause he got me a job right at the same shoe store where he was working. We worked side-by-side every day, him selling shoes and me working at the cash register and helping our boss with inventory.

Our new boss, Mr. Finklestein, was an elderly gentleman who, as Curtis liked to say, ran the store like a naval captain would run his ship. We got to know him real good, as you can imagine, with both of us being there six days a week, and we respected him because he was fair. He kept giving us more and more responsibility, and before you knew it Curtis and me was practically running the place. Mr. Finklestein said it was good to be able to get away from time to time and tend to other business. We both got a raise, and when we sat down and figured out how much we'd be making, we figured we just might be able to get ourselves a car before too long. Now I knew what to do with the money in the jars.

"I have a surprise for you," I told Curtis. "Oh, you're going to be so happy."

I told him that he had to close his eyes and just sit there for a minute 'til I could go get something, and then I rushed across our little room and got down on my stomach and pulled out three bags of coins from under our bed. I put them in front of Curtis and told him to open his eyes.

"I've been saving ever since Mama and Grammy told me to," I told him. "This is money for a rainy day. There's eighty-one dollars and thirty-five cents there. How much does it take to buy a car?"

I had never seen my husband stumble over words and be left with nothing to say, but that night he was speechless.

The next day we went out and found ourselves a car and ran to our boss and asked him if he would consider loaning us the difference between what I had and how much it cost. He said he'd give us the money and deduct payments from our pay each week, and, by golly, that afternoon we had ourselves our first automobile. It was a black Ford, two years old and in good shape. We walked around and touched almost every inch of it, and we told each other we was beginning to live our dream.

We drove all over town that day, squealing and shouting like we was kids. We drove fast and we drove far. We stuck our arms and our heads and even our feet out the windows just to feel like we was running with the wind itself. We felt downright powerful. After a while I asked Curtis to pull over and get out. He asked me what was wrong.

"Nothing," I said. "I just want you to change seats with me. You're going to teach me how to drive. Right now." And I climbed in behind the wheel. "Now. Tell me what I have to do."

It took a while, but after several bumpy starts and stops and lots more giggling, we took off. I took to it like a duck to water, as they say, and I drove 'til my body ached, my hands was numb, and the tank was empty. Going fast with the wind in my face and having control of a machine with so much power gave me a sense of freedom I'd never dared to imagine. I thought for sure we'd be going places now.

But it wasn't more than two months 'til Curtis lost his job again. He said there was no explanation for it. I quit mine out of respect for him and because I didn't see how I could go on working for a man who had just fired my husband. From time to time I asked Curtis what could have happened to make Mr. Finklestein turn on him like that.

"To hell with him," he said. "We don't need him."

We lived for several weeks on our combined final paychecks.

Curtis never got down. He said that, heck, we was missing my family anyway and that it was probably time we tried to find jobs closer to Newark. Somehow again through friends, he found himself a job selling insurance in Delaware, Ohio. I went to work at Hackle's dress shop right in the center of town and became manager in about six months.

With both salaries and the money I'd saved again, we was able to rent our first house. It was tiny, but it had two floors. We didn't use the second one; it just felt good to have that space above us. We didn't have much furniture so we made the little living room that faced out onto the street our bedroom and blocked it off from the rest of the house with bright curtains Mama made us, and we draped them across a bar we put up. We scattered the rest of our things around the kitchen and felt real homey. It was a place I looked forward to going to at the end of the day. I thought we was finally settling down.

One Thursday on our way to work, we drove past the bank, and I just happened to see a sign that said "Last Chance To Buy Lottery Tickets – Drawing Friday."

I screeched at Curtis to stop the car, and he slammed on the brakes so fast I almost bumped my head on the windshield.

"Nothing's wrong," I told him. "Just let me get out and you circle back around for me. I'm going in there, to the bank, and I'm going to buy us one of those lottery tickets."

"Nellie, that's a waste of money," he insisted. "There's no way we're going to win a lottery. Now get on back in here. Come on now."

But I was already halfway across the street and stopped long enough to tell him that we had just as good a chance to win as anybody else, and, besides, I had a feeling about this. I bought the ticket and stuffed it into my purse.

Now, one of the things we liked to do on Saturday mornings was treat ourselves to a donut and coffee down at the little eatery at the end of our street. The same people showed up every week, and we was all friends now. The Saturday after I bought the lottery ticket, we went into the eatery, same as usual. People must have been looking for us 'cause right away when we stepped through the door, someone yelled, "There they are!" And everyone in the place stood up and started clapping and yelling, "Congratulations! Congratulations!" We didn't know what the heck was going on.

"Haven't you heard? Don't you kids read the paper? You two won the lottery. No kidding. You won the whole thing. Three-hundred dollars. Couldn't have happened to a nicer couple. Congratulations."

Well, all over town people was talking about us. Everywhere we went, people came up and shook our hands and congratulated us and carried on. We was supposed to work later that day, but when we went in, our bosses told us to just take the day off and enjoy the happy news.

We went home and sat at our table and talked about what to do with all that money. We decided to give seventy-five dollars to Mama so we set that aside. Then we thought we should take ourselves out for a nice dinner. We counted out the money for that and put it in another pile. We both needed new shoes, and I needed some underwear so we made a pile for that too. Curtis didn't want to know how much we had left. He said he wanted to be surprised some day like he had been with the car money, so I filled up more jars.

We had us lots of friends. Sometimes it felt like we had too many, but that was just me. People was always around, but I didn't feel like I had time enough to get to know any of them real good like I knew friends back home. Curtis was an entertainer. He drew people to him natural, and he was happiest when there was a crowd around. My girlfriends was always anxious to come over to our place, and sometimes I wondered if it was to see me or get a glimpse of him. It was clear they wanted to know how we was together, and some came right out and suggested that he must be real good in bed. I put on a smile and acted all mysterious and tried to keep my face from getting too hot.

When all of us was together, I had trouble keeping up with the constant chatter. Didn't matter. Most of it was kidding and joking about personal things or other people, and I didn't feel inclined to be a part of it. Truth is, a lot of nights I'd go to bed and think about the time all of us had just had together and worry about what I had contributed. I felt a little bit like dreary wallpaper around a room full of beautiful things.

Curtis joined some organizations where he thought he could make some good contacts to sell his policies to, and he got to know a lot more people there in town. He said he had to go out from time to time at night with his new business friends to cement the relationships. That's the way he put it. Sometimes he asked me to go along, and I did, but mostly he went out by himself.

Some nights he was out real late. I'd try to wait up for him, but I usually ran out of things to do. I'd go out on our little porch and look up and down the street for him. Then one night I remembered how Mama used to do the same thing looking for Daddy, and I made myself quit it. I'd go to bed and cuddle in beside him when I felt him come in.

The only news in the papers and on the radio those days that we was in Delaware was the war in Europe. I didn't know a lot about it. To be honest, it didn't seem to have much to do with me. Then President Roosevelt started saying how we might have to get into it to help our good friends—our allies, he called them—and Curtis and me and all our friends got pretty nervous.

When the government announced that they was going to set up a military draft system, Curtis was sure he'd get drafted, and he decided to do anything he could to get from being called up. At the time, his daddy was working in Dayton for the government, helping design some parts for some special plane and he had some good contacts. We agreed that, hard as it would be, Curtis should ask his daddy if there was any way he could help us get a job with the government to keep Curtis from getting drafted. Mr. James got right back to us and told us he could get Curtis a job in sales in the men's section at a huge PX Center at Wright Patterson Air Force Base. We moved.

We lived pretty good there in Dayton because even when rationing began, we could get about anything we wanted at the PX. Our luck doubled when a job opened up in the administrative office and they hired me for it. I counted cash several times a day and got deposits ready for the bank, checked receipts and entered in the books they kept what stuff we had to sell, filed all kinds of papers, and just did all kinds of stuff.

Oh, how I loved that job. I was in an office on the second floor. Curtis worked down on the first floor, but I could easily see him whenever I wanted to because the whole front wall of the office section where I was, was all glass. The officers treated me with respect, like a real lady, and I felt even more important than I had back on my job at The Sparta. Me and the officers had coffee at our desks together, and they told me about their families and showed me pictures of their children. Curtis and me wasn't there for more than a couple of months when things started to go bad again.

Now you know how friendly Curtis was with everybody. It was just his nature. Most people was friendly right back, but at the Center, from the very beginning, there was hard feelings between him and one of the lieutenants I worked with. Curtis said he thought the Lieutenant was jealous of him because he was making so many friends so fast.

I knew that the Lieutenant was dating one of the girls down where Curtis was working. I saw them leave together several times, and they looked to be pretty close. Well, the problem was that the girl and Curtis was always talking together when they wasn't busy. Sometimes they had their breaks at the same time, and they would step out for a smoke or a cup of coffee together. I saw it. So did the Lieutenant. But we didn't talk about it.

One day, right out of the blue, Curtis was called into the office of the officer who was over the entire PX. I watched from my desk upstairs. They was in there a long time when the Lieutenant was called in, too. I got real nervous. Pretty soon Curtis came out of the office looking like he did when he was fired from the shoe store in Newark, and I knew something awful had happened. He looked up at me and motioned for me to come down. We stepped outside 'cause everybody was watching us.

"I'm fired." That's all he could say. "I don't know why. They didn't give a good reason. I just have to clear out right this minute. "My God, Nellie, what are we going to do?"

I walked back through the PX and right up to the offices, and I could feel all the eyes on me. This time I was going to find out for myself what happened. Curtis tried to stop me, but I wouldn't hear it.

"Why has my husband been fired?" I asked the officer. "I just don't understand it. He's done a good job, hasn't he? I mean, he's a good salesman." I was talking louder than I should have, but I couldn't help it. "He doesn't know why you let him go, and I think we deserve to know the reason."

"Nellie, we're sorry for you that this has happened," he said, and looked sad. "We gave Curtis the reason why we let him go. Today isn't the first time we've talked to him. Maybe he just isn't able to share it with you right now. That's between the two of you. But we want you to know that this has no impact on your job whatsoever. You've performed very well. We need you, and we want you to stay on with us."

I went back down to where Curtis was waiting. People was standing around watching to see what would happen next. My face and neck was bright red, I knew, but I held myself tall. We decided again that since they was letting one of us go the other would go, too. We was a team. I marched right back to my boss and quit on the spot. Curtis and me walked out hand in hand together, and we never looked back. I told Curtis that the Lieutenant said that he had explained why he let him go. Curtis told me that was a lie.

I wanted to believe him.

We was out of money, and we couldn't find work. We had to do something. Anything. We knew there was no point in asking his daddy for help again. Soon as he found out about the lost job—and he would—he'd be furious. I couldn't ask Mama, of course. She barely had enough for herself and the little ones. Help eventually came unexpected from the newspaper.

Everywhere, all over the states, cities was holding dance contests and marathons. They was big events, and they brought some excitement to a nation worried about where it was going with the war. If you won the contest or was the last one standing at the marathon, you had a chance to win big money. Neither one of us had ever been to one of those things, but when the big news came that there was going to be a dance contest in Dayton, Curtis decided that we should enter it.

He had earned himself the nickname "Rubber Man" from our friends for the way he could move when he danced: he could bend and dive and rotate his body like soft, smooth rubber, and he was as light as a feather on his feet. He got our entry money from those friends, and he promised them that when we won the contest, they'd all get their money back. And, as usual, they believed in him.

I was terrified. Oh, I knew how good he was, but I wasn't sure I was up to matching him. And I wasn't sure dancin' my way to money was the way to go. I was glad Mama was in Newark and wouldn't have any way to find out what I was about to do.

Curtis decided I had to have a pretty dress to wear: something that would really make us stand out from the rest of the dancers, and he came up with a bright red one with a deep neckline that showed a lot of my cleavage. I thought about Old Phoebe and how she called me a harlot. A harlot would have loved that dress. I looked in the mirror and didn't like what I saw lookin' back. Bea popped into my head, and I turned away so I couldn't see myself. I was so far away from bein' a lady.

I tried to put up a good argument as to why I shouldn't be wearing something like that and why we shouldn't be dancin' for money, but Curtis said the dress would attract all the attention of the men judges, and the other men in the audience wouldn't be able to keep their eyes off me. That only made me feel worse, but, as usual, Curtis' logic outdid mine. We was practically desperate for money, and there was no room for me to be squeamish. I prayed to God that He'd forgive me for what I was about to do.

The big night finally came, and all our friends was there, along with most of the rest of the town. Curtis was walking on air, confident we was going to win. I locked myself in the bathroom and listened while he talked to me through the door. He told me how good I was at dancing, how he believed absolutely that I was the best gal there and, besides that, I was the prettiest. He told me that I should just look at him the whole time we danced and never look out at the crowds watching. He convinced me that we was going to win and have that money to live on for a while.

And so I lost myself in the music and his smile. We danced. Oh, my, how we danced. I followed his lead easy, but I was careful with my moves because of that dress. It showed too much. It was Curtis who entertained. He twirled and twisted and jumped and landed on his knees. He was enjoyin' himself, and he was downright beautiful.

Each time the music stopped and the judges came around and eliminated people, we held our breaths 'til they passed us by. Finally, there was just three couples left on the floor, and it was up to the crowd to decide which one was going to be the lucky winner. We tried to get our breath back and ignored the sweat pouring off of us. The other two couples got lots of applause, and Curtis and me held hands tight, and he whispered that if we didn't win, it didn't matter 'cause we had done our very best. When the judge held his hand over us, the crowd exploded. We had won, hands down.

Just like when we won the lottery, the first thing we did was put some of the money back for Mama. Curtis left it up to me to work out a budget for the rest. I put a little aside again for our rainy day.

The dance money didn't last long and there wasn't any jobs so there was only one thing left for Curtis to do. He took me back to Newark and my mama's home, and he enlisted and was sent to Indianapolis for infantry training. The Burke Golf Factory was converting to make ammunition for the war, and I got myself a job there. I was back in the same building where my daddy had worked so long as a janitor and where I had sold candy bars as a young girl.

I really had gotten nowhere.

I didn't take any precautions on the days just before Curtis left, and I don't know why. Maybe I wanted to get pregnant. Maybe I didn't. I didn't sit down and think about anything right then. Things was so hectic, and I was feeling so bad and so scared about him going away and all that, well, for whatever reason, I made a mistake, and I got pregnant. Just like that. Curtis was so happy, but the full force of what I had done hit me hard. My husband was about to go off and fight in the war, I was living with my mother, and I'd probably be fired soon as my boss found out I was having a baby.

I was thin and strong and was able to hide my growing belly pretty good up half-way through the sixth month, thanks to Grace and Mama. Grace figured out how to make my blouses and skirts look normal and good when it was time to make them bigger, and Mama sewed them up and made them look like new. There was a limit to what we could do, though, and my boss finally had to let me go. He promised me that as soon as the baby was born and I could get back to work, he'd take me back.

Mama called Curtis when I was taken to the hospital, and he was given a thirty-six hour leave to be with me. He rushed into the maternity ward just in time and hugged me and gave me kisses and announced to all the other women in there that he was going to have the most beautiful baby in the world. He entertained everyone and had us all laughing, even the nurses.

When the pains came, though, he felt them too, and with each of my contractions he hurt more. Why, he hurt so much that the nurses was spending as much time with him as they was with me, and finally they had to tell him to leave and wait out in the hall 'til it was all over. Before long, a nurse I hadn't seen before came rushing in and told me not to worry about a thing, but Curtis had fainted out in the hall and was in his own room down from where I was. She assured me that they was monitoring him and he'd be fine.

Our baby girl was born one week before he was sent to Europe. We named her Bea.

Bea was treated like a little sister there in my mama's house, like a little baby doll, and I had to remind myself from time to time that she came from my body, that she was mine. Mama treated her like one of her own and loved her with the same kind of love she had had for all of us. I wondered at the size of her heart. I knew I would never be able to love another child of mine as much as I loved Bea.

On days off, I took my little daughter to Idlewilde Park and showed her the ducks on Dream Lake there. I placed her tiny little self up on the low branches of trees and told her to listen to the birds' songs. We sat by the lake, and I showed her the pretty ladies with their colorful dresses and told her she'd be a lady someday, too, just like them. We sat in Mama's garden together, and I talked to her about the colors of the lilacs and the tulips and forsythia, same as I had done with Baby Carl, and I pointed out the delicate butterflies whenever they decided to let themselves rest in front of us.

I took her to visit Patty and all my other friends so she'd understand how important friends are, and I made sure she had a big birthday party to celebrate her first year in this world. At night, I worried about how I could make sure she grew up strong and independent and proud, and, unlike me, well educated. Bea was going to be everything I had always wanted for myself. She was going to be somebody.

Within two years, there was six stars pasted in Mama's parlor window: five of them was for her five sons, and one was for her son-in-law who was off somewhere in France.

The war brought Phoebe home from the hills, and she brought a woman about my age along with her. Janice was her name, and she was from West Virginia. Her family, Phoebe explained, was a good church-going family of some means out there in the hills and had been one of Phoebe's sponsors when she was evangelizing. In fact, Phoebe had lived with them for close to a year. I wondered what made her leave such a good situation. I couldn't imagine it was because she couldn't wait to be back home close to her family, even during war-time. She didn't give us an explanation, and Mama decided we shouldn't push her too much. There we was again, stepping lightly around Old Phoebe.

Bless Mama's heart, she took Janice in same as she did all of us. She had saved most of the lottery money and money from the dance contest we had given her, and we was all able to live off that, the little bit I had saved from Burke, food coupons, the small allotment I got from the government, and money I was able to get by selling some of our gasoline rations. Phoebe no longer had any kind of job at the church. Janice had nothing to contribute. We managed.

Janice was the timidest person I had ever met. She appeared to want to disappear into herself. She clung onto every word Phoebe said, and I felt terrible about how Phoebe sometimes treated her. Clearly she had the upper hand and told her little friend exactly what she could and could not do. I couldn't tell how Janice felt about Phoebe. Couldn't tell what it was that kept her there with her. But they was together constantly, always whispering to each other. When one went out for anything, the other one went too. The two of them took over me and Bea's sleeping place in the parlor, and we moved into Mama's room. None of it felt natural. I kept my mouth shut. We had too many other things to worry about.

With Phoebe back, us women and the little ones went back to eatin' supper pretty much in silence again. I fretted with Mama about her letting Phoebe have her way with us again, but poor Mama was just tryin' to keep peace and not cause trouble in front of our guest. It was a hard time for all of us, and the less arguin' among us, the better, she said.

It was hardest on my little Bea. She was at that jabberin' stage, when everything is fun. Her antics at the table made us all want to laugh, everybody but Phoebe. I was always havin' to "shush" Bea and whisper to her to be a "good little girl." She, of course, didn't understand and thought she was doing something wrong. I couldn't stand it, and after a while, me and her ate our dinners alone in the parlor.

Janice had been with us five months when a letter came for her. It was the first she had received, and it had been forwarded from the church. I beat Phoebe to the mailbox that day, and when I called for Janice and told her she had a letter, she rushed to get it. Phoebe was right behind her. After Janice finished reading, Phoebe took the letter from her, read it, and tore it up. The two of them had some words, and, finally Janice left the room crying.

Then one day about a week later, when I was getting Bea ready for a morning walk, Janice came over to me like she was goin' to talk, but real quick-like she brought a letter out of her pocket and handed it to me and asked me if I would mail it for her. I said that I would and thought about how frightened she looked.

Within two weeks, a big black car pulled up in front of our house, and a tall older man in a dark suit got out, checked our address, and walked up across our porch. I was at the door before he knocked.

"Hello, Ma'am," he said. "I'm Evan Dougherty. I believe my daughter Janice has been living here."

I said that yes, she was here, and I asked him in. I thought, Hallelujah, he's come to take her home, take her away from Phoebe, and maybe we'd finally find out what all this is about.

I could tell Mr. Dougherty was a real gentleman by the look of his suit and his polished shoes, and when I left him to go find Janice, I wished I'd had some notice he was coming so I could have spiffied the place up a little for him.

When she came into the parlor, he took her in his arms and held her tight and kissed the top of her head, and my heart hurt with memories of my daddy doin' the same thing to me. When he let go of her, he looked at her hard like he was tryin' to make sure she was all right. When Mama hurried in, wiping her wet hands on her apron, and introduced herself, his manners was perfect. Phoebe hid in the shadows, watching.

Mr. Dougherty told his daughter to get her things and said he was taking her home.

"You can't make her go." Phoebe's voice came out of the shadows.

"*You...*" He looked hard in her direction and then at the rest of us spread out over the room. I could tell it was an effort to control himself. "I have nothing to say to you. I'll pray that you can find peace within yourself."

It took just a few minutes for Janice to pack her things, and in a few minutes more, her and her father was in their big black car headed back to West Virginia.

My family all just stood watching until the car was out of sight, and finally Clyde got up the nerve to ask Phoebe what all of that was about. She told him to mind his own business and spewed out gospel at him. Her eyes was wild.

"Somethin' bad has happened here, Phoebe," Clyde said. "That's pretty obvious. I don't know what went on out there in West Virginia, and I don't know what you did to Janice, but I want to tell you that things are going to change around here. We're tired of how you're always preachin' at us, and we're not going to take it anymore. Obviously, Janice decided not to take it either."

"You don't know what you're talking about!" Phoebe shouted at him. "You don't know one thing. Don't you tell me what I can and cannot do in my own home. I am a woman of the church, and don't you forget it. Why—"

"Cut that out!" Clyde yelled right back. "This isn't your home. It's Mama's, and don't *you* forget it. And don't talk to us about the church. You're not any more involved in the church these days than the rest of us. Maybe even less."

"How *dare* you. You have no right to talk to me like that. Just who do you think you are? Mama, tell him—"

"You leave Mama out of this," he warned her. "I'm talkin' direct to you, Phoebe."

"You're nothing!" she yelled. "None of you! You don't know anything! And you don't understand a thing about me."

"You can just go to Hell, Phoebe," Clyde told her. "Just go straight to Hell."

"I *am* in Hell," she screamed and crept back into the shadows.

We lived each day the same: washing, mending, cooking, clipping coupons, and watching for the mailman. Each night we all got ourselves around the kitchen table and wrote letters to all our men. The letter-writing always ended with prayers by Mama for their safe return. We went to bed early and got up early, and the days and weeks became a blur, with nothing to mark one from the other.

Curtis wrote beautiful letters to me about how much he missed me and what wonderful things we'd do when he got back home. And he even wrote poems for Bea, and I pasted them in a pretty little book I made for her so she could look back at them some day and know how much he loved her and thought about her. I wrote him about Bea and how happy the three of us was going to be when he got home. He wrote back with all of his plans for new businesses and the pretty things we'd have someday. We sent pictures to each other, and I pasted his on Bea's crib so she would remember who her daddy was. "Daddy" was the first word she tried to say.

Finally the war was over.

The day it was declared, every single church bell in every single church in every county rang all day long. The Square filled up with neighbors and friends and strangers, and I think we all felt that, finally, we could all start living again and that our lives would be better than they had ever been before. There was so much hope and joy in the air that you felt you could reach out and touch it. Phoebe said it was the presence of God we was feeling, and for once I agreed with her.

PART 8

Curtis and me decided to stay put in Newark, and for a good year we lived right there in Mama's house. He found a job at a furniture store and started taking classes to learn radio electronics through books sent through the mail, but he quit the course early on and said that he could do better if he started a business of his own. We got ourselves a G.I. Loan, and he opened up a parts store for automobiles.

Curtis didn't want me to work, and I thought I'd enjoy taking care of our new little house we bought and being a good wife and mother, but, truth is, it wasn't what I thought it was going to be. My neighbors could talk for hours about washing diapers and baby food and such. They could go on and on about what was the best cleaning liquids or laundry detergents, and they actually took pride in the creases they ironed in on their husbands' pants.

They took pains getting themselves ready for when their men got home from work, and I figured I should do the same as them, but I couldn't figure out what they did that took so long. We all had the same parts, far as I knew, and I cleaned and polished all mine, same as them, but I finished faster and had to look for other things to do.

I went down to our shop practically every day with Little Bea to see if there was something I could help with. But Curtis laughed and told me that he didn't need any help, that all I needed to do was to keep taking care of the house and our daughter. Those was the best jobs I could ever have, he said, and I couldn't argue about that. I worked hard at it, but, well, it didn't do much to fill me up.

The business grew, and pretty soon Curtis talked to me about maybe having to hire someone to help manage the office. I thought about that and came up with a plan.

" Let me be your office girl," I said. "I know I could do the work just fine. Why, with one job or another, I've done all those things that you need doing. I helped Bea with the books at her shop, and that's really what I did at the PX, remember? And I already know all your sales people. I could help manage them. Remember how I scheduled at the Sparta? The best part is that you wouldn't have to pay me. We'd work together like the old days."

"Nellie," he said, and he was frowning, "you have a daughter to take care of. What would we do with Little Bea?"

"Well, I could do a lot of the book work and the scheduling at home. I wouldn't have to come in but maybe a few hours a day, and she could come right along with me. She's a good girl. Why, we could keep some of her toys right there in a corner in your office. She wouldn't be in your way. We could work it out. Come on, honey, say yes."

He said no. For the first time in our marriage, he turned me down on something important. It wasn't two weeks before a pretty young blonde woman was sitting in his office doing the job I wanted.

At first Bea and me just kept popping into the shop like we always did when we was out for a walk, but after a while it was plain to see that Curtis was just too busy to visit much so we stopped going. Truth is, it was just too hard to go in and see Curtis and the girl, Nancy, working together and sharing stuff that I wasn't a part of.

Then one night Curtis came home and said that Nancy had left in a huff several days ago and never showed up again, but he'd just hired someone named Trish to take her place. I dropped by several days later to meet her. She was maybe even prettier than Nancy had been. That night I teased Curtis about whether a girl had to be pretty to do that kind of work. He wasn't amused.

Curtis kept growing. I stayed the same and wondered what had happened to us. Truth is, there was little left of "us." He joined the Chamber of Commerce and the Masons, and I spent more nights alone. When the town organized a variety show to raise money for charity, Curtis tried out for singing and dancing parts and got chosen for several spots in the show. He was shinin'. I felt flat. I was determined to be happy for him and worked hard on the house to make everything perfect for him to come home to.

For two solid weeks there was rehearsals almost every night. I got babysitters a couple of times so I could go down and watch and Curtis seemed happy to see me. He introduced me to everybody, but there was so much going on and so many people around who was all friends to each other that I felt like an outsider.

Most nights I fell asleep before he got home. When I managed to stay awake, he was so excited and energized that he almost seemed not to notice me, or he was just too tired to talk and headed straight for bed. I told myself I had to do something to make me more interesting to him, but I couldn't think what that something might be.

I told Curtis I wanted to look for a job after the show was over and things settled down a little.

"I want to be involved in something," I told him. "I want to contribute to our future. Remember how we walked around The Square together when we was first married? And how we talked about what a strong team we'd be, and how we'd work hard to make our dreams come true? Well, I want us to be that team again. I want to work with you."

"You're doing the most important thing in the world," he told me, smiling and pulling me to him. "You're managing a home, and you're raising a beautiful daughter. Maybe it's time we add to our little family. You have the babies, and I'll take care of you. What do you say?"

He was talkin' down to me, and something flared up in me.

"But I don't want to be taken care of," I told him. "I want to help you take care of us, like I used to do. I know I don't have to work, but I want to work. I wish you could understand."

I could tell from his voice that he didn't understand. Not at all. He told me that women with children didn't work and brought up again how he was surprised that I wasn't ready to have more children, and when I reminded him that I'd had children to take care of all my life, he walked away, sayin' how havin' your own children is different.

I needed help to work all this stuff through in my mind and called Grace and Mama to arrange a time to get together. I tried to act like nothing special was going on, and they was good not to ask me any questions. After a little while of just sitting around in Mama's kitchen and catching up, I said casual as I could that maybe it would be fun to bring out the Ouija Board.

We had a lot to ask the spirits there in the kitchen. Grace asked if her new beau was the man she would marry, and the answer was "no." Mama asked if Phoebe was going to stay out there in Tennessee where she had moved and keep preaching, and the spinner moved to "yes" and spelled out the word "woman" too. I wondered about that one, and I could tell they did, too, but we all three let it pass.

When it came time for me to ask my questions, I tried to act real casual about it and said I was wondering if I should have another child. The spinner didn't move. I went on and asked should I get a job? No answer. Mama and Grace stopped looking at the board and stared at me. I tried hard to put the next question right.

"Is Curtis happy?" I asked, and the danged thing just went around in circles.

As Mama walked me to the door, she asked if I'd like to have a little heart-to-heart with her.

"I'm not ready yet, Mama. Maybe later. Not yet."

I was lost.

One beautiful spring afternoon I made up my mind to shrug off how I was feeling and get happy again. I figured now that winter was over, things would look better. Me and Bea walked around the neighborhood, and I cut some forsythia that was growing in splotches in the alley at the side of our house. We sat ourselves down in our backyard, and I wove the branches into pretty little crowns for her and told her stories about princesses. She chased a robin and showed me her somersaults, and we sat forever and watched the ants crawl on the pink peonies growing along the fence.

When we went inside, she played dress up from the box of clothes and jewelry I had put together for that purpose. She smiled at herself in the mirror and looked at me for approval. I remembered that first time back at the general store when the new owner told me I was pretty and how I started looking in mirrors to see if it was true. I told Bea how pretty she looked.

Watching her doing her pretending took me back to when I was a little girl so many years ago, and I wondered how and when it was that I stopped pretending and dreaming. When had I lost my imagination, my belief that all things was possible? I wanted that innocence, that joy back, and I wanted to keep the child in Bea alive forever. That could be my greatest gift to her.

It was close to supper time when we stopped our playing, and I called Curtis to see if he'd be home on time. He said he'd be a little late because he had been so busy all day and he had some catching up to do. I asked him to hurry home as soon as he could so that maybe after supper the three of us could go for a ride and get us some ice cream cones.

Soon as I hung up, I got a great idea. I phoned the girl down the street and asked her to come over and have dinner with Bea so that I could walk to the shop and ride back home with Curtis. I fixed my hair real nice, put on some fresh lipstick, and changed into the dress Curtis liked best on me, the yellow one with the full skirt and lace on the bottom.

When I got to the shop, one of the fellows who worked for us was just walking out the door, and I could see that he was surprised to see me.

"Well, hi, Nellie. What are you doing here?"

He laughed funny-like and apologized for saying that. He started to walk back inside and get Curtis, but I told him I'd just go on in and surprise him.

He looked back at the office and talked louder. "Well, he has some work to do. I know that."

The man was acting really strange. I thanked him and circled around him and went inside.

I walked down the hall to his office, opened the door, and peeked inside. There was a small light turned on at the desk, and I had to squint my eyes to let them adjust to the soft dark. Curtis was sitting in his chair at his desk, and the new bookkeeper was sitting on the desk facing him. Her foot was in his lap, and his hand was up her leg.

The girl jumped up and had some trouble getting her shoe back on. Curtis had some trouble getting himself out of the chair. He walked over to me. To this day I can't believe the words that came rushing out of my mouth.

"I'm sorry," I said, backing out of the room. "I shouldn't have barged in. You said you was working, but I just thought I'd surprise you and we'd drive home together."

I was babbling, and for whatever reason, I was blaming myself for what I had just seen. I was acting like a fool, but it was so hard to get my mind around what had just happened. I ran away to the street and sucked in the sun and air and was surprised to find that everything out there was normal. I asked myself over and over how could this be happening. Why would he do this to us? I walked and tried to make my mind go blank, because I wasn't ready to think yet.

I heard my name and looked up and didn't know for sure where I was. Curtis was driving slowly beside me in our car, telling me to get in, and when I motioned him away, he stopped the car and got out.

I allowed myself to be put into the car, but I couldn't talk, and Curtis didn't try. When I got home, I paid the sitter and busied myself with Bea.

Finally I found my voice. "I don't understand. I just don't understand."

I held my breath and waited for him to explain things to me, but he didn't. I didn't force him because I was too afraid of where words might lead us. The spirit inside me was sayin', "Be sure about what you want to say. Words can't be taken back once they've been allowed to get out."

The girl was gone. Curtis came home one night and said he was looking for a replacement. He didn't seem concerned at all about it, and I acted like I wasn't either. It was easier that way.

After several days, I asked him if he'd found anyone for the job, and when he said no, I asked him again about me working with him. This time he said yes, and I forced myself to push back the questions I had and just be happy with his decision.

Finally, I was going to contribute. I kept telling myself that I must have been wrong after all about what I thought I saw there in the office. My husband just proved that he loved me and wanted to be with me. Everything was going to be fine, I thought, and I could be me again.

My dear mama was a saint, I'll tell you. My two youngest sisters and my little brother was still living there at home with her, and when I couldn't get anyone to watch Bea right away, she said that having one more person there from time to time wouldn't make any difference to her. Besides, she said, she'd enjoy having more time to spend with her granddaughter. It was the best thing that could happen. I didn't feel guilty about leaving Bea with a stranger, and I got to see Mama most every day.

I can still picture her standing there at the end of her sidewalk, holding Bea's hand and watching for me. A big pot of coffee and sugar cookies fresh from her new oven was always set out on the old kitchen table for us to enjoy while we talked about our day.

I thought things was shaping up to be real good. Everyone at the shop was happy and working hard, and Curtis praised me and told me he had been a fool to try to keep me at home. He said he was relieved to have me take over so much responsibility, and he felt good that Bea was spending time with Mama.

Then the phone call came.

"Do you know where your husband was last night?" The woman's voice was soft and taunting.

It took me a while to get the question registered in my head.

The woman laughed. "I know where he was. How can you be so naïve?" And before I could answer, she hung up.

It was impossible to think of anything else but that call. I repeated it over and over in my mind, and I tried to convince myself that whoever had called had the wrong number. I didn't say anything to anyone about it.

The other call came two weeks later. This time I recognized the voice.

"Nellie, are you happy?"

"Why are you calling?" I asked.

It took some time for her to answer. "Don't you know? Can you really be so stupid, little housewife?"

I know you'll find it hard to understand, but I still didn't want to believe what my mind was telling me. I was thinking with my heart. Curtis was showing me so much love that I didn't think it was possible for him to have any left over for another woman.

One night a month later, when Curtis was out to one of his Mason meetings, I got a call from George. He seemed to know that Curtis was gone and asked if he could come over. I tucked Bea into bed and fixed some coffee so me and my brother could have a real nice visit. But the minute he came in the door, I could see he was all worked up.

"Nellie," he said, "I've put off telling you this for too long. I should have dealt with it a long time ago."

Oh, how I didn't want to hear what was coming next.

"Nellie, that goddamn..." He took a drink of coffee and started all over. "Sis, I'm sorry to have to tell you this, but it's high time you know about it. Everyone else in town knows. God, honey. I don't want to be the one to hurt you, but..."

"What?" I said. "What is it? Just spit it out for cryin' out loud. You're scaring me."

215

But, of course, I already knew what it was about. I knew I was about to be more embarrassed than I had ever been in my life. Embarrassed and shamed. All because of my husband.

"Curtis is a lyin' cheatin' son-of-a-bitch, Nellie. There it is. You have to know the truth. He's been seen up on Horn's Hill with another woman. Not once, Nellie, many times. People are talkin' about it all over town." He banged his hand on the table. "Dammit. John wanted to go and beat the tar out of him, but what good would that do? Nellie, honey, you have to get him under control. You have to talk to him about this and put an end to it once and for all. He's a father, for God's sake."

I was numb now. This was something that was impossible to imagine, and it was true.

"Who knows about it? Who's telling the story?"

"What? Well, what difference does it make who saw it?"

"Who told you?"

"Sam. Sam, the guy who works at your shop. He was up there with his kids this past weekend. Nellie, it was in broad daylight. They was going at it like a couple 'a...well, they was in his car and...Sam was talking about it tonight at the pool hall. He's a son-of-a-bitch, too, for talkin' about it. I'll tell you what; we should tie into him, too, for being such a big-goddamn-mouth."

"Who did Sam say the girl was?" I asked. But I'd heard her voice, and I knew.

"That girl who worked for him just before you took over the job."

I stepped out of myself for the second time and felt I was watching someone else playing a part. I put my arms around George and thanked him for being such a good brother, and I told him not to worry, that I'd find out the whole story. I was even surprised by how calm I was.

But his final words hit me hard.

"Nellie, it isn't the first time. He's known as a rounder all over town. Honey, for God's sake, get that man under control."

Getting *myself* under control would be the first step.

I had to heal.

After George left, I walked outside and looked up at the stars and

216

told myself how beautiful God's world was. I took my shoes off and felt the cool, wet grass between my toes. And I bent down and put my cheek next to the velvety smoothness of the flowers in my small garden. Finally, I sat down under the big old oak tree and went through everything that had been happening between me and Curtis over the years. And I made myself face the truth that I'd known all along.

What I didn't know was what to do about it.

Every question that came into my head was followed by another. I wondered if it's possible for someone to change, to be able to throw out parts of what makes him who he is. Could someone like Curtis, with so much passion inside, be expected to be happy with just one person's love? Did I have the right to insist that he give up a part of his needs for me? I thought about my own mother and father. Was Daddy's passion for life simply too big for my mama to match? Was that why she tolerated his need for more, and should I do the same? Was that what married people had to do, to give up part of themselves for each other? Bea made a decision not to do that, and look at the pain that it caused. I didn't know if I had the courage to be like either her or my mama.

Another question was sitting back there in my head, one that I was having trouble acknowledging. What could my man do to fulfill me? I'd tolerated my loneliness. I'd stopped dreaming. And I no longer knew who I was. I realized right then that the only people in this entire world who gave me absolute joy was Mama and Bea because I could count on their constant love.

The phone calls stopped, and my brothers never mentioned the incident at Horn's Hill again. I allowed life to go on and tried to close the door on the hurts inside me and allow the scars to fix themselves. I worried every time Curtis was gone at night. I had no self-respect.

I never pushed him away when he needed me, but it wasn't lovemaking. He closed his eyes, and when it was over, we turned away from each other, and I tried to sleep. I felt used, and it shamed me. I could have been anyone lying there under him.

Curtis outgrew the business and decided to go to work for a big company that sold securities. I didn't understand exactly what that was, even though he explained it to me lots of times. All I knew was that the new job took more of his time away from me and Bea.

To fill my time, I started going to flea markets and garage sales and antique auctions. I looked for green see-through dishes that matched and sparkly vases to put flowers in. I got good at buying at fair prices and figured if I ever ran short of money, I could just sell everything all over again. I became a collector.

Our house looked real pretty, and it made me happy that my friends liked to come there to visit. It wasn't long before they started hinting that if I ever wanted to get rid of this or that, to let them know. I began buying for the purpose of selling. Word spread, and in no time at all, I started getting calls from ladies in the good neighborhoods in town and out in Granville, telling me they heard I had antiques for sale and asking me if they could stop by and see what I had. Before I knew it, I had me a business going.

When the ladies came, I welcomed them at the door just like I would have in a shop down on The Square. I shook their hands when they introduced themselves, and I chitchatted just a minute before I asked them if they'd like some tea while they looked around. Sometimes, if one of them had been there before, I brought out little sugar cookies for her on my green dishes so she'd feel real comfortable and take her time looking around. I used words like "delicate" and "lovely" and "transparent," and I smiled at myself for imitating those other ladies I had learned so much from: Mrs. Barry, Mrs. Tildredge, and my wonderful friend Bea Taylor. My own little Bea enjoyed going out places with me to buy our pretty things, and my customers knew her well and talked to her when they came over. I liked it that she was feeling so comfortable bein' around ladies like them.

I bought and sold, and I made money, and I put every cent I made in envelopes and jars around the house. I had me a rainy day savings again. And I had me a new dream.

I called Mama to talk to her about it, and she met me and Bea down on The Square. There was a spark in her eye, and she was smilin' real pretty.

"Mama," I said. "I know what I want to do. I know what I could be good at, what I could make some money doing and be respectable. And you and Bea could be a part of it. We could all work together."

I was gushing, and the ideas flowed out from me.

"We'll open a tea shop and we'll serve coffee and tea and your sugar and cinnamon cookies. We'll bake Aunt Lizzie's German Chocolate Cake and Grammy's donuts too. We'll put fresh flowers from our gardens in little glass vases in the center of the tables in the summers and pinecones in baskets in the winter. Why, we can sew us up some pink tablecloths for the tables and matching curtains for the windows. And this is the best part. Besides giving all those lady shoppers something to sip and munch on, we'll give them something to consider buying. We'll sell antiques and other pretty things we find and fix up from yard sales. When Bea gets older, she can help us and learn to manage things so she can have her own business someday. Oh, Mama, we can work together and have fun doing it."

Finally, I stopped and took a breath. Mama's eyes was twinkling, and Bea, who was sitting on her lap, was clapping her hands together, imitating my excitement. Mama said it was a grand idea. She'd help bake and she'd make her garden bigger so we wouldn't run out of things to put in those vases. She could work at the cash register to give me more time to pay attention to the customers.

"Where would you want to put your tea shop, Nellie?"

"Turn around here, Mama, and look across the street, right over there kitty-cornered from us."

The space was right next door to where The Fashion Ladies Shop had been, and a big "For Lease" sign was in the window. I told her how I was working on saving the money to open up soon.

Mama called me that night and asked me to stop by the next day. She had something for me. I went over the next morning and found her working away in her garden. She told me she was getting it ready for

Nellie's Tea House. I sat on the grass by the bed of roses while she went inside to fetch something she had for me.

First, she handed me a poem Grammy gave her a long time ago when she was young and was considering something. I read it aloud:

Someone said that it couldn't be done,
But he with a chuckle replied
That "maybe it couldn't," but he would be one
Who wouldn't say so till he tried.

So he buckled right in with a trace of a grin
And if he worried, he hid it.

Somebody scoffed: "Oh, you'll never do that"
"At least no one ever has done it."
But he took off his coat and he took off his hat,
And the first thing we knew, he'd begun it.
With a lift of his chin and a bit of a grin,
Without any doubting or quiddit.
He started to sing as he tackled the thing
That couldn't be done and he did it.

There are thousands to prophet failure,
To point out dangers that wait to assail you.
But just buckle on in with a bit of a grin,
Just take off your coat and go to it.
Just start in to sing as you tackle the thing
That "cannot be done" and you'll do it!

I couldn't do nothin' but grin. Then she reached back behind the lilacs and brought out a bouquet she had just made. It was tied up with a pretty bow.

"We'll make some bouquets like this to put at your desk in your new place, Nellie."

Finally, she reached into her apron pocket and pulled out a little silk purse and handed it to me.

"It's the last of Grammy's mad money, honey," she said. "I can't think of anything she would rather have me do with it. Now, you go follow your dreams."

Curtis asked me to stop what I was doing there at the house. He thought it looked cheap for us to be buying things and then selling them out of our own house and having strangers coming in and out; he didn't want neighbors to think that we needed the extra money. I didn't feel like arguing with him. Wasn't any point in it 'cause he always won any of our disagreements. Besides, this time I didn't care. I had me a dream, and I was determined to make it come true. Selling things in our home had been a first step. I was going to keep those pretty things I had and put them out real nice in me and Little Bea's new shop, and Mama was going to be there to help me.

I wasn't ready yet to explain it all to Curtis.

I decided right then and there that I had to take matters into my own hands and start my daughter out early on her way to getting really smart so she could make her way in the world better than me. We visited every store and park and field I could find so I could teach her what I knew about things. When we ran out of places to go, I decided we needed to start in on some book learning. I headed for the library.

Now, I hadn't been in a library my entire life, and I wasn't sure just exactly what I was going to find there, but Bea and me walked in anyway, and I pretended to know what I was doing. The calm and the coolness of the place settled over me the minute I walked in, and I stood for several minutes in the middle of that big room with its long tables and benches and rows of books and just took it all in. I watched people reading and teaching their own selves just because they wanted to. No one took notice of me at all, and the nice lady behind the help desk didn't act the least bit surprised that I didn't know how to find books to read to my daughter. I accepted the ones she told me was good, filled out the lending card, and walked out with nine books of my own to enjoy with Bea.

Our reading times together at night after suppers was something we both looked forward to. It wasn't like me teaching her; we was learning together, and we was having fun doing it.

Pretty soon, I started picking out books just for me to read when Bea was in bed, and I couldn't believe how much I liked to read about things on my own, when I didn't have to. I brought out the little notebook my old friend Bea had given me, and I wrote down new words I learned and names of places I had never heard about. And the sound of how words went together proper started coming to me, just like Bea said they would.

Me and Bea, why, we were getting real smart together, and we practiced what we were learning on each other. Sometimes we read just to allow us to make believe, and other times we read to get smart about things.

We were well on our way to be successful business ladies, and I felt alive again.

One day Curtis came home and told me how he'd pretty much made as many contacts as he could in the communities around where we lived, and that he'd have to expand his territory. I didn't know how to argue with him, and, the truth be told, I thought things would be easier with him being gone more. Maybe his indifference wouldn't hurt so, and I wouldn't be reminded as much about his lies.

He started visiting other towns and was gone two or three days a week, and after a while, he kind of settled down in Cincinnati during the week, and me and Bea stayed put. We agreed not to move because he didn't know how long he'd need to be there, and he knew I wouldn't want to leave Newark for good. I went along with his way of thinking, and I praised him for how good he was doing, and for how well he was taking care of us.

I got myself cleaned up and had the house looking real nice for him every Friday night when he got home. Something inside me still hoped that Curtis would change his ways and we could go back to the way we were when we first met. I was still in love with the good parts of that loving young man I met all those years ago. I thought if I could be pretty enough and interesting enough, then things could be good between us again. And I wanted him to want to be a good father to Bea.

Often times, though, it was very late by the time he got home, and he was too tired from the drive to talk. He'd give me a quick kiss on the cheek and go on up to bed and tell me we'd talk in the morning. I'd swallow down the big lump that came up into my throat and push aside the heavy feeling that would pop up in my heart.

More than once I sat at the kitchen table, drinking coffee 'til the early hours of the morning, wondering what to do. Having him there at home with me and knowing that he was so far away in spirit hurt, yet knowing what he had done disgusted me and made me terribly mad. The worst thing was worrying what would happen to Bea if I didn't have him to help provide for her. It scared me. For the first time, I really understood the truth of what Mama had gone through all those years.

We'd been living our lives like that for close to eight months when I got a new message of shame. Patty called and asked me to take a walk with her out at Moundbuilder's Park. She got right to the point.

"Honey," she said. "There's stuff going on that you don't appear to know about, things about Curtis and what he's up to there in Cincinnati. I'm sorry to be so blunt, but it's time you get yourself down there to Cincinnati where your husband is living and bring him on back here to live with you and Bea. Nothing good can come of a man having the kind of freedom you're allowing yours to have. My gosh, Nellie, don't you ever worry about what he might be doing when he's away from you?"

"No," I lied. "I don't worry. I trust Curtis. He's good to me. We have a wonderful life. Why, I—"

"Nellie," she said, interrupting me. "I know better, and so do you. I'm sorry, honey, to be the one to bring you this news, but someone has to tell you. Nellie, he's showing pictures of some woman who he's seeing down there in Cinci. Showing *pictures*. Do you hear me? Weekends when he's down at the pool hall with his buddies and he gets a few drinks in him, he brags about her. Last week him and two of your brothers got into it down there, and people had to break it up before it became a real fight. They threatened to beat the shit out of him. I imagine it will be a while before he shows any more pictures around. But you'd better get your butt down there and put an end to it once and for all. He either needs to get his beautiful ass back home here or you need to get yours down there. One of you has got to change locations."

The next day, I dropped Bea off at Mama's, borrowed George's car, and headed down to Curtis' other home. I talked to myself all the way down there about what I was going to say to him, but no matter how many times I practiced, I sounded like I was begging him or being selfish and downright bitchy.

Finally, I pulled off the road and took out some paper and a pencil and made notes as to how I might put things. I listed the lies, the excuses, and all the little things Curtis had done that made me feel small. I made a list about the ways we were the same and the ways we were different. I listed all the bad things about me and Bea living with him in Cincinnati, and all the bad things about making him come back home to Newark. I tried to think about what I could do to make things better between us, and it was clear, looking at that list, that I needed big ideas. But I didn't have any.

I thought how I was letting him humiliate me, but then I worried about how I'd take care of my little girl by myself. And I remembered Bea's pain when she told me about leaving her husband and what it had cost her, and I couldn't hold back the tears. I was paralyzed by indecision. Finally, I just looked up at the big old sky and told God it was all in His hands because I just simply did not have the answers.

When I pulled down the street where Curtis lived, I still didn't have any firm idea what I would say to him, so I figured I'd just let the words come out the way they wanted to and see what happened. I parked the car and sat there, holding tight on the steering wheel, and decided to try to pray one more time. I asked my own special God to help me finally get things right, to show me a sign to help me know what I should do, and to help me find a way to put an end to all this hurt.

No one was at the house. It was a duplex, and my knocking brought Curtis' neighbor outside. She was an elderly woman, tiny and soft spoken. I introduced myself to her, and it was plain to see that she was flustered when I told her I was Curtis' wife. She was friendly, though, and she invited me inside to wait for him. We chitchatted for a while, and she decided she'd make us some tea. And when I looked at my watch, she said there was plenty of time because they usually didn't get home until close to six. My mind couldn't get away from the word "they."

"My, oh my, Miss Nellie," she said as she poured the tea. "You're going to have a big surprise when your young hubby walks up those porch steps."

I held my breath while she put her thoughts together.

"You see, dear, there's another woman living there. I thought she was his wife, naturally. And, long as I've gone this far, I think there's something else you ought to know before they get here.

"An ambulance was here a couple of weeks ago. Took her to the hospital. She had a miscarriage, is what I heard. Thought you should know." She reached out and tapped at my hand. "Sorry, honey."

The neighbor got up and went somewhere. The clock ticking on the wall was too loud, and the evening shadows creeping around the curtains on the neighbor lady's kitchen window was gloomy. Words from people who loved me came into my head: "Keep a close rein on him... get control...he's a son-of-a-bitch...going at it...in broad daylight... showing pictures...we'd like you to stay on, Nellie, but...a man like that needs...don't get trapped, honey...follow your dreams...he'll be a handful."

So many people knew. They had all told me, but I hadn't listened.

Outside somewhere a car door slammed. Then another. The neighbor lady stood next to me and whispered, "They're home, honey."

225

I stood and looked out the window. Someone had put there, on the ledge, a small glass jar filled with a few pieces of grass and a tiny crooked twig. A lid, with little holes punched in it, was screwed on tight, keeping whatever was inside all bottled up. Tiny beads of moisture streaked down the walls of the jar. I picked it up and looked through it. A delicate and beautiful butterfly lay there, slowly fluttering its wings.

"My grandkids caught it," she said. "Put it in there so they could watch it and see how pretty it is close up."

My breath got caught in my throat, and I felt the tears roll down my cheek.

"It will die in there," I said. "You can't bottle up a butterfly. Butterflies have to be free."

I kept the jar in my hand, and the lady and I walked out together down her porch steps and over to a small tree with pink blossoms. I bent down on my knees in the warm grass and held the jar in my lap. Slowly I took the lid off and waited for the butterfly to escape, but the tired, poor creature didn't understand that she was free.

"You don't have to stay in there," I said, and the words caught in my throat as I tipped the jar over. "You're free. Free to fly again."

The butterfly lay in the moist grass and ever-so-slowly fluttered her wings, and then, suddenly, she rose up into the dark green leaves and disappeared in the deepening dusk.

The neighbor lady and I stared deep into each others' eyes.

"You'll be all right," she said in a low voice. "God bless you, child."

It was hard to walk up to Curtis' porch. My feet didn't want to take me there. I didn't have to knock. He was waiting for me. I could barely see the other woman in the shadows behind the window. I understood her fear.

"Nellie," he said, "it isn't what you think. I can explain."

"Shhh," I told him. "I know you can explain. You've always been able to explain, and I've always believed you. But not this time."

I touched his lips and ran my fingers through his soft blond hair and knew the memory of doing those things would be with me for a long time. My kiss was soft on his cheek.

"There's nothing left to be said. I will never forget you. I hope you won't forget me." I could barely whisper, "Goodbye, my husband."

His voice came out jagged. "What will you do?"

I reached the bottom step and turned around to look at him one more time.

"Lots of things," I told him. "Lots of wonderful things. But the first thing I'm going to do is find me and Bea a big old tree to climb."

If I am not for myself, who is for me?
And if I am only for myself, what am I?
And if not now, when?

Hillel

Forgiveness is the answer to the
child's dream of a miracle by which
what is broken is made whole again,
what is soiled is again made clean.

Dag Hammarskjold

Printed in the United States
82712LV00008B/43-90/A